MJ James fell in love with books at a very young age. Books were the one thing in the world that made sense and provided constant companionship. MJ was diagnosed on the autism spectrum at the age of 24. After their diagnosis, they went on to earn a BA in Psychology and an MS in Developmental Psychology. They are the parent of three incredible humans.

## Connect with MJ James

www.MJ-James.com

Instagram @MJ_James_Writes
TikTok @MJ_James_Writes
Twitter @MJ_James_Writes

# Trigger Warnings

In-Between can deal with some tough topics, including rape, and family abandonment. These are, unfortunately, very common with autistic women. I attempted to handle the topic with care, but it is still a potentially emotional topic.

HAPPY READING!

# In-Between

## MJ James

Developmental editor services provided by Fiona McLaren
Proofreading editor services provided by Aaron H Arm
Cover design by PurpawArt

ISBN: 978-1-958175-00-2

www.mj-james.com

*For Aunt Ruth who always encouraged
me to keep writing.*

*And Aunt Debbie who taught
me to embrace my uniqueness.*

# Chapter One

Alicia did not plan on being a receptionist at the age of thirty.

According to her life plan, the plan she created on her sixteenth birthday, she should have been in her last year of graduate school, about to walk down the aisle with a PhD in Engineering. Except that thirty-year-old Alicia learned that life does not go according to plan.

Whenever Alicia became overwhelmed with the ringing phones, she turned and looked at her son's photo, right next to the laminated phone script. Then she knew it was all worth it.

"Monty Investment Group, how may I direct your call? I will transfer you to him right now.

"Monty Investment Group, how may I direct your call? Ms.

Broadman is at a conference. Would you like me to transfer you to her voicemail? Yes, she will be monitoring it. I will transfer you right now.

"Monty Investment Group, how may I direct your call?"

"Can I speak with Ms. Henry?"

Alicia froze at the sound of her name. Her heart was racing, and her voice caught as she finally spoke. "This is Ms. Henry. How may I help you?" She already knew who was on the other end of the line. None of the clients ever bothered to ask her name, and she had no personal acquaintances who would bother to call her at work. No, this was another call from her son's school.

"Ah yes, Ms. Henry. There has been another situation at school with your son, and we need you to come."

"To whom am I speaking?" She tried to keep the frustration out of her voice. This was the third phone call this week.

"This is Ms. Simpson, the school nurse."

"What type of situation has there been this time?" Alicia picked up the pencil and prepared to write on the message slip. She would add this note to the pile of other ridiculous phone calls.

"It would be best to discuss that when you arrive at the school."

"As you have probably noticed, Ms. Simpson, I am currently at work. So, if you plan on calling me in for yet another set of arbitrary complaints, then this can wait until I come and pick up my son."

"Well, I would think that your son's safety would be more important than your work." The high-pitched voice drilled into Alicia's head.

"I was not under the impression that my son was unsafe, as I had left him in your and your colleagues' care. Surely if something had happened to my son, you would have told me right away instead of insisting on vague hints. The last time the school requested that I leave work, I arrived to find that your only grievance was a fully grown garden that you somehow think my son created. Losing my only source of income because your school has an overactive imagination does not seem to be about my son's safety."

Alicia found her gaze focused on the potted fern plant. Watching the light from the front windows shine on its glossy fake leaves usually calmed her. Today it wasn't helping.

"Your son has run off, Ms. Henry. Maybe it is worth your time to come now." The voice seemed almost satisfied to be delivering this news. Alicia hoped that she was interpreting the situation wrong. No educator should be happy to tell a parent they lost a child, even if they didn't like the parent.

"What do you mean he has run off?" Alicia was yelling now. "Why are you just now telling me?"

"If you remember, I told you there was a situation. You are

the one insisting we have this conversation over the phone. His class was walking back to the classroom, and your son never made it inside. We have, of course, attempted to locate him. However, it looks like he has left the school grounds."

"You lost my son, again?" The front door opened and one of the investors walked in, decked out in his Brioni suit. Alicia ignored the frustration brimming inside her and smiled at the man. He walked past the desk to the hallway behind her and pushed the button for the elevator.

"He ran off," the nurse said on the phone.

"He has never run off." Alicia tried to keep her voice low and professional so it would not carry to the elevator. "However, you seem incapable of knowing where he is. The last time you told me he was missing, I didn't even make it out of work before you called back and told me he was in the library, exactly where he was supposed to be. The time before that, he was sitting at his desk, doing work when I arrived."

Alicia looked down at her watch and saw that it was now just barely after twelve-fifteen. The elevator arrived and the man stepped in and disappeared. Alicia's voice began to rise again. "Didn't lunch end just a few minutes ago? Can you send someone else to look for him and make sure that he did not stay out on the playground equipment?"

"Ms. Henry, he did not return from PE."

"PE? That was thirty minutes ago. You're just telling me

now?"

"As you said, we wanted to make sure he was actually missing before we called you. Are you going to come to the school, Ms. Henry?"

"Can you send someone to the classroom to make sure he isn't back at his desk?"

"I assure you that Kenny is nowhere on the school grounds. We have not simply misplaced him."

"That is what you said last time," Alicia mumbled before disconnecting the call.

She took a deep breath. Then she tried to assess her options. It was the second time this month that she had to leave work early to go to the school. Yet, if her son was missing, she had to go.

The lines were ringing. Alicia picked up each in turn and put them on hold with a curt "hold, please." Then she got up and walked to her boss's office.

Her boss was the director of customer relations, but Alicia had yet to see him talk to a customer. When she walked into his office, his cowboy boots were propped on his desk, crossed at the ankles. They looked out of place next to his blue suit pants. His body was draped over his chair, and she briefly wondered how it managed to hold his frame. His eyes were closed, and she could hear a brief snort when he breathed in. He was asleep again.

"Excuse me, Mr. Norm."

He did not stir, so she spoke a little louder.

"Mr. Norm, I need to leave for the day."

At this, he finally woke up and looked around until he noticed Alicia waiting at his door.

"Mr. Norm, I need to leave, please. There is a problem with my son's school, and I need to go. I took care of all of the filing and the records. I will put the phones on voicemail and will check it first thing when I arrive tomorrow."

"You need to leave again? This is the problem with hiring a woman who has a child. They never seem to take their work seriously."

Alicia was tired of being ripped in two. The school berated her because she needed to work, and work tore her down for taking care of her son. But right now, her son was missing and that was all that mattered, so she pushed down the resentment and tried to keep her voice as meek as possible. "I'm sorry, but the school just called to tell me that my son is missing. They do not know where he is."

"Will he appear if you go to his school?"

"I. . . well. . . I would love for that to happen. But, either way, I need to go."

"If you go, then don't bother coming back."

"What do you mean?" Alicia said.

"I mean, you are fired."

"You're firing me because my son is missing?"

"I'm firing you because you do not make this office a priority. If you truly cared about your work, then you would show the same dedication to your job as I do to mine. This lack of loyalty is unacceptable."

Alicia clenched her fists and held them at her side. She saw his row of golf trophies lined up on his bookshelf and wanted to fling them against the wall. She wanted to take the visitor's chair, which she had spent so much time sitting in while he talked down to her, and smash it to pieces. Yet, none of that would help her son. So, she bottled all the rage back inside herself and spoke as evenly as she could manage. "Fine, I will be by tomorrow to pick up my last check."

"Don't bother. I will have it mailed to your house."

Alicia turned around, grabbed her purse, and did not even bother taking the phone calls off hold or turning on the voicemail. *Mr. Loyal-to-his-Job can figure out how to do it all on his own.*

# Chapter Two

Alicia tapped her two index fingers against the car steering wheel. She allowed herself to do this until the count of thirty. Then she stretched out her fingers and balled them into fists. She closed her eyes and took two deep breaths. It didn't help. The anxiety still crawled over her, settling like a stone in her gut. She couldn't breathe. She was losing control, drowning in the stress of losing her job and now her son. She latched on to the thought of her son. She could panic later when he was safe at home, tucked into bed. Finally, Alicia unhooked her seatbelt and got out of the car.

She glanced around the schoolyard and noticed the large pile of rocks stacked halfway to the school roof. A sigh escaped her at the sight. She continued walking into the main office. She had no idea where her son would have gone off to or why and she tried not to let her mind race with all the possibilities. Until she knew more, she would not worry about what might be. Instead, she focused on putting one foot in front of the other.

She walked into the front office and headed towards the long counter that separated the administrative desks from the cramped lobby.

"Mom."

Alicia turned to the bench against the front wall, and all the tension released from her body. There was Kenny in his worn blue jeans and superhero t-shirt that were a bit too undersized after his recent growth spirt. She collapsed in front of her son who was sitting on the office bench, reading one of his books, his black backpack at his feet.

"I'm so glad you're safe," she said, gathering Kenny up into a hug, scrunching his book between them.

Alicia felt the presence of someone right behind her. She was not surprised to see the light grey pantsuit with the perfect creases that could only belong to the principal. Alicia looked up to see her blonde bobbed hair, small nose, and thin clenched lips. Alicia took in her body language and realized that the principal was upset. *Why would the principal be upset when she was the one who had lost her son?*

"I think we should talk in my office," the principal said in a clipped voice. Alicia knew that it was not a request but a demand.

"Do not move. I will be out soon." She looked at her son, taking in his slightly disheveled brown hair and his rosy cheeks that were just starting to hint at the man he would become. He lifted the tattered paperback up and was lost in the story, his leg slightly bouncing under the bench. She was hesitant to leave, afraid that he would disappear again if she left him alone. But she tore herself away and followed the principal through the raised counter and back to her compact, tidy office.

"Where was he?" Alicia did not even wait until the door was closed before she asked her question.

"He was found at his desk. We need to discuss your son's continued behavior."

"What do you mean, my son's behavior? You called me and told me that you lost my son. Now you tell me he was where he was supposed to be. I just lost my job because I had to leave work to find out that you hadn't noticed a boy sitting at his desk. We need to discuss the school's behavior, not my son's."

"Why don't we sit?" The principal gestured to the folding chairs across from her desk as she took her seat, placing her folded hands on top of an open file. "There have been numerous incidents this year. Kenny's behavior is troubling. If something is going on at home, it would be better to let us know so we can support him here."

Alicia ignored the chair and instead stood with her arms folded, glaring at the principal. "It seems to me that the problem is this school, not my son. Within the last six months, I have had to pick him up five times. One time was because you accused him of growing vegetables, another time you accused him of fixing a kid's broken arm, and three times now, you have lost him while he was where he was supposed to be. Do you have any idea how ridiculous this sounds? And now you are saying that somehow his home environment has impacted your school's sense of reality?"

"Ms. Henry, I understand that it is difficult being a single parent. There is no male figure in his life." The principal started sifting through a file on her desk, not bothering to even look at Alicia.

"What would a father figure have to do with you losing my son?"

"Then I understand that you have your difficulties. Perhaps that may be impacting Kenny as well."

"What difficulties?" Alicia finally sat, her left hand raised to her neck, her fingers needing her tense muscles. Then, realizing what she had done, she quickly moved her arm back down, focusing on keeping both her hands rested on her knees. She was not sure where this was going, but the conversation seemed to have gotten out of her control. It seemed so evident that the school was calling her for the most random things. No one could believe that her son was capable of what they were accusing him.

"It says here in his records that you are on the autism spectrum."

"Yes, do you think that Kenny is as well? A team evaluated him in preschool, and they did not see anything that would lead them to believe he is on the spectrum."

"I have seen that report." The principal shuffled around some more papers and then finally looked up to Alicia. "I do not think that Kenny has autism, but have you considered how he may be impacted by being raised by a mother who does? Is there no one else who could help out? A grandparent or siblings? I know it must be difficult for you as well, and you mentioned that you just lost your job."

Alicia stared at the principal, her body frozen. She wanted to defend herself. The principal needed to be told how out of line that comment was, but her words were locked behind the wall of her anger. Then she took a deep breath and let her body relax. Finally, she found the words, and they came flowing out.

"Ms. Johnson, this conversation is now over. If you continue to call me for fabricated reasons, our next conversation will involve a lawyer where I will be suing you and the district for discrimination. I may be a single mother with autism, but I take good care of my son.

"All you have are records of offenses that no one would believe. I have a pile of ridiculous notes that the school keeps sending home. One accused him of ruining someone's science experiment by making seeds grow right after they were planted. Another said that he made all the children believe that there was a fire-breathing dragon on the playground. Last week, I received a note that my son created a six-foot-tall pile of rocks while taking a math test. Unless you're accusing my son of doing magic, I suggest that you talk to your staff about the ridiculous accusations and stop harassing my boy, or I will make it my mission to make sure that you are no longer at this school."

Alicia stood up and walked out, trying to keep her hands still and her breathing even. She found her son still on the bench and gestured for him to follow her. Alicia heard the receptionist calling her on the way out but was too frustrated to care what else they wanted to tell her. She was silent as they walked to the car. Her son let her cool down before they spoke, but she heard his feet shuffling behind her.

Alicia opened the back door and watched while her son climbed in his booster seat and put on his seatbelt.

"Are you ready?" she asked.

"Ready," he answered, following their routine. He tried to give her a big smile to help cheer her up, so she reached in and kissed him on the cheek before closing his door and going to her seat.

"Are you OK?" she asked as she started the car, a light gray compact vehicle that she had since college.

"I'm OK. Are you OK?"

"I'm fine. Your principal just made me upset. Were you hiding today?" Alicia backed the car out of the parking spot. The parking lot was small, and Alicia had to concentrate on how much space she had. It took her several attempts at pulling in and out of the spot before she finally managed to straighten the car. Kenny waited until they were moving before he spoke.

"No, I was right there, but everyone acted like they couldn't see me. Ms. Roth sent out Terry and Tommy to find me. I started screaming right by her. I thought she would get mad at me, but she just walked away into the class. Finally, she saw me again, and she got so mad that she called the office to come and get me. I was at my desk the whole time, so I don't know why she was mad."

"Do any of the adults at school talk to you about me having autism?" Alicia waited for a few cars to pass and then pulled out of the school parking lot. They continued down the residential road.

"Sometimes. They said something about it today. I told them that it makes you a better mom. You always remember to cut the crust off my sandwich, and we are always on time for everything. Plus, you play with me all the time. Most everyone else's parents ignore them."

"Ms. Johnson seemed to think it made me a bad mom. I told her that she had to stop getting mad at you for all this made-up stuff."

They stopped at a four-way stop and Alicia glanced back at her son. His face was staring down at his closed book. Then she looked in all directions to make sure there were no cars and counted three seconds in her head before continuing through the stop sign.

"I'm sorry," Kenny said.

"You said you didn't run away in class."

"I didn't."

"Then you don't need to be sorry. I don't know why they keep saying you are doing all this stuff, but we will find a way to make it stop."

They pulled into the parking lot of their apartment complex and into their assigned spot. It was a nice parking lot with enough space in-between the rows of cars for two cars to drive next to each other. They were lucky, as the owner still lived onsite and ran the apartment. He had taken a chance on renting to them when no one else would. Alicia glanced back at her son. He was now hunched completely in his seat.

"Is there something else I should know about?" she asked.

"Some of the stuff happened."

Alicia's eyes widened slightly at her son's comment. "What do you mean?"

"They said I built the pile of rocks. I didn't. I was sitting at my desk, trying to take the multiplication test."

"They are getting mad at you for what someone else did," Alicia said.

"I don't know."

Alicia turned off the car and got out. She opened the back door and squatted down next to her son's seat. "If you were talking a math test, then you couldn't have made a pile of rocks. Someone else must have done it, and they seem determined to blame you for every weird thing someone has done this year."

"During the test, I was picturing rocks in my head to figure out the problems. Then, when we went out to recess, there was a giant pile of them." Kenny reached over to unhook his seatbelt, not looking at his mom when he spoke.

"Can rocks be moved with minds?" She reached out to him, rubbing her hand down his arm, but he still did not look up.

"No," he muttered as he stood up from his seat, swinging his backpack on his shoulder.

"Sometimes, when people keep telling us things, we start to believe they are real."

"Yeah, OK," Kenny muttered as he pushed past her to get out of the car.

Alicia locked up the car and followed him, making sure that he stopped and looked both ways before he crossed the parking lot. They walked up to their apartment in silence, which was on the bottom floor of the two-story complex. The doors all opened into a courtyard that had been covered completely in concrete.

There were a few plastic benches and potted plants that had seen better days scattered around. They moved occasionally, but Alicia had never seen anyone actually using them.

As soon as Alicia got their door open, Kenny walked past her and placed his backpack and shoes in their assigned spot. Then he went and sat down on the orange couch they had managed to acquire from a neighbor. She stared at him, at a loss for what he was feeling or how she could help him. "Do you want to keep talking about it?" she asked as she closed the door.

"In my books, magic is real. Could it be real outside of books?"

"It would fun if magic was real. If you could wave a wand and wish for anything, what would you ask for?"

"How about spaghetti for dinner?" His shoulders started to release and he looked towards Alicia for an answer.

"Spaghetti, again?" She shook her head at him in a playful manner. "Didn't we just eat that two nights ago? I think we have had too much spaghetti."

"No," he laughed. "You can never have too much spaghetti."

"Ah, well, in that case, I guess your wish is granted. Spaghetti for dinner it is, but first we have the best part of the day."

"Reading time?" Kenny asked as he raced over to his backpack to pull out his book.

"Yes, reading time." Alicia picked up her library book from

the arm of the couch and sat down. Kenny lay down next to her, putting his head on a pillow next to her and filling up the rest of the couch with his gangly legs. Keeping with their normal routine was calming, even if Alicia could not focus on the pages.

# Chapter Three

Alicia tried to make the morning as normal as possible. She got up and made Kenny breakfast while he sat on the couch, reading. As usual, she had to pull him away from the tales of mythical monsters to get him to the table to eat his eggs and toast. While eating, they played their favorite breakfast game of guessing the animal that the other one selected.

"Is it a mammal?" Alicia asked.

"Yes."

"Does it live in America?"

"No."

"You picked another tricky one, didn't you?" Alicia tried to keep a playful expression on her face, but her thoughts kept drifting to her lost job and her son's school.

Kenny giggled. "You're not going to get this one."

"Does it have fur?" Alicia tried to imagine the worst that could happen. *Without money, we would lose our apartment. But on the bright side, that would mean Kenny would have to transfer schools.*

"Of course, it is a mammal."

"Right, good point. Keep eating." Alicia moved around the kitchen, cleaning up the breakfast mess as she thought. "Does it live in the savannas?" *There has to be someone willing for us to take over their couch.* It had been a while since she had to ask.

"The savanna?" Kenny looked confused.

"Like lions and elephants."

"Oh, no. It lives in the rainforest."

"Thank you for the free clue." *Whatever happens, it will work out. Maybe it won't be easy, but we will get through. We've managed so far. What matters is right in front of me.* She tried to focus back onto her son.

"You tricked me, but you still won't guess this one." Kenny had stopped eating, his food spilling out his of his grin.

"Finish eating," Alicia said, "so that I can keep guessing." Kenny returned to his ketchup-covered eggs and stabbed them with his fork until he got some to stick. Then he deposited the food in his mouth without enthusiasm.

"Is it a type of monkey?" Her son was growing so fast, and

she wanted to enjoy every second of it.

"It's not a monkey, but it is a primate."

"Thank you for another free clue." The grin on Alicia's face was no longer forced.

"Oh no," Kenny said, putting his hand up to his forehead. "You keep tricking me."

"I think you are being nice to me since your animal is so hard. So, a primate that is not a monkey." Alicia started making his lunch as she thought. "Is it a gorilla?"

"No, it's not a gorilla." Kenny ate the last bite of his eggs and took his plate to the sink.

Alicia put his carrots and sandwich in his lunchbox and then moved over to the sink to wash off the plate. "Is it an ape?" The familiarity of their morning routine gave her comfort.

"It's not an ape. You are not going to get this one for sure."

Alicia moved to the pantry and pulled out a fruit strip and rice crispy bar. "Orange or apple?" she asked.

"Apple." Kenny had now moved to the couch in the connecting living room.

"Cut or not cut?"

"Not cut. I don't like it when it goes brown."

"I know, but sometimes you don't like it when it is whole. I think you stumped me again. I don't know any other primates." She paused and watched him as he tied up his shoes. He had insisted on tied laces at the start of the school year, officially declaring the slip-on shoes she bought him babyish.

"You give up?"

"I give up."

"It's an Aye-Aye."

"What's an eye-eye?" Alicia asked as she closed his lunch box and moved it into the living room.

"No." Kenny started laughing again. "An Aye-Aye. It's like a lemur, and it lives in the rainforest. It has big, weird eyes."

"Was yesterday library day? Go get your backpack." Alicia grabbed her nice purse, the one large enough to hold her resume.

"It was computer day," Kenny yelled from his room. "I looked up animals no one has heard of."

"Well, it was right. I have never heard of that at all. You are just so smart."

"Don't worry, Mom. You'll win one day." Kenny wandered back to the couch with one hand holding his unzipped backpack. In his other hand was his jacket.

"How about you put on your jacket, and I'll pick up these papers that fell out? We need to leave, or you won't have time to play before the bell rings."

"Mom, did you lose your job again?" Kenny asked.

"Why do you think that?" Alicia asked.

"You only wear those clothes when you are looking for a new job."

"There you go being smart again. Let's get in the car." Alicia helped shuffle him out the door and turned to lock up. "Things did not work out at the office. I'm going to go and look for something else today. So you don't need to worry. Everything will work out."

Kenny was quiet as they walked to the car. He didn't speak until they pulled out of the parking lot. "If we don't have any money, you don't have to buy me any Christmas presents."

"That is sweet, Kenny Bean, but Christmas is not for another two months. It's too early to worry about presents."

"It's never too early to care about presents." He flashed her a wide grin that she saw in her rearview mirror.

"I am the luckiest person alive. Do you know why?"

"Because you have me for a son."

"You are right."

Kenny's smile was short-lived. "I'm sorry, Mommy."

"What are you sorry for?"

"For causing all this trouble. I don't mean to do any of it; I don't. It just seems to happen."

"Kiddo, none of this is your fault. You didn't do anything. It's just your school telling stories."

"Yeah, OK." He dropped his gaze and lost his easy smile.

Alicia turned onto the street of the school's main entrance and had to put all her focus on driving. She stopped at the back of the line of cars heading to the drop off. Orange traffic cones were placed in front of the school, creating a lane where cars could pull up, let their kids out, and then drive off again. Except it rarely worked out that well.

While they were waiting to move, a white SUV drove up beside them and parked in the middle of the road. The passenger door opened, and a kid no older than six got out and walked in front of their car without a glance. The car door seemed to close on its own before the parent drove off, nearly hitting another group of kids crossing the road.

Alicia noticed the principal was standing outside on the grass in front of the school building. She was talking into her walkie-talkie while the fifth-grade safety patrol students opened car doors to let their peers out. It did not take long for the principal to notice Alicia, and her already dark look turned into more of a scowl. Alicia kept her face blank, which was pretty typical for her anyway. Then she looked back at the principal, making eye contact. Alicia counted in her head: one… two… three… four. Four seconds of eye contact was normal for most individuals. When the principal did not pull her gaze away, Alicia continued making contact. Five… six… seven… eight… nine. Finally, the principal turned her head and talked into her walkie-talkie. Alicia never understood why people insisted on looking at each other in the eyes. It felt intrusive, but at least this time, she had won.

Finally, they arrived in front of the school. A young boy in a neon orange vest grabbed their car door and tried unsuccessfully to open it. Before he could try again, Kenny leaned against the door, helping it unstick. "Goodbye, Mom," he said as he hopped out of the car. Then he moved the other student out of the way to make sure he closed the door so it would stay latched.

"Goodbye, Kenny Bean," Alicia said, but he was walking away before she even finished speaking.

Without her son, the car suddenly felt smaller, and her responsibilities pressed down on her. She headed out of the drop-off line, determined to do her best to improve their situation.

# Chapter Four

Alicia didn't see the club until she was right at it. Her mood deflated, and she started to hyperventilate, cursing herself for getting lost on the way to the temp agency. She couldn't breathe. She couldn't see. All she could manage to do was pull to a section of metered parking, right in front of her personal hell.

The club was the reason that she did not come downtown. When she was still pregnant, she had gotten lost looking for an apartment she was supposed to tour. She drove down this same street. The panic gripped her, and she slammed on her brakes, causing another car to rear-end her. Alicia couldn't breathe, and she couldn't think. When she finally began to have control over the panic, she was in an emergency room. Thankfully her baby was fine, but it was over a year before she drove again. She never went back downtown. Alicia took another deep breath. She was better now. She could handle this. If only she had followed the damn directions.

The club was tucked in between a clothing boutique and a pay parking lot. It looked so much smaller than she remembered it. It was just a bunch of siding that seemed added on to the rest of the center. She could not imagine how something so lifeless could have taken away so much of herself.

She should never have gone to the club that night. In the past, she had always said no when her roommates tried to drag her out of the house. They begged and pleaded to try to allure her with how much fun she would have. All they wanted was a designated driver allowing them to party together. Their idea of fun was so different from Alicia's. She enjoyed the quiet of the house while they were out. She could curl up in the living area with a book without worrying about being disturbed. The club was loud and bright. You had to stand shoulder to shoulder with other people.

She usually spent the hour they took to get ready rebuking their attempts to get her to join. Except she had just had her last final. Her third year of college was finished, and she would be coming back a senior. Two of her roommates were graduating, and one was taking a year off to visit Europe. She had no illusion that they would keep in touch with her, and she wanted one memory where she felt like she belonged. So, she decided that she would go.

They got all dressed up in makeup and skirts—two things Alicia typically avoided at all costs. Her face itched from the caked-on makeup. The clothes were too tight. The black mini skirt, borrowed from one roommate, was combined with a nearly see-through top borrowed from another. Alicia had second thoughts just looking in the mirror. Trying to drive without a skirt riding up didn't help.

It didn't take long before her roommates left her for the dance floor. Now she sat abandoned at the table with half-empty glasses as company. There was no personal space in the club. Even sitting, she was constantly being touched as people walked by. Others leaned against her as they talked or even danced. People sat down at the tiny table without even asking, taking advantage of the one free chair. They would laugh, talk, and even make out before getting up and moving on. Strangers were everywhere, but her roommates were gone. She hadn't seen any of them in at least half an hour.

She saw the flash of green when he sat down. Alicia lifted her head from her drink to the dance floor, pretending to be looking for someone who had just slipped off to pick up a new drink or use the restroom. If people thought she was with someone, then they would hopefully leave her alone. It seemed to work. No one had so much as glanced in her direction in a while. The new arrival, though, was staring at her. It made her skin prickle. Alicia glanced up briefly and saw him looking straight at her. She looked away again and fixed her gaze onto the dance floor.

The brief contact hadn't allowed her to see much. He was wearing a green suit that stood out against the dark clothing of the rest of the club. His lips were lifted in a sneer, making Alicia feel almost like prey. She wanted to move, but she had no idea where to go. She stood up and peered into the darkened club, searching for even one face that she recognized. There was no one. She had to choose if she was going to run or stand her ground.

Alicia sat back down and turned toward the man. She opened up her stance, appearing larger than she was. Then she turned and met the man's gaze. She didn't look him directly in the eyes; she only did so when it was absolutely necessary. To look a complete stranger in the eyes was barbaric. Instead, she gazed at his nose and lips, just close enough to be acceptable. The man's skin almost seemed to glow under the club lights. It was a flushed combination of green and purple that made her a bit ill to keep looking at, but she did.

The man's lips were thin and never moved from a sneer that seemed to show that he was better than everyone else around him. The most overconfident people were also the most insecure.

Most men just had to be shown you were not easy prey, and then you had to give them an out that didn't make them lose face among their fellow males. At least that is what her books on body language had told her. Except the man didn't back down after the first few seconds. He kept staring and, if anything, looked even more amused.

He seemed to be a few years older than her, probably in his late twenties or early thirties. His suit grew uglier the more she looked at it. It was bright green on the surface, but it was traced through with darker green in a lace-like pattern. His hands were placed on the table, gently clasped like he was waiting patiently. The man's face was on the ugly side with his weird skin and thin lips. His hair was an inconsequential brown that didn't seem to lay flat. She caught a brief glimpse of his eyes and nearly gasped. They were a light brown, minor enough. However, they seemed filled with assurance, like he had nothing to worry about because the entire world belonged to him.

He never stopped looking. He just sat relaxed, in no hurry, and gave no signs that he planned to ever get up and walk away. Alicia knew it was too late to leave now, but she was too afraid to move away from him also. She felt her heart beating fast, and her breath started to catch. She had to keep control, so she began to count in her head. It had always calmed her. One… two… three… she reached two hundred and fifty-three before he finally spoke.

"Want to dance?" he asked.

"No, thank you. I'm saving the table for my friends."

"It seems they left you here while they get to have all the fun. That isn't fair at all. Come dance with me."

Her hands were clutched tight around her untouched soda, but he grabbed at her left wrist and began to tug her towards the dance floor.

"No," she screamed. She pulled back on her wrist, holding on to the table with her other hand, but he was stronger than her and determined to pull her away.

Alicia felt someone brush press against her back. "Help me," she said. She looked up to see a face so pale it nearly glowed in the club lights. She jerked away towards the man in the green suit who used the opportunity to pull her further away from the table.

"Let me go," Alicia demanded, but the man just laughed and tightened his grip.

"Excuse me, sir." Alicia looked back at the pale man. He stood rigidly with his hands straight at his side. His hair was nearly as pale as his skin, but his eyes were a bright blue.

"Perhaps it would be best if we found you another dance partner," The man said.

The smile dropped away from the man in green, and his face darkened. "How dare you question me. Are you loyal or not?"

"Yes, sir, you know that I am."

"Then stay out of my way."

The man in green caught both of Alicia's wrists and wrapped them around her. He began to drag her again, this time towards the bar rather than the dance floor. She screamed and kicked, and when that did not work, she bent her legs and dropped to the floor, but the man in green just lifted her like she weighed nothing. Everyone went on like they could not see what was happening, everyone except the blue-eyed man. She looked at him, forcing herself to make eye contact, and pleaded for him to help her. He looked back. His face seemed indifferent to what was happening before him.

"Help me," she pleaded again.

He moved slightly, and Alicia felt a brief glimmer of hope. Then, just as suddenly, he pulled back, returning to his stoic stance.

She fought as she was pulled out to the side of the club. She remembered that it was dark, and there seemed to be no one around. The moon was bright in the sky, giving just enough light to see the garbage lying on the ground. When the man in green tried to kiss her, she bit him, drawing blood. She remembered him hitting her, but she must have blacked out. She had no other memory until she woke up the next morning, still at the side of the building. Her clothes were torn, and her body hurt everywhere.

When Alicia tried to stand, her ankle protested under the

weight. She propped herself up against the building and leaned on it until she walked out to the street. It was empty this early in the morning, but she could see traffic a few streets ahead. She walked slowly, leaning on what she could until someone noticed her and called for an ambulance. She spent a night at the hospital being lectured by grown men about drinking in excess even though she had no alcohol in her blood. One month later, she found out that she was pregnant.

# Chapter Five

Alicia focused on her breathing; nothing else mattered but her breathing. She had turned off her car, and now all she heard was the flow of traffic behind her. Alicia tried to find the rhythm in the sound and tune it out. Then she tried to relax her body. She was safe; no one was hurting her.

It had been over two years since her last major panic attack. She thought she had them under control, that she had finally taken back her life from the night that had changed everything. At first, she couldn't go out in public. She never made it back to school. She had moved back in with her parents and shut herself in her room, only going out for doctor visits and therapist visits. She worked hard to pull herself together, knowing that she had to be strong for her child, more than her parents had been for her. She would love her child no matter what. She knew what it was like to grow up different, and she would not let her son feel the pain of rejection that she felt from her parents.

She got a job, one that paid just enough to let her save and move out. It was a patchwork of dead-end jobs that fired her when she lost the cheap childcare she could find or when a panic attack happened at work. She was moving up, improving her life. It may have been slow, but they were finally doing OK. Except now, she was unemployed again. Then she found herself back in front of the place that had taken so much from her.

Staring at the building, she couldn't help but wonder. Why had no one seen her get dragged out of the bar? Did no one care, or was there more going on? It was a question that had been nagging at her mind for years. Now she wondered if this was something that could help her son. Could her son conjure up a dragon, heal a kid's arm, or make a garden suddenly sprout a full crop? It was ridiculous; her son didn't have magic. The school must be delusional. But sitting in front of the building, she couldn't help but wonder. What could it hurt to ask? Most likely, nothing would come of it. It was nearly nine years ago. If she left without trying, would she blame herself for not doing everything she could for her son? Maybe something else was going on that night.

Even as she thought it, she knew that it was a desperate act. Magic only happened in the stories that her son read, but didn't she owe it to her son to at least try? But try what? It was then that Alicia noticed the delivery truck parked in the parking lot. She got out of her car and walked over to the side of the building.

Her heart began to pound again. There, right up against that wall, was where it all happened. Alicia kneeled, trying to catch her breath before she passed out. She could feel his hands on her again, and the hopelessness threatened to overwhelm her. *I survived*, she told herself. *I choose to keep surviving.* She told that to herself until she started to believe.

When she could breathe again, she noticed the side door propped open. If there was someone making deliveries, then there was someone inside the bar. She owed it to her son to at least ask if anyone knew his father. It was improbable, but maybe if he was a regular they would remember. Or maybe there had been other girls, ones who came forward and left an impression and would lead her to more information. However, as much as she was doing this for her son, she also knew she owed it to herself to finish facing this demon. She had made it this far, and she knew she would be strong enough to finish.

Taking another deep breath, she walked into the bar.

From the outside, the club looked like it would be no bigger than a small grocery mart or clothing store. Then she stepped inside and the room opened up. The ceiling was high and had exposed pipes running the length of it, like a warehouse store. In the back there was a stage large enough to hold a full band. The floor was empty, and all the tables and chairs were stacked against the wall, next to the bar. It was brighter than she remembered, with sunlight streaming in through the door and the windows high up on the wall. Without the music and flashing lights, it seemed less ominous. But the size still didn't seem right—there was too much distance to the far wall. They must have designed it well.

"I'm sorry, but we are closed. We won't be opening for hours." Alicia started at the voice. She looked around and finally found a man standing behind the bar, holding a box of bottles. He had on a tank top that highlighted tattoos running up his arms and under his shirt to his chest. She was caught up looking at the designs before she remembered that would be considered rude.

"Oh, I know. I was hoping you could help me," Alicia finally said.

"Did you leave something?" He put the box on the counter and then bent down to pull out a battered cardboard box.

"What? No. I just had a question about someone who used to come here." She stood unmoving except for her eyes that drifted to the bottles lining the shelf, as they occasionally glistened in the light reflected from the metal pipes.

"Are you a cop?"

"No, nothing like that. I, I know it is not likely. I'm just looking for my son's father. I met him here about nine years ago." She reached into her pocket to grab her phone but pulled her hand out when he started stepping back. "Sorry, I was just grabbing my phone."

"Right, of course," he said, but he stayed where he was, watching her closely until he saw the phone. Then he seemed to relax slightly. "That is a long time to be asking about someone."

"I know it isn't likely. My son has a medical condition, and I need to find out some information about his father. I don't want anything from him except to ask some questions that may help my child." Alicia hated lying, but for some reason, this did not feel like a lie to her.

"You have a picture?" He moved towards the bar and held out his hand for her phone. At the invitation, Alicia stepped towards him.

"I have my son's picture. I know it is not much, but he looks just like him." Another truth that Alicia had tried hard not to think about over the years. She pulled out her phone and opened her photo gallery. It was all pictures of her son. She picked the one with his smiling face and handed over her phone. "It was May, not quite nine years ago. The man was dressed all in green with the same brown hair and the same easy smile. Is there any chance you know anything about him?"

The man took a long look at the picture and then turned

to take her in. "I'm sorry, but I can't help. Unfortunately, I don't recognize anyone who looks like your son."

"Thank you anyway. I knew it was a long shot. Can I leave my number with you in case anybody thinks of something?"

"Yes, sure." He reached below the bar and pulled out a pad of paper and a pen. Alicia wrote down her first name and her cell phone number. Then she wrote down the date, hoping that that may help as well.

"If anyone thinks of anything, we will give you a call."

"Thanks again." She walked out of the bar, wishing, not for the first time, that she was better at reading people. She was pretty sure that he had lied. But people were so complicated, it was hard to know for sure.

# Chapter Six

Alicia sat looking over her steering wheel at the parking lot, clutching her extra-large coffee. It had been months since she had indulged in something so unnecessary. When driving around didn't calm her nerves, she decided that caffeine would work better. Instead of making her jittery, it always made her calmer. It was almost noon, and she hadn't even managed what she thought would be the most challenging task of the day.

The temp agency sat in a strip mall surrounded by clothing and craft stores. She watched the people, mostly women, walk in and out without a care in the world. Alicia wasn't so naive as to think that she could spot people's problems plastered on their faces. However, it was nice to momentarily indulge in a life where she had nothing more pressing in her day than to pick out a new pair of jeans for her son. Although, he did need new jeans; his current pants were already creeping up his ankles. Hopefully, he wouldn't have another growth spurt until she managed to find a new job. She looked down at her four-dollar coffee with guilt, unable to swallow the last few sips.

Alicia was gripped with fear. Some of the anxiety was old, a trauma that she thought she had overcome still fresh and raw. Some of the fear was new, such as the fear of how she would now support her son. She had managed to tuck some money away, but not even enough to pay rent for next month.

Alicia felt the anxiety creeping over her, taking away her ability to breathe.

She tapped two fingers on the steering wheel, counting to thirty slowly, breathing with the count. The anxiety hadn't stopped, so she allowed herself to do it again. She paused at the end of the second time, but knew she had to do it a third time. You could do it once, or you had to do it three times. If you didn't stop at three times, you couldn't stop until you did it ten times. It had been a while since she had to do it ten times, longer still since ten times wasn't even enough.

After three rounds, she extended her fingers, stretching them, and then curled them into fists.

She was exhausted. Not the exhaustion that made her want to sleep, but the kind that ate away at her. It was too much to think about the past and too much to think about the future. She was tired of trying to be who everyone wanted her to be and failing at it repeatedly. If it weren't for her son... but there was her son, and she was all he had.

Alicia looked in the rearview mirror, fixed her hair, put on some lipstick, and pretended to look normal. She opened the car door, double-checking that she had everything she needed. Then Alicia readjusted her outfit to make sure everything was on straight and as professional-looking as possible. Then she turned and walked towards the building.

The front of the temp agency was made entirely of glass, allowing her to see what she was walking into before she ever opened the door. The office was full of white desks made out of inch-thick wood, making the space overly bright. There was a larger rectangular white desk right where she would walk in. Behind it were square-shaped white desks lined up in a row against the white back wall. In between, there were white tables with chairs. Even the carpet and walls were white. The only color belonged to the silver legs of the chairs and then the people. The office seemed to capture the sunlight and use it to create its own glow.

Briefly, Alicia thought about going back to her car to pick up her sunglasses. Then she shook off the suggestion and walked inside.

"How can I help you?" The receptionist had a wide grin,

silky brown skin, and tight black locks. Alicia felt herself grinning back, and the tension started to release from her body.

"Hi, I am here to look into getting a new position."

"Then you came to the right place. Have you been here before?"

"No, I've never used a temporary agency before."

"There is a first time for everything. Did you fill out the paperwork online?"

"Oh, no. I did not know that I was supposed to."

"No worries, follow me."

The woman led Alicia to the side wall where there were three more square white desks. Each desk held a silver computer monitor.

"Sit down here and follow the prompts on the screen. It will ask you to fill out the paperwork and then have you take some basic assessments so that we can gauge where you will be the best fit."

"Thank you," Alicia said as she sat down at one of the desks and began working on the computer.

It was nearly two hours before Alicia finished with all the assessments. First, she had to retype her entire resume, even though it was all there, ready to hand to the center. Then it went into an even more detailed analysis of her capabilities. They asked about software that Alicia had never heard about. Feeling inadequate in her skills, she finally just checked everything she recognized.

She did not realize that that meant she had to prove that she knew about the various software. She had to pass tests on everything that she had marked. Thankfully, most of the software was relatively easy to figure out, and she was sure that she passed. But by the time she looked up, it was two, and her son got out of school in less than an hour. Alicia tried not to worry. She had to keep going the best she could. If she ran out of time, she would excuse herself to get her son. She talked herself through this as she walked back to the receptionist's desk.

The receptionist had her wait at another white chair, this time at the front of the office. It was not very long before one of the recruiters from the back of the room escorted her to their square white desk. It started well. The recruiter was impressed with her testing scores. It shortly went downhill. She didn't have a lot of experience. Her period of time at jobs was not very long. She never finished college. Her requested work hours were not very realistic. It ended with a firm handshake and the recruiter telling her, "We will call you if we have something come up that is more part-time. It happens, and it is harder to find people who only want part-time work. So, there is a chance."

Alicia left the temp agency deflated. She was so proud of how hard she had worked to pull herself up, but it did not seem to be enough.

She would have to go out tomorrow and try to find another

retail job. She could also put in for waitressing, but the hours while her son was at work didn't pay very well. It was why she had moved into an office job. Alicia was lost in thought, trying to plan out her next move and not let the anxiety overtake her. She wasn't sure why she even looked up. Maybe she felt the man looking directly at her.

He was standing next to a black SUV parked a few spots away from her car. The man's eyes were covered with dark sunglasses that contrasted with his light blond hair. The hair reminded her so much of that night. It wasn't common to see such sun-bleached hair this far north, but it probably would not have triggered her if she hadn't been to the club earlier in the day. She tried her best to ignore the man as she walked back to her car.

# Chapter Seven

Tuesday night was Taekwondo night. Twice a week, they headed home from school, picked up dinner, and changed into their uniforms. When they arrived at the training center, they placed their food in the back room, and Alicia sat down and relaxed for the first time all day.

She was safe here. This center was where she reclaimed her life. She had arrived broken, so scared that she couldn't even manage the Master Instructor touching her without pulling back. Her son was still growing inside her, and she knew she had to pull herself together to take care of him.

Master Kang must have taken pity on her. Most of the time, Alicia was the only woman in the center. Often, she was one of only a few adults on the mat. Master Kang had paired her up with the kids, knowing that the grown men caused her anxiety to spike. He never touched her, often demonstrating how to fix her form by using other students.

Before Kenny was born, Master Kang let her know that one of the teenage black belts would watch her son when she was ready to come back to train. When he found out that she was having trouble making ends meet, he offered to let her help out with classes in exchange for training. She got her black belt, then her second-degree black belt. Now, after more than eight years of practice, she was a fourth-degree black belt. Besides her son, it was the one thing that she felt like she had accomplished.

Now she came in twice a week to take over the classes and give Master Kang some time to catch up on paperwork. She trained hard, and no matter what stress she walked in with, it was gone by the time that class was over.

After tonight's last class, Alicia walked out to see Kenny laying on the waiting room floor with an iPad in front of him. He was lying between the few rows of plastic chairs that were set out for parents to watch the classes. It was a tight space for the three rows of chairs, but the majority of the space had been covered in red and blue mats for training.

"Did Master Kang let you use his iPad again?"

Kenny gave her his trademark grin and went back to watching the screen.

"I hope you don't mind." Master Kang walked out of his office in the corner. It occupied just enough space for a desk and a few chairs. He had changed out of his uniform already and was now dressed in a pair of black jeans and a black t-shirt. The shirt was a little too tight and clung to his chest, toned from his years of training. He was older than Alicia by nearly ten years, but she couldn't tell by looking at him. He could easily pass for his mid-twenties.

"You didn't have to let him."

"I figure with all the help he does around here, it is the least I can do to pay him back." He grinned at her, the kind that made his entire face light up, and then navigated through the chairs to stand near her. They were close to the same height, but he still leaned down slightly to speak to her. "Besides, what kid wants to hang out here all day?"

"I do," Kenny yelled. He put the iPad down on one of the chairs and ran through the chairs, his own training making him extremely nimble for an eight-year-old. He threw a side kick at Master Kang, which was easily avoided. Then the two moved to the mats to fake spar. Alicia watched them for a few minutes. They were laughing as they moved. Kenny ran around then darted in close to try to use his shorter legs to land a kick. Before he could, Master Kang had his leg up to lightly push him away. Then it would begin again.

"OK, boys, time to put up the chairs." Alicia began stacking up the chairs. They stopped playing and began to help her. Together they put away the chairs, vacuumed, and cleaned off the mats.

"Are you done for the night?" Alicia asked Master Kang.

"Almost. I have a bit more work to do. But if you are available, I could take you two out to eat."

Alicia remembered their brief year of dating a few years back. She loved him, in her own way, but she never felt butterflies or desire to do more than hold his hand. She had tried to make it work, but it was too much for her and not enough for him. So, they broke it off. He had been with other women since, who had felt threatened by their friendship. So, they took a step back from that as well. Alicia missed having him as her best friend, but he deserved more and she didn't want to stand in the way of that.

"Thank you, but we already ate."

"Well, that is at least a different reason than you gave me last week."

"It's good to change it up."

"If you wanted to change things up, you could take me up on my offer. It would be good for you to have a break."

"This is my break." Alicia tried to smile. But as much as she liked Master Kang, she also didn't like this conversation twice a week.

"Kenny, finish up. It's time to go."

He was in the backroom again, washing down the table and sweeping the floor, his regular nightly help.

"He told me what happened," Master Kang said.

"What do you mean?"

"About your job."

"Oh, even he doesn't know what happened."

"He told me that you lost it."

"Well, yes. But it will be OK."

"You know, things have been doing pretty well here. I could use some extra help."

"I appreciate it. I do. But I turned in some applications today. I think I will be getting a callback soon."

"Well, you know the offer still stands. We are family, and I will always be here for you."

"Thank you, Master Kang. I appreciate it."

"Please call me Christian."

"How are things going with Bridget?"

"We broke up a month ago."

Alicia put her hand on his arm. "I'm sorry. Why didn't you tell me?" She looked at him, but when he didn't say anything, she finally understood. "You broke up over me?"

"She told me that I needed to choose between her and you. I told her that was like asking me to abandon my sister."

"But if you thought of me as your sister, then we wouldn't

have a problem," Alicia said.

"Exactly." He pulled her towards him, and she rested her head on his shoulder.

"If it would be anyone, then it would be you," Alicia said.

"I know."

"I'm sorry I can't be what you need."

He stepped back from their hug, moving his hands to the side of her arms. "You are more than enough, you both are. You are perfect just the way that you are."

"Finished," Kenny said as he walked back in the room. The two adults moved apart from each other.

"Just remember that you have a job here if you want it."

"I know," Alicia said. She walked away to grab their stuff from the corner of the office "We should go."

Kenny took his backpack from her and then reached up to take her hand. He turned around and gave Master Kang a small wave as they went to the door.

At the door, Alicia paused. The Taekwondo studio was in a small shopping center, where all the other businesses had closed long ago. There should only be two cars in the parking lot, except tonight there was a third. It was a black SUV, similar to the one she had seen earlier in the day. It was parked a few spots over from her car.

"Is everything OK?"

"Yes, I'm sure it is nothing. There is just another car in the parking lot. It looked like a car I saw earlier, but I'm sure I'm wrong. It has been a long day."

Christian walked up to the window and looked out. "Let me walk you out just to be sure." He waited until Alicia stepped back and then went outside. He stopped and stared at the car, which chose that moment to reverse out of the spot and leave the parking lot.

"Maybe I should take you home," Christian said. Alicia and Kenny had followed them out of the center and were standing beside him on the sidewalk.

"I think you scared them off. Imagine how terrified they would be if you were still in uniform. Besides, I need our car." She started walking with Kenny towards their car. While she helped her son into his seat, Master Kang came and looked over their car. She shut her son's door and paused before opening her own.

"What are you looking for?"

"I want to make sure they didn't do anything to your car."

"You know nothing about cars. How would you know?" She let out a small laugh.

He walked over to her and went to put his hand on her arm, then stopped himself. "Will you text me tonight when you get home, just to make sure you're safe?"

"Yes, I promise."

"See you Thursday," he said.

"Thursday," Alicia said as she opened her door and got inside the car. As she pulled out of the parking lot, she saw him standing on the sidewalk, watching them.

"When are you just going to marry him?" Kenny asked.

"What? Where did you get that idea?"

"You like him, right?"

"As a friend. Why do you think we would get married?"

"I don't know. It would be kind of nice to have a dad. Why not Master Kang?"

"I'm sorry, bud, but I'm not getting married anytime soon. So, you are going to have to deal with just me a little bit longer."

"Don't worry, Mom. You're enough."

When they arrived home, Alicia made sure to let Christian know they were safe. She thought back to what it was like to go out with Master Kang, to have him hold her hand and kiss her goodnight. As much as Alicia enjoyed being with him, she didn't think she wanted that kind of relationship with anyone. But was that just another way that she was letting Kenny down?

# Chapter Eight

The next day, Alicia walked away from the counter, feeling overwhelmed. It was the third store that had told her that they no longer accepted paper applications.

"You need to go on our website," a well-intentioned store manager told her. "Once you do that, I will be sure to look it over. We don't have anything open right now, but it could change."

Except she didn't have a computer or even internet access. They were luxuries that she couldn't afford. So, she tried filling out an application on her phone. It was an inexpensive pre-paid phone, but it was a smartphone. Although, after thirty minutes on the store Wi-Fi, trying to get the website to let her fill in the required fields, she wasn't sure it was all that smart.

Overall, the day was long and mostly unsuccessful.

Tomorrow she would have to go to the library and use their computers to job search. Today she was done. She arrived at the school early enough that she was only the second car in the pickup line. She sat imagining going home and taking off the flats that pinched her toes or the slacks that rubbed her legs raw. She would get Kenny and then get barefooted and in sweats in no time.

She was imagining indulging in a bubble bath when she saw movement out of the corner of her eye. She looked towards her driver's-side window and saw two large eyes staring at her. She let out a gasp, and her hand moved to her chest in surprise. It took her a few heartbeats before she could breathe again. Alicia wasn't sure how long it took for her to register the blonde hair and the gray suit and recognize it as the principal. It must have been too long. The principal was looking at her like she was annoyed. Grudgingly, Alicia rolled down the car window.

They spent a few seconds staring at each other. Then, finally, Alicia realized that she probably should have issued some greeting, but the principal had already started speaking by then.

"I am so happy that you asked Kenny's uncle to come to class today. I do think that it will be good for him to have a male influence around. I can only imagine how difficult it must be for you to be a single mother. It is great that you have someone willing to help out and become a role model."

Alicia stared at the principal, trying to have the words make sense inside her head. "Kenny doesn't have an uncle. I'm an only child."

"Well, yes, Kenny seemed a bit surprised by him as well. I assume that he is your boyfriend. I think it is great that he is willing to step in and help when he is not his child."

"Someone came to see Kenny?" The words did not make sense to her even as she said them, so she tried again. "You think my boyfriend came to school to hang out with my son?"

This time the words clicked inside her head and with them came a flood of anger. First, some crazy car following her, and now some uncle showing up at her son's school. She rolled up the window as the principal was still talking, shut off her car, and got out.

"You cannot park here. This is the pickup line."

"Screw the pickup line. Tell me exactly who was hanging out with my son. Is he still here?"

As Alicia raced towards Kenny's classroom, the principal tried to keep up. "He came in to help out in the classroom. He said he was Kenny's uncle, and you asked him to come in since he has been having some problems in school. He was such a delightful young man. I was thrilled that you had found someone so nice to be involved in his life."

By this point, Alicia made it to the classroom. She flung

open the door. It opened into the back of the classroom, and—at the sound—all the children turned and looked at her. They were grouped together in fours and angled so each student would be able to see the classroom. Alicia scanned through the children until she found Kenny was sitting at his desk, very much surprised.

Alicia continued looking around the room. The desk at the back of the room was empty. The only adult was sitting in front of a white board on a high stool. She held a book in her hands, but her eyes were looking straight at Alicia. Her son was safe.

Alicia walked into the classroom and knelt and hugged her son before realizing that this probably wouldn't be very good for his class reputation.

"Is something wrong?"

Alicia looked up to see Ms. Pearson standing over her. She was in her late twenties, but had already taken to wearing sweater vests. Her current one was bright pink with two grey kittens woven into the pattern. She pulled back her frizzy brown hair into a ponytail that had strands falling out.

"No," the principal began, but Alicia soon cut her off.

"Yes, something is wrong. You let some strange man in this classroom. You did not even bother to call me and verify that he was authorized to be near my son. You have no idea who this man is. It wasn't just my son you put at risk. It was every child in this classroom. Who knows why he wanted to gain access to a third-grade classroom?"

The children began whispering, and Alicia did not doubt that they would be telling their parents all about the events of the day. The principal would get a lot of angry phone calls, and this time they wouldn't just be from her.

The teacher looked from the principal to Alicia in confusion. "Volunteers are not allowed into the classroom unless they have passed the school district's screening. He had a pass, so I assumed he was authorized even though I did not have any notice that he was going to come into the classroom to help."

"Yes, well..." the principal stammered. "In this case I decided an exception should be made. I am very concerned about Kenny, and if someone was going to help, I wasn't going to make him wait until all the paperwork was finished."

"You let an unregistered adult into my classroom?" The teacher's voice took on a stern tone like she was lecturing a student.

"Now, now, there is no need for that." The principal moved from her normal condescending tone to one trying to prevent a catastrophe. "We had no way of knowing that Kenny did not know this gentleman. He knew quite a lot about your son. It seemed natural that he was already a part of his life."

"Did Kenny say that he knew the man?" Alicia asked.

"He seemed a little surprised," the teacher said.

"Did anyone think to call me to verify his story?"

"We did not want to bother you at work," the principal said. She shifted her weight around, and her words fell flat.

"What work? You have already caused me to lose my job, and now you are putting my kid at risk." Alicia's voice began to rise again.

"Perhaps we should take this to the office."

Alicia looked at the children and realized that most of their tiny bodies were all turned towards the adults. The majority of the children seemed to be amused, like they were watching a play put on just for them. A few seemed to be more concerned about the conversation, and one little girl in a bright blue dress sat with her hands clenched together and tears falling down her cheek.

"The office would be good," Alicia said. "Kenny, grab your stuff and come with us, please." Once they were out of the classroom, Alicia reached down and gripped Kenny's hand, afraid to let him go. Before they made their way down the hallway, the bell rang, and soon they were walking amid a swarm of children eager to head home.

When they finally made it to the office, the principal turned and looked at Alicia. She just waited silently, like this was all Alicia's fault and not the school's.

"Did you take ID? Do you have any idea who this person was?" Alicia asked.

"He just said he was his uncle. Since you do not have any

brothers, I assumed that he was a new boyfriend. I came out of my office when he came in. He seemed like a nice guy. He was well put together, and I was impressed that you had managed to do so well."

"You do realize that he is not my boyfriend. He is some strange person that you let into the third-grade classroom without any idea who he was."

"Oh, right. Well, Mildred,"—the principal gestured to the office secretary—"had him put his name in the visitor log and then escorted him to the classroom."

"Do you think that maybe we should look at what he put in the visitor log?"

"Yes, that is a great idea," the principal said.

Alicia did not understand how the principal could be so dense yet still feel that she should always talk down to her.

While the principal was walking to get the visitor log, the office door opened, and in walked in one of the other moms of a child in her son's class. She had red hair that ran down the length of her back, and even in jeans and a t-shirt she looked completely put together. Alicia recognized her instantly. She was there for every school event and was always helping in the classroom. Alicia would have been grateful, except Kenny said that her daughter was the biggest bully in their class. She was continually putting everyone down and getting away with it because the school was afraid to lose the mom's support and, more importantly, the checkbook. Somehow, she had spearheaded the new playground last year and got all the teachers iPads.

"I just heard that a strange man was wandering around the campus."

The principal turned to the mother, Alicia now forgotten.

"There is nothing to worry about, I promise. It was just someone coming to help out in the classroom. He was an uncle of one of the other students."

"Are you sure?" the mother said. "I heard that there was a man over at King Elementary just about a month ago. He was a sketchy older man who was trying to pick up one of the children. It turns out he had a record. You remember me talking about this at the PTA meeting?"

"Yes, I remember. But I assure you, it was not the same man. This gentleman was younger, probably in his mid-thirties. Tan skin and light blond hair."

"Wait, did you say light blond hair?" Alicia said.

"Yes, well, it was a little closer to white, actually, but it is good that you do recognize him. See, there is no cause for concern."

Alicia grabbed onto the office counter for support. The room seemed to spin, and it took her a moment to orient herself enough to respond. "There has been a car following me around for the last few days. The driver matched what you just described." She hadn't imagined it, and now the school had given this person direct access to her son. Alicia's reaction must have penetrated even the principal. Her carefree manner was gone, and she was finally paying attention to Alicia.

"I think we should call the police," the principal said.

Alicia was unsure how much the police could do at this point, but what would happen if she didn't report it and the situation worsened?

"Yes, I think that you should."

# Chapter Nine

"Have you seen him before?"

The policeman knelt in front of Kenny. It put the policeman directly at eye level. Alicia couldn't help wondering if this was in a training manual or just something this officer did naturally.

Kenny shook his head back and forth.

"Did he say anything to you?"

"He said that he knew my mom. He asked if I had been having problems in school, and he kept asking about them."

"Anything else?"

"Not really. We were doing math, and the teacher asked him to help us, but he wasn't any good."

It had taken over an hour before the police had even shown

up at the school. The officer was middle-aged, but his chest filled out his uniform. Alicia tried to stare at his buzz cut and large ears rather than the gun strapped around his waist.

There were only a handful of people around by the time the officer had arrived. The other mother had left to go care for her children. Kenny had already grown bored and hungry and was ready to get on with his day. Alicia couldn't blame him. What use would the police be if it took them this long to start asking questions?

The police officer stood up and beckoned Alicia and the principal over to the side of the office.

"What sort of problems has he been having at school?"

Alicia couldn't tell who he was addressing. The officer wasn't looking at anyone in particular, and he did not use either of their names. Alicia was about to open her mouth to say something when the principal finally spoke.

"Kenny is an unusual kid. Things happen around him, and we are not sure how he does them."

"Exactly what kind of things?" the officer asked.

"He convinced a group of kids on the playground that a fire-breathing dragon was chasing after them."

The officer just stared at the principal.

"He runs away from school. No one can find him, and then he sneaks back to his desk and pretends that he has been there the entire time."

"Is this what he has been getting in trouble for?"

"There was another time that he caused an entire garden of plants to grow suddenly—" The principal had a desperate edge to her voice like she was begging the police officer to understand precisely how abnormal Kenny was as she listed off all the strange happenings.

"He got in trouble for a fire-breathing dragon and magical growing plants?"

Alicia couldn't help feeling a bit vindicated. Someone else outside the school's realm also thought that they were full of wild stories. It didn't make up for them making her lose her job, but it did make her feel better.

"That is exactly what he has been getting in trouble for," Alicia said.

The officer looked at Alicia and then at the principal. He seemed at a loss for words before he finally collected himself. "Well, that is not why I am here. Do you have any idea who this man was and why he was interested in Kenny?"

"He asked about the occurrences. He seemed very interested." The principal's voice was so low that they could barely hear.

"You talked to the man?" the officer asked.

"Yes, I walked him to the classroom, but I saw him again as he was leaving. He asked me to tell him more about what had been going on. He seemed very concerned. I just wanted what was best for Kenny."

"You discussed my son's educational record with a stranger?" Alicia's hands were balled into fists at her side, but she kept her voice even, aware of the officer next to her.

"I thought he was trying to help." The principal had deflated from her usual confident self.

"There seems to be a lot more going on here than just a man wandering on campus. Unfortunately, I can't help with all of that. But we will increase patrols around the school and keep an eye out for anyone matching this description. If anything else happens, let us know."

"Thank you," Alicia said.

The police officer nodded and then looked at the principal who had walked away and started talking to the staff.

"Good luck," the officer whispered as he left the office.

Alicia took Kenny's hand, and they walked out to their car, still parked in front of the school. It must have been a nightmare navigating around it for pickup.

As they drove home, Alicia kept looking at every car, expecting a black SUV to start following them. Then she realized the man could just as easily be using a different car now, and she began looking at every driver as they drove past. If a vehicle followed them for too long, she made a random turn, watching to see if they followed.

She knew that she was letting her anxiety take over. She also knew that she was awful at deviating from her regular driving routes. It wasn't long before she had them both hopelessly lost. She turned on her GPS and followed it all the way home. If he knew where Kenny went to school, then he probably already knew where they lived anyway. Not that the thought made her feel any better.

*Why is he interested in my son?* Alicia thought. *Why now?* Her mind kept going back to her visit to the bar. She couldn't help feeling like she started something that she didn't understand.

Kenny had not talked since they left the school. He walked from the car to the house and sat on the couch, staring blankly at the wall. A look of helplessness had replaced his carefree manner and cheerful grin. Alicia sat down next to him and pulled him into a hug.

"None of this is your fault. I won't make you go back there until we know you're safe."

"Mom," Kenny whispered.

"Yes, Kenny Bean."

"There is something that I didn't say before. The man, he told me a secret and told me not to tell anyone."

Alicia's breath caught. Finally, she managed to say to him in a relatively normal tone, "You know that I am the one person you can say anything to, no matter what. You can especially tell me secrets."

"He told me that he was going to help me so I could learn to control everything."

"I don't understand. Control what?"

"All the powers, so they don't just happen. He said I could learn to make them happen."

Alicia sat down next to him and wrapped her arm around him. Her son thought that he had powers. She worked on controlling her voice so that he wouldn't hear her skepticism. "How was he going to help you with your powers?"

Kenny didn't speak at first. He sat staring at his hand that was rubbing against his legs. When he did speak, Alicia could barely hear him. "He said that he was going to take me to a place where there were more people like me. He told me he would take me to my dad."

# Chapter Ten

Kenny was sitting in the living room where Alicia could see him as she moved around their apartment. She had gathered up enough clothes for a week and thrown them in the washing machine. Then, she got Kenny's backpack and took out all his school items and put in some things for him to do. It was hard to decide what to pack. She wasn't even sure where they were going. They had next to no money, and she had no friends.

She could go to her parents' house. They hadn't technically disowned her when she had decided to keep Kenny, but they did make it clear that they had no desire ever to meet their grandchild.

What would happen if she showed up on their doorstep now?

Alicia looked at her son, quietly sitting on the couch watching TV. Maybe she was overreacting? Could she take the chance if she was not?

All she wanted to do was help her son, and now the man in the green suit was sending people after them. Going back to the club had been a mistake, one she did not know how to fix. She grabbed the rest of Kenny's toys, including his cars that he swore he was too old for even though he played with them constantly, and a few of his favorite books.

While she waited for the wash, she checked her bank account and gathered up the emergency cash she had been saving away. She even checked the couch for loose change. But, unfortunately, they didn't have much.

When the bags were packed, she put them by the front door and went to the TV. The TV set was small, bulky, and only got local channels. They rarely turned it on, so when she leaned over and turned it off, her son looked at her in horror.

"It wasn't finished. You told me I could watch the show."

Alicia put her hand to her head and closed her eyes briefly. Then she walked over and sat down next to her son. "I know, but we need to talk for a few minutes."

"Is this about my dad?"

"This is about the man who came to your school."

"You told me you don't know who my dad was." Kenny looked straight at her when he spoke.

"I still don't know." Alicia reached to put her hand on his shoulder, but he moved away from her.

"But the man knew. He said that he could tell me. He said that he is like me and that I could meet him."

Alicia saw the tears falling out of his eyes and wanted to do anything to make them go away.

"Kenny—" She waited while he composed himself. "Sometimes, there are bad men in the world. They want to hurt us, and they will tell us the things that we want to hear most in the world to try and trick us."

"Was my dad a bad man?"

Alicia sighed, unsure of how to best proceed. "I do not know if your dad is a bad man, but I know that he did bad things. He did things to hurt people, and more than anything, I want to protect you."

"OK," Kenny said. He moved closer to her and allowed her to wrap him in her arms.

"We need to go away for a while. We are going to have a little adventure. If you could go anywhere in the world, where would you go?"

"I would go to the Grand Canyon." Kenny spoke into her shoulder.

Alicia couldn't help but smile slightly.

"Why would you pick the Grand Canyon?"

"Because it is so big that it has a river running right through it, and in the pictures, it is red. Red is my favorite color." Kenny pulled away as he spoke and used his arms to animate his words.

"All excellent reasons. OK, we will go to the Grand Canyon." Alicia figured Arizona was as good as any place. Also, it was far away from where they were now. "OK, Kenny Bean, go grab your jacket and let's start our adventure."

"No, we can't go yet," Kenny spoke matter-of-factly. There was no anger or even defiance in his voice.

"We need to go now. Let's see how far we can drive before it gets dark."

"It is not time yet, Mom. He hasn't come."

"Who hasn't come?" Alicia felt chilled by her son's words.

"I am not sure. It doesn't tell me things that clearly."

"Who is telling you that they are coming?"

"No, Mommy." Kenny laughed at her like she had gotten something so wrong that it was silly. "It isn't a who. It's the ground, but it doesn't talk like people. It just sometimes knows things and only things that affect it. Like if an earthquake is supposed to happen."

Alicia sat on the couch and faced her son at eye level. She tried to recall what she knew about delusions and hallucinations and realized that she did not know anything. All Alicia knew right now was that her son was making no sense. That, and she was scared. People were out to kidnap him, and now he said that the earth was speaking to him. Maybe the school was right to be

Alicia tried to figure out the best way to get her son out of the house. She couldn't see any weapons on the man, but she could be wrong. He also hadn't moved any further into the bathroom, but he didn't need to. He would be on them before she could do anything.

"Maybe a dead house plant that came back to life. Perhaps you have seen things that shouldn't be here, like a lost toy. Or maybe he was playing hide and seek, and no matter how much you looked for him, you couldn't find him. Did he heal someone, maybe a cut you received or a scraped-up knee?"

"You were at his school. Who knows what you talked with them about?"

"So, there have been incidents. Which one?"

"What do you mean, which one?"

"What type of magic does he have?"

"You are not seriously telling me that my son is some kind of... witch."

"Am I a witch?" Kenny ran out from behind Alicia and straight up to the man, grasping his hand. Kenny pulled away from the man's hand, realizing that it was red and swollen from the door.

"Enough," Alicia said. "You need to leave my house right now."

The man held up his hand. The swelling and discoloration were now completely gone. Kenny sat down on the bathroom floor, a sheen of sweat on his forehead. Both Alicia and the man knelt to check on him. Alicia put her hand on his forehead, checking his temperature.

"Are you OK? What happened?" Alicia asked.

"That was nice work," the man said. He held up his healed hand for everyone to admire. "That must have taken a lot out of you. Most healers couldn't manage that untrained."

"What the hell just happened?" Alicia said, this time towards the man.

"You can heal." The man ignored Alicia and talked to Kenny like they were the only two in the room. "You mentioned a dragon. Can you do illusions also?"

They soon found themselves surrounded by multiple versions of the light-haired man. He was standing in the shower, walking in the hall, brushing his teeth at the sink, and one was even sitting on the toilet with his pants thankfully pulled up. Kenny just started giggling, and even the man finally cracked a slight grin. Alicia seemed to be the only one not amused.

"That was impressive. A master healer and illusionist. Even the king could not have pulled that off at your age, and he had the best tutors available."

Alicia put her hand on the wall to steady herself. She closed her eyes and opened them again. When she still saw multiple versions of the man, she tried to find a logical explanation. Except that there was only one. Her son could do magic. She watched the illusions wandering around the bathroom and froze when she saw her son standing in the middle of them. He was smiling, the kind that filled up his face and radiated joy. It had been a while since she had seen him this happy, and it was all her fault. She didn't understand, and he had paid the price. She straightened up and shook off her self-pity. Her son could do magic. Now she knew, and they could finally move forward. Except the man was still standing inside her house, the face that had haunted her nightmares for so many years.

"He's a witch," Alicia said.

"No, he's an elf. A half-elf."

"An elf? My son is not a little green man."

"I think that would be aliens."

"You're telling me that my son is an alien?"

"No, like me, he is an elf, not an alien."

"That is ridiculous. You expect me to believe that you are an elf? Where are your pointy ears?"

"I believe you are thinking of Vulcans."

"No, elves definitely have pointed ears. You do not have pointed ears. Your ears are distinctly human."

"I assure you that my ears are elf ears."

"Then what happened to them? Did you hide them or cut the tips off?" Alicia's face crunched up in disgust.

"I didn't need to. Elf ears look just like human ears. You have read too many fairy tales." The man's voice raised as he spoke.

"I'm sorry, how was I supposed to know?"

"Your son is an elf, well, a half-elf. You can believe it or not believe it. I did not believe it until recently, either. I would not have thought that he could have magic, but he does." The man paused and took a moment to recenter himself. Then he knelt down and spoke to Kenny. "What other illusions have you managed?"

Kenny started talking about the dragon swooping over the playground when Alicia interrupted.

"What do you want with him?"

The man tore his eyes away from Kenny and looked at Alicia.

"Who are you, and what do you want with my son?" she repeated.

"My name's Sadar." He held out his hand towards Alicia and waited through the awkward pause while she stared at him, not moving to shake it. Finally, he withdrew his hand, stood up, and continued, "I was called when you came to the club. I figured you were trying to pull some scam to get back at him for, well, for what happened. I was surprised that you had a son, and he looked so much like him. I figured I should look into it more. To find out that the king has a son and a half-human one at that. Honestly, it was impossible to believe."

"And now that you do believe? What do you plan to do now

that you know this king person has a son?" Alicia had not softened once. She did not like how close the man was to her son or her son's apparent ease with him.

"Now, he needs to be trained. I can take him to the king, and he can have tutors provided for him. They will teach him how to use his magic. He can live among his people."

"What are you talking about? He is among his people. He is staying with me. I don't care how rich that man is, he can't have my son."

"I mean, I guess you could come too. At least so you can see that the kid is safe." Sadar said it in such an offhanded way, like he thought that she would let him walk off with her child.

Alicia moved over to her son and pulled him gently away. Kenny, now showing concern on his face, moved willingly to his mom.

"Let me repeat myself. You will never take my son away from me. Now get out of my house."

Kenny gripped his mother's hand tightly. The house began to shake. The toothbrush holder fell off the sink and bounced off the laminate floor. Alicia was shocked at the sudden earthquake. She had never been in one before and tried to remember what to do. Before she could respond, Sadar took over the situation.

"It's OK, buddy." He held his hands up in the universal gesture of *I'm going to do no harm*. "I won't take you away from your mom, I promise. I want to help you learn to control your powers. We do not have to go anywhere if you don't want to. I can help you right here. Do you believe me?"

As Kenny slowly nodded, the earth began to stop shaking.

"Did he do that?" She looked at Sadar and then glanced at her son. "Was that you?"

"I'm sorry, Mama," he said.

Alicia picked him up and hugged him, rubbing his back to calm him down as much as herself."

# Chapter Twelve

Alicia set down the three plates of spaghetti on the kitchen table.
She had hoped that the familiarity of cooking the dinner would
help to ground her. Except her mind was still spinning through
everything that had happened in the last few days and every sign
of magic she had missed over the last six months. Her body
hadn't calmed down either. Every time there was a noise or even
if someone shifted in their seat, she moved, ready for action. At
least now she had a kitchen knife, safely in its sleeve, tucked in
her jeans' pocket.

Kenny practically attacked his food even though he had been
eating almost nonstop for the last hour. *Magic must take a lot out
of him. Magic, how could her son have magic?*

Sadar sat across from Alicia. He picked at his food as if he had never seen heated-up sauce poured over noodles. It may not have been the grandest of meals, but she'd a rough night. He should be happy that he was even still inside her house. It was a decision that she already regretted. She didn't trust this man, but he seemed the only way that she would get any answers.

"If you don't like it, I am sure you can go somewhere and find something more to your taste."

"I'm sure it is excellent." He picked up a big forkful of spaghetti and watched as they fell back onto the plate.

Kenny began laughing, and Alicia relaxed a bit at the sound.

"No, you have to twirl them like this." Kenny dug his fork into his remaining strands and twisted until they began to circle around. "Once you do that, they'll stay." He brought the fork up to his mouth. The bite was so big that half the noodles fell back to the plate. "That's how you do it," Kenny said, the food still half hanging out his mouth.

"Chew, then talk," Alicia said. Kenny chewed and swallowed and began to devour the rest of the food on his plate.

Sadar picked up his fork again. He tentatively put it in the pasta and twirled it like Kenny had shown. When the noodles collected around the fork, he held it up in triumph. Then he put it in his mouth. He finished chewing and then nodded in agreement. "This is excellent indeed."

Kenny grinned at him and then turned to his mom. "Is there

any more?" His plate was empty except for a few stray pieces.

Alicia slipped her plate over to her son.

After Kenny finished the second plate, Alicia sent him off to shower and get ready for bed. It wasn't their regular routine, but nothing about today was turning out as expected. Alicia picked the plates up from the table and went to put them in the sink. She needed to wash the dishes, but she would have to turn her back on Sadar to do so. That was something Alicia was not willing to do. Instead, she just placed them in the sink and went back to the table.

"He's a good kid," Sadar said.

"He's the best. That is why I won't let you do anything to hurt him."

Sadar ignored the hostile glance sent his way and continued. "It must have been hard raising him after everything."

"Don't you dare talk to me about that night. You were there and let it happen. You are every bit the monster that he is. You are here because something is going on with my son, and I have no better choice than you for now. Do not think for one minute that I trust you."

The words exploded out of Alicia, as they often did when she was trying to regain composure. She found herself clutching her fists so tight that her nails were biting into her skin. She began rocking slightly in her chair. When she noticed, she stopped and tried to focus on her breathing instead. All the anger and hurt and feelings of violation came back to her. This man before her had watched her be hurt and did nothing. Now she needed him to help her son. The idea turned her stomach.

"I didn't have a choice," he said.

Alicia tried to look for any sign of regret in Sadar's face, but it was fixed in a neutral expression. It just made Alicia angrier.

"You always have a choice. You made yours."

"I'm blood bound. I did not have a choice."

"Blood bound—what the fuck does that even mean?"

"When I was a child, no more than a toddler, I already displayed strong Earth magic. I was also confirmed to develop illusionary magic as well. Only once in a generation does a non-royal develop two types of strong magic, and to have my Earth skill be as strong as it was is rare. There were rumors that I must have had a bastard royal relative at some point in my family line, but one could not be found.

"I was taken from my family and chosen to be a guardian for Queen Elentri and King Taro's son. I was given ancient oaths that were tied to magic and sealed with my blood. My life no longer existed outside of serving the royal line. I have no other purpose."

Alicia just stared at him, "What the hell are you even talking about? First elves and now kings and blood magic? You're telling me it was magic's fault that you just stood and watched him drag me off? Your magical oaths froze you like a statue making you unable to move?"

"No."

"Then I guess you had a choice after all."

Alicia walked away down the hallway to help her son finish getting ready for bed.

# Chapter Thirteen

Alicia placed a kiss on her son's forehead and then untangled his limbs from around her waist before sliding off her bed. Her son was lying in the middle of the full-size bed. Alicia pulled the covers back over his sleeping form. Then she picked up the knife and her bedroom door key from off the nightstand. She made sure to lock her bedroom door on her way out.

Her bedroom was at one end of a short hallway. The other end of the hallway was her son's room, with the bathroom in the middle. In between was a passageway that led to the living room and kitchen. Alicia stopped in the open space and watched Sadar. He was sitting in the middle of their couch. His legs were opened wide, and each arm branched along the couch. He was facing away from her, towards to blank TV, but she was certain that he knew she was there.

She turned and walked into the bathroom and opened a slim linen closet and pulled out her son's spare set of sheets and an extra blanket. She touched her pocket, feeling the reassurance of the knife, and walked into the living room.

"I hope that you don't mind dinosaurs. He loved them when he was younger, and it is the only extra sheet we have. The blanket isn't all that warm either, but it's all we have. Well, except the blanket on my son's bed, and you are not using that." The words came out in a nervous rush before she could get her mouth to stop talking.

"Thank you. I'm sure they will be fine."

"We don't have extra pillows. You will have to use the couch pillows. But you should have a pillowcase for that." She put the sheets and blanket on the arm of the couch and walked back to the bathroom. She pulled out the matching dinosaur pillowcase and tried to get her hands to stop shaking. She finally bunched them into fists, with a side of the pillowcase stuck in each hand, and pressed them into the temples of her head. Then she released her hands and walked back out.

Sadar was standing with his nose wrinkled in confusion. On the couch was the top sheet splayed out in a haphazardly manner. In his hands were the bottom sheet and the blanket. He stood immobilized, as if unsure.

"You have put sheets on a bed before?" Alicia asked.

"This is not a bed. It is a couch."

"Well, it is what we have to offer. If you want something else, then you are more than welcome to leave."

"I cannot leave the prince unguarded. Now that I know he exists, it is my responsibility to see him to safety."

"What prince?" Alicia asked.

"Your son is the prince. Even in the human world that is what you call the offspring of a king."

"I thought his dad's name was King. Are you telling me you think he's royalty?"

"He is royalty. Our land is ruled by a king who keeps us safe from the human world."

"Put those down." Alicia gestured to the bedding in Sadar's hands. He reached out to hand them to her, but she stepped back away from him. "On the couch please. Also, can you just walk over by the kitchen?"

She waited until he had stepped away and then leaned over to start putting on the bedding. "Where exactly is this land of elves?"

"It is a bit difficult to explain. It is here, in the same place. Except a little removed."

"Like a different dimension?" She had finished the bottom sheet and was working on tucking the top sheet around the edges.

"No, not like that. A long time ago, elves lived alongside

humans. They stayed hidden until the human population grew so much that we no longer could. So, our first king used his illusionary magic to create the In-Between, a world that reflects the human world. It is anchored in the human world, but lives side by side with it. Elves with illusionary magic can slide between the two worlds."

She had finished putting down the blanket and stuffing the square couch pillows in the rectangular pillowcases. Yet, neither of them moved. "Why didn't the elves just stay and live with humans?"

"We tried. Humans were jealous of our magic and became violent. It was better for everyone for us to go."

"You have this magic to slip between these worlds?"

"I do."

"You could have taken my son right out from under me and I wouldn't have been able to follow."

"I could have, but your son has the magic to come right back. I'm pretty sure he has accidentally traveled between worlds before. If I had truly believed he was half-elf, I probably would have taken him from the school."

Alicia thought back to the flimsy lock on her bedroom door. If this was all real, then what could stop him from grabbing her son while she slept?

"I won't take him," Sadar said, as if reading her mind. "At least, I won't take him without you. I already promised him that.

Besides, it isn't quite what you think. My magic isn't strong enough to let me slip through wherever I want. I have to use doorways, places where our worlds are more connected."

"You could be saying that to make me let down my guard. Then you would take off with my son."

"I wouldn't do that. Kenny's too special. It will be easier to just take you with us. Once you know he is safe, you can come back to the human world."

"He is not going. You are not taking him."

Sadar took a step towards her, and Alicia moved off the couch and pulled out the knife from her pocket. She held it up to him, even though the knife was still in its protective sleeve.

"It's OK. We don't have go anywhere, at least right now. I get why you don't trust me to protect your son."

"I don't understand why you want him so bad. Can't you just leave us alone? That man must have other kids running around here. Go see if one of them wants to go with you."

"There are no other children. I don't know how your son exists. Elves and humans cannot have children, and the king recently made sure he wouldn't have any elven offspring either. Kenny is his only kid."

Sadar said this in such an offhanded way, yet the implications hit Alicia immediately.

"What do you mean that elves and humans cannot have children?"

Sadar froze, realizing what he had just admitted. "It has just never happened before. It is why I thought you were trying to get attention, why I never expected to find an actual elven child."

"You mean half-elven child."

"Yes."

"He is my child. I was pregnant with him for the full term. I gave birth to him. He is my child."

"I was not trying to imply otherwise. Kenny is not a full elf. He feels like an elf, but he doesn't at the same time. As far as I know, he is the first of his kind."

"How did it happen? If it never had before, why now with me?"

"I don't know. Maybe it can happen. It just has never happened before. After all, elves do not reproduce as often as humans. Most elves stay in the In-Between. Only a few go to the human world. Maybe we just assumed that it was not possible when it was just improbable."

Alicia heard him say the words, but even she could tell he did not mean them. Kenny had always been her miracle, the most fantastic thing to have come out of the most horrible experience of her life.

"Hopefully, when I work with him, I will have more answers for you."

# Chapter Fourteen

Alicia woke up. She was sitting up in bed, next to her son, with a book still held in her hands after finally tiring out that night. It was dark outside. A glance at the clock showed it was a little after one in the morning. Kenny was still, and the house was quiet. What had woken her up?

Then she heard a scuffling noise by her front door. Were those footsteps? Was that the sound of someone trying to open her front door? Her heart started pounding and her mind started cycling through all the horrible things that could be happening. Any other day she would have walked herself through her breathing techniques to calm her anxiety. She would have told herself how unlikely it was for someone to be trying to enter her house. Yet tonight, she had a strange man sleeping on her couch, and she was willing to err on the side of paranoid.

She went to her bedroom door and listened. It was quiet, but she still hesitated before unlocking the door. *You are a brave strong woman*, she told herself as she took a deep breath, but even then, she only cracked open the door. Just enough to peek through. Except she could not see anything but darkness.

Alicia wanted nothing more than to go back to bed and pretend that there were not shuffling noises outside her house. Before she had her son, she would have happily hidden in her closet, hoping that everything would turn out OK. She didn't have that option anymore. She went back to the nightstand and picked up her cell phone, slipping it in her pocket. Then she picked up the knife, sliding off the protective sleeve, and walked into the hallway. More sounds came from the front door, so she carefully peeked into the living room. The couch was empty.

Alicia found herself slipping into the same midst she had while training. She was focused and ready. So, when she saw movement coming from the kitchen, she had gone to a fighting stance and was slashing out before she had even fully processed the situation. The dark figure moved faster and had caught her wrist before the knife made contact. She moved her body weight to break the grasp when she realized the figure was Sadar, and there was still noise coming from the front door.

"We need to go," he spoke quietly, letting go of her

wrist.

"What's going on?" she asked.

Voices carried through her door. They were deep voices that spoke a language that Alicia could not understand. There was a crash against her door, and then the noises stopped.

Alicia went to speak, but Sadar put his finger to his lips again and then pointed at Kenny in the bed. When Alicia just stood there staring at him, he started moving his finger back and forth between Alicia and Kenny. Alicia stared at him, baffled at what he was doing. Finally, Sadar gave in and spoke in a light whisper.

"We need to leave. Go grab Kenny."

Alicia walked over to the bed and began to pick up her son. She stopped, realizing that the knife was still in her hand. Her fingers froze around the handle, unwilling to let it go. She could feel herself shutting down, all the fear blackening the edge of her awareness. The knife was her only source of protection, but she pushed back at the panic and dropped the knife on the bedside table. Then she reached for Kenny, picking him up slowly, trying not to wake him. He curled into her and settled into her arms. Alicia then headed back to Sadar. Her eyes widened when she heard a noise on her front door again.

Sadar motioned them into the bathroom. The window slid open soundlessly, and Alicia couldn't help thinking that she was glad that she had gotten it unstuck earlier in the night. Sadar stuck his head out the window, looking around. Then he went feet first out the window and made the four-foot drop without a sound.

He was gone for a few seconds, a few very long heartbeats before his head reappeared in the window. He tried to reach for Kenny, but Alicia backed up out of his reach. She waited until Sadar moved before, still holding on to Kenny's sleeping form, she climbed so her legs were sitting on the windowsill. She slid them both through the window opening and then dropped down to the ground.

"Take him to the end of the block and wait for me," Sadar said. Then he disappeared to the front of the apartment building.

The window had let them out on a small grassy area in front of the parking lot. The lot was lit by a lamp on each side, but one of the lamps kept fading out and then popping back at full luminosity. Even then, they were barely bright enough to allow Alicia to make out the shadowed cars.

The night was quiet, with just the occasional buzz of a car driving on the nearby freeway. Alicia put her back against the apartment building with her drowsy son tight in her arms. She just needed a second to think. *Why would someone break into my apartment if they had already sent Sadar after us?* But her thoughts were interrupted by screaming from her apartment. Their words were thick with frustration and malice. Then there was a loud crash, causing Alicia to jump. There were more crashes, and Alicia was fairly certain they were tearing apart her apartment.

She glanced down at her son, but he had fallen back asleep. Alicia tried not to jostle him as she kept low against the building, walking towards the street. The complex was nestled around single-story houses. The cars were all tucked up in the driveways, and the lawns were nothing but manicured grass. The only objects were fences that barely went to her waist. If anyone looked, they wouldn't be able to miss her. So, she walked steadily towards the end of the block, trying not to be visible but also not appear suspicious if anyone happened to see her.

At the end of the block, just around the corner, there was a large elm tree. The leaves were mostly raised off the ground, but the trunk was large enough for Alicia to feel like it was at least sort of hiding. When Kenny began to stir in her arms, she let him down. She swung her arms around in small motions, trying to get her muscles to stop hurting. He was too big for her to be carrying him now.

"What happened?" Kenny said, voice thick with sleep.

"Quiet, we don't want anyone to hear us if they are trying to find us."

"Who were they?" Kenny tried to keep his voice down, but it still felt extremely loud to Alicia.

"I don't know." She pulled out her cell phone and began

to type out a text message to Christian. Alicia thought about all that had happened in the last day and decided to keep it short. *Someone tried to break into our house. We are safe.*

"Where is Sadar?" Kenny asked.

"He told us to meet him here. I am not sure where he is." Alicia realized that she was waiting for a man that she did not trust. For all she knew, he could have staged the whole situation in their house. Maybe this was all part of a plan to get them to leave.

Alicia was still deciding what she should do when a silver four-door car pulled up in front of them. Alicia grabbed Kenny's hand and tried to get him up running. But before he had moved, the car window came down, and Sadar appeared.

"Get in."

Alicia took a last look around and, without a better option, helped Kenny up. This time he moved faster and was in the back seat where his booster seat was placed. Alicia looked at Sadar questioningly. He just stared back wordlessly.

Alicia helped Kenny get his seatbelt on and then hopped in beside him. She had barely clicked her seatbelt before the car was moving again. Alicia tried to keep quiet. Her thoughts were racing through her head, and the world no longer made any sense. It lasted for less than ten minutes before she finally caved in.

"Who the—" Alicia looked at Kenny, still wide awake,

and changed her words midsentence, "heck were those people?"

"I don't know."

"What do you mean, you don't know? I just left my house in the middle of the night. I just shimmied out of a bathroom window with my kid, and you don't know who was even at the house. Maybe they weren't there for us at all. Maybe it was just a drunk neighbor going to the wrong door." But even as she said it, she knew she was wrong. She remembered the anger in their voices and how they had ransacked the house.

"I know they were elves, and they were doing more than just waiting outside your house. I think it was just two people. They were using Earth magic and masking their movement. That is what woke me up, which means that they did not know I was there. They must have thought it was all humans or that Kenny wouldn't know what he felt when they used their magic."

"Why? I don't understand why they would come for us."

Alicia felt the vibration of her phone. She pulled it out of her pocket and saw Christian's photo across the screen. She went to answer it, but before she could, the phone was ripped out of her hand. Alicia looked up to see Sadar leaning back from the driver's seat with only one hand on the steering wheel. The other held her phone.

"Hey," she managed to say, but he had already rolled down his window and threw her phone out of it. "Why the hell did you do that?"

"Mom," Kenny said, his eyes wide.

"Why exactly did you just steal my phone and throw it out of the window?" She tried to keep from yelling, but the frustration still bit into her words. "That was a friend of mine—I need to let him know that we are safe."

"Do you know how easy it is to track a cell phone?"

"No, I don't. Do you? You could have asked me to turn it off. Did you need to drop it on the freeway? Do you think that someone is going to hone in on my phone to find us?" She looked out the window. It was dark outside, but the streetlights illuminated the road enough to show that there was no one driving next to them. "I think you could have waited at least a few minutes and we would have been fine."

"Turning off the phone would have been an acceptable solution." Sadar spoke as if every word was dragged from him.

"It is a bit too late for that now." Alicia looked back longingly. She didn't have any of the numbers memorized, but at least the Taekwondo studio's number was published. "Where are you going?"

"Right now, I am just driving as far away as possible."

"The Grand Canyon," Kenny said.

Alicia looked at her son in the night glow. He was wide awake, enjoying the lights streaking off the side of the freeway. He looked eager and excited, like this was the start of a grand adventure.

"I don't know about that," Sadar said. "I think we need to lay low for a while and figure out where we need to go next."

"I thought you had that all worked out. You seemed to know what to do before those elves showed up."

"Yes, Kenny needs tutors. I need to figure out the best place for us to go now."

"You seemed pretty set on taking him to see his father. Is that where we are heading?"

"I think that is the best place for him to go. For now, we will find someplace to lay low."

Alicia studied Sadar as he drove. He looked straight ahead, his face an unmoving mask. But Alicia had learned how to navigate the world without naturally being able to read people. She had to learn to pay attention, and sometimes it was what people didn't say that was important.

"You don't know where he is, do you?"

"He trusts me. I have been by his side since he was born. I have devoted my entire life to the royal family," Sadar growled. His hands tightened around the steering wheel until Alicia was afraid it was going to break.

"I guess that answers my question."

Alicia, realizing that she had pushed enough, or perhaps too much, decided to keep her mouth shut for the time being. They kept driving. Kenny, lulled by the motion of the car, fell back to sleep. Alicia watched as they started to leave the city behind. The road turned into a four-lane road and the only light was the headlights of the cars.

Her mind started looping the events of the last few days like a reel of a movie on repeat. She was missing something. Why didn't Sadar know where this king was if he had stood by his side for so many years? Who could possibly have broken into their home? But there was another idea, one that Alicia could not brush off. She told herself that there was nothing she could do to change the situation, but for all her trying to talk herself down, the question blurted out of her mouth anyway.

"Where did you get this car?"

"What?" Sadar seemed startled out of his own contemplation.

"The car—where did it come from?"

"I stole it."

"You stole it? Wow, you don't even have remorse, do you?"

"Look, what did you expect me to do?" Sadar glanced back at her as he spoke. "We could not have taken your car. Elves may not live on this side, but even we have connections. How long do you think it would be before they found us?"

"That doesn't make it right." It came out as a whine, and realizing it, Alicia slumped further into her seat.

"Did you want to be caught?"

"No," Alicia said, but she also knew that she could never

justify stealing a car.

"I did what I had to do to get us out of there. The world is not as black and white as you seem to think it is. Everything is not good or bad. Everything is mostly areas of gray, and you do what you need to do to get by." Sadar stared straight ahead as he spoke, and Alicia wondered if he was talking more to himself than to her.

"That sounds like a way of justifying anything. If there is no right and wrong, then the world turns into chaos." Alicia stared out the window at the calm of the night. She could see the lights of a town in the distance, and she wondered about the families going about their normal everyday routines. She relaxed at the thought.

"The world is chaos. Everyone is out to help themselves and do what they need to do to get by."

Alicia found the idea depressing. However, she also could not argue with it. Instead, she continued to focus outside the car. The side of the freeway was now surrounded by large evergreens that hid the lights of the town completely from view.

"They won't notice it is gone," Sadar said, mistaking her quiet for disagreement.

"Who won't notice?" Alicia was startled by the continued conversation.

"The couple that I took it from. I left them an illusion of their car, so they won't even notice it is missing."

"If you can create an illusion of a car, why don't we just drive that?" Alicia asked.

"Magic is difficult to explain." Sadar paused before continuing. "I can create an illusion of a car and leave it. It becomes separate from me, but it won't work. It will last for a time and then fade away. Other illusions can help modify something already in existence, but that requires contact with the magic user. It also requires a connection that is not illusion. I couldn't just create a working car without something to build it upon."

"Then why leave the illusion?" Alicia asked. "Why not just take the car? Either way, they will wake up in the morning and not have a working vehicle."

"It's better this way. It gives us more time to drive before they notice it is missing." Sadar seemed to sense Alicia's frustration because he hurriedly continued. "Besides, this way they will think it is a mechanical failure and send it in for repairs. They can get a rental and continue on their day. It is much easier on them than the vehicle just going missing. Besides, I am careful who I take it from. I try to do the least damage as necessary."

"None of that makes it right," Alicia grumbled.

"No, but I did the best I could in the situation. If you have a better idea, then I am all ears."

# Chapter Fifteen

It was nearing lunchtime when Sadar pulled off the freeway. The exit was seemingly in the middle of nowhere with just a gas station, a diner, and a hotel. Sadar drove into the hotel parking lot and shut off the engine.

The hotel was small, just one story with no more than twenty units. There was a sign, badly in need of a new paint job, that declared it was the Desert Rose Inn. But the inn was surrounded by fields of grass and not a flower in sight.

"Shouldn't we drive further?" Alicia asked.

"Do you have somewhere you want to be?"

"Only as far away as possible from the people who want to kidnap my son."

"Here is just as good as anywhere. As long as they don't know where we are, we will be safe."

Alicia unhooked her and Kenny's seatbelts and slipped out of the car. She saw her bag on the floor of the passenger's seat and reached in to grab it. She moved it to the seat and opened up the small duffle bag to pull out her wallet. She had packed it the day before, right on top of the bag so that it would not be forgotten. Yet it wasn't there. She moved around her clothes, shifting through them. Then she opened the two side pockets, finding them empty.

She looked up to find Sadar watching her from the driver's seat. He reached into his pants pocket and pulled out her wallet. It was a cheap cloth wallet with colorful dots on a dirty white background, but at that moment it was her most prized possession. She ripped open the velcro that held it closed, and looked inside. Her driver's license was missing as well as her bank card. Even her grocery card was gone. All that was left was the thirty-six dollars she had in cash and a selection of coins.

"I didn't want you to use your card and lead them straight to us."

"Did you throw them out on the freeway as well?" Her words came out with a sting. She was so upset that her body started to vibrate with the anger. "I need my cards. How am I supposed to go get us a room without ID and a way to pay?"

"I destroyed your cards. But you don't need to worry.

I'm an elf, remember?" Sadar opened his hand and had a perfectly passable driver's license with his picture and some random name on the ID. "It will be easier if it is just me that goes in, in case something isn't right. Wait here for me, and I will be back shortly."

Alicia stood back up as Sadar got out of the car and began to walk across the empty lot to the entrance. He was an imposing figure, even from the back. He was tall with a muscular build, and he walked with a stride full of self-confidence. He did not, even once, look back to check that they were staying by the car.

"I'm hungry," Kenny said. He was still in the back seat and had opened his backpack. The contents were spilled across the seat, and in his hand was one of his toy cars.

"I know. We should be able to get you some food as soon as we get checked in." Alicia looked at the steering wheel and was not surprised that the keys were not there. She looked around, trying to figure out where they were. There were a few cars across the street at the gas station and restaurant, but none were facing her way so that she could see their license plates.

The gas station was a common chain that had a row of pumps for cars and a few for trucks. The restaurant looked like it was right out of a movie about a small town. There were large white letters on the top of the roof that read May's Diner. There were windows all around the building as well as a red and white awning. There were a handful of cars in the parking lot, but in front were two bicycles, which left Alicia hopeful that there was at least something else near here.

Alicia jumped when Sadar reached out to hand her a key card. She hadn't noticed him walk back towards them.

"Should we put our stuff away and get some food?" Sadar said.

"I think that's a good idea. If we wait too long, Kenny may break down and eat the car." Alicia tried to act casual, and not like she was just plotting how to get as far away from him as possible.

Sadar looked in the door at Kenny who was currently driving his cars around the back seat. "I think we can do better than cars. I bet that restaurant serves burgers."

"Yeah," Kenny cheered, the hunger momentarily forgotten and the adventure remembered.

"Which room is ours?" Alicia asked.

"We're in room 204. I wanted it on the second floor so that I can see out, but it is right by the stairs if we need to leave in a hurry."

"Wait, we're sharing a room?"

"What did you think? We cannot travel as a family and get two separate rooms."

"We aren't a family."

"We are to anyone who sees us. If they see a man and a

woman driving with a child and do not think they are together, that will call undue attention. For better or worse, we are now a couple."

Alicia glared at him and grabbed their bags. She waited for her son to get out of the car and then walked to their room. She opened it up to find two full-size beds, a TV, and a bathroom. Kenny immediately took off his shoes and climbed on the bed furthest from the door.

"Can I sleep here?" Kenny asked.

The bedspread was a faded brown flower pattern that had seen better days. The room looked shabby, with walking paths worn into the carpet. The TV looked similar to the one they had at home, small and boxy. At least the room looked clean. There was no dust, and when she pulled down the bedspread the sheets were white and unstained.

"Absolutely. So, I guess this makes this my bed as well." She put the bags down at the end of the bed and then lay down, glad to be able to stretch out. It may not have been the most glamorous place, but the beds were at least comfortable.

Sadar walked in a few minutes after. He was carrying the car seat and a small bag that Alicia had not noticed anywhere before. He took one look at them stretched out on the bed and put away his bag in a drawer under the TV stand.

"You all look comfortable," Sadar said in disapproval.

Kenny grinned up at Sadar and then moved around,

making the top half of the blankets a jumbled mess.

Alicia grabbed her bag, took out a clean shirt and her brush, and went into the bathroom. She changed her shirt and then combed her hair. She looked at herself in the mirror and felt the panic taking her over. She closed her eyes and took a few deep breaths. She could do this. No matter what, she would keep her son safe. Then she walked out of the bathroom.

"Who's ready for some burgers?"

# Chapter Sixteen

"Here you go." The middle-aged woman placed a kid's hamburger, fries, and chocolate milkshake in front of Kenny. Then she put another hamburger and fries in front of Alicia. Her eyebrows rose as she placed the third hamburger in the middle of the table. "Enjoy your meal."

"Thank you," Alicia managed as she watched the pink polyester uniform skirt stick to the back of the waitress's thighs as she walked away.

Kenny had already taken the ketchup bottle and covered all his food in red. It had moved to his hands and then his face as he began to eat. Alicia remembered to breathe. There was a bathtub back in the hotel, so it didn't matter. If the worst her kid was doing was making a mess and chewing with his mouth full after the last couple of days, then he was doing amazingly well. She took a handful of her fries, added them to his decreasing pile, and was rewarded with an open-mouthed grin full of half-chewed hamburger.

Alicia ate a few of her fries as she glanced at the door. Sadar could be back at any minute. He hadn't told her where he was going, but she guessed that he would be getting rid of the car they had driven and picking up a new one. The thought was unsettling, but more importantly, she wanted to talk to her son before he came back.

"So I was thinking," she said. Kenny glanced at her to let her know he was listening. Then he went back to giving most of his attention to his food. "I'm not sure that we should stay with Sadar for much longer."

"Why?" A fry fell out of Kenny's mouth when he talked, and Alicia could not help but cringe. "Sorry," he said and closed his mouth to finish chewing.

"I am not sure that Sadar is a good person. I don't want him taking you to see this king. I think he may be trying to take you away from me."

"Is the king my dad?" Kenny asked.

"Yes, I think he is."

"You said the king isn't a good person. If he wasn't a good person, then why did you have me with him?"

Alicia knew that it was an innocent question, but it filled her with sorrow. She wasn't sure how to explain how much her son was loved and wanted, and also explain how he came to be. She knew one day she would have to tell him in more detail, but not yet. "That is complicated. Someday I promise I will tell you. But, for now, will you trust me that he is not a good person but that I love you so much and am so lucky that you are my son?"

"Will you trust me, too, Mommy?"

"With what, Kenny?"

"I know you don't like Sadar, and I'm not sure if he is a good person or a bad person. I don't think he knows if he is a good person or a bad person. I think he still has to decide. But I need him right now. I have all this stuff inside me, and I'm scared that I will let it out and hurt everyone. Sadar has it also, but he keeps it under control. I think he can teach me how. Can we stay with him until he teaches me? I promise if he decides to be a bad person to let you know, and we can leave."

Alicia looked at her son and wondered when he got to be so wise. "I'm sorry, Kenny. All that was happening to you, and I had no idea. I kept telling everyone they were making it up, but you needed my help, not my dismissal."

"Even I didn't think I had magical powers. Well, maybe I wondered a little. So, we can stay?"

"We can stay for a bit longer. But not too much longer; I still don't trust him."

Suddenly, Kenny started waving his arm and then screamed, "We are over here," even though only a few other diners were in the restaurant. Sadar could have easily found them, but Kenny probably wanted to make sure she knew to stop talking about him. She had one sharp kid.

# Chapter Seventeen

Alicia could hear them when she stepped out of the shower.

"What do you feel?" Sadar asked.

"There is a place a little ways away. It seems breakable. If I tried to move it, the whole area would crumble."

Alicia had slipped away to freshen up when they had started their training session. She had turned on the shower water and listened at the door, making sure that Sadar would not try to kidnap her son as soon as her back was turned. It made little sense for him to help them escape and then take off with her son, at least until he knew where he was going. Even so, she knew that she did not trust him.

"That is a fault line. Do you know what that is?"

"We learned about them in school. It is a place where two parts of the Earth meet."

Alicia dried off and put on her pajamas, the flannel ones that almost looked like a t-shirt and pants. If they did have to run tonight, she would be able to wear these out in public.

"Very good. You mustn't touch fault lines. You probably wouldn't make too much damage this far away, but then I am surprised you can even feel it. It is best to leave them alone. What else do you feel?"

"I feel the earth whispering."

Alicia stepped out of the bathroom and found them sitting on the floor between the bed and the TV. They covered the walkway, but she could climb onto the corner of the bed without getting in their way. Sadar glanced at her briefly. Kenny sat with his eyes closed, looking like he was far away. Alicia noticed a rock the size of a quarter on the floor between them.

"What do you mean whispering?"

"It is talking, but not in words. It feels like a hum inside of me that makes sense. I make it turn into words."

"What's it saying?" There was a note of concern in Sadar's voice.

"It is telling me that I need to train and control my powers."

"Does it talk to you often?"

"I think it always has talked to me. I didn't realize that not everyone could hear it. But when I realized, I tried not to listen.

That just made it worse. That's when things started to happen. Do you hear it?"

Alicia looked at Sadar, wary of his answer. It didn't seem healthy that her son was hearing voices.

"Everyone feels the earth differently." Sadar spoke to Alicia as much as Kenny. "Illusion magic has always been my strongest magic. But I have heard those that are extraordinarily strong in earth magic talk about the power as though it communicated with them."

"So it is real?" Kenny asked.

"It is real."

Alicia let out a sigh of relief. She sat at the edge of the bed, wanting to watch her son train. How could she have missed this? There were so many little moments that came back to her. Not just the school complaints, but times that Kenny had known when something was going to happen. She had written it off as coincidences. It was the only logical explanation for her. She relied on logic to navigate the world, and it had made her miss what was happening to her son.

She had always had difficulty with abstract concepts. Either magic existed or it did not. Three days ago, she believed it did not exist, but that no longer fit. She now knew that there was magic in the world, and that her son had the ability to use it. She wished she had figured it out sooner, but who would have stopped and thought that it was magic?

"Do you see the rock in front of you? No, don't open your eyes. See it in the same place that you can feel the earth. Do you see it?"

"Yes," Kenny said after a small pause.

"Good, I am going to lift it."

Alicia noticed the rock lift an inch off the hotel floor.

"Did you feel that?" Sadar asked.

"Yes."

"That was just a little power. You would have to be pretty close to feel that. If I used more power, then people could feel it from farther away. In the In-Between, everyone has magic. No one pays attention to people using magic since it is everywhere. However, here no one has magic, at least not strong enough to be felt unless you were right next to them. What do you think would happen if you used a lot of magic?"

"They would feel it?" Kenny sounded uncertain.

"Yes, they would feel it and would know where we are. Normally when we train, we see how strong you can be. For us, we are going to see how controlled you can be. Can you pick up the rock? Make sure not to use too much power."

Alicia saw the rock lift again, except this time it went past an inch and straight up to the ceiling. Sadar looked up, and Alicia was sure that he intervened before it made a hole in the plaster.

"That's enough," Sadar commanded. His face had a flicker of shock. He helped the rock drift slowly back to the ground before he spoke again. "That was a lot of energy you used."

"But I barely used anything. How could anyone feel that?" Kenny pouted.

"It is all right, kiddo. You did well in your first lesson. It is really important not to use any magic until I can teach you what a little magic is. You are already pretty strong, and you haven't even been trained yet. A little for you is a lot for everyone else. Do you understand?"

"Yes, I think I understand," he sighed dramatically.

"Great, now off to bed with you."

Kenny opened his eyes and looked around like he had forgotten that he was sitting in a hotel room.

"I have some pajamas in your bag. Why don't you go change?" Alicia said.

While Kenny took the pajamas from his mom and went into the bathroom, Alicia watched Sadar. He sat unmoving, staring at the rock on the ground. He was completely unreadable to Alicia, and she wasn't sure how to feel about what she just witnessed. She opened her mouth to ask him, but Kenny already came bounding back in the room, dressed in his space pajamas. He raced over to the bed and jumped on it.

"I did, I did," he squealed.

"I'm not so sure. You are going to have to brush them extra good in the morning. How are we supposed to find all the blankets now that you have scattered them all over?"

"I guess I could sleep on the other bed."

"Ha, you are not going to destroy yet another bed." Alicia bent over him and began to tickle him. "My son, the destroyer of beds." She reached over and gathered the blankets as best she could and tucked them around him. Then she leaned down and kissed his forehead. "Sleep tight, my little man."

He reached out and hugged her and then turned over to go to sleep. She had tucked him in this way ever since he was little. She knew he didn't need it as much as she did, but she appreciated that he still let her do it.

# Chapter Eighteen

Alicia had lain down next to Kenny until he had fallen asleep. Once Alicia was sure that he was out, she slid out of bed and went to pack up their bags. If something happened in the night, she wanted to be ready to leave. Getting their items together was a way, even if it was a small one, of controlling an out-of-control situation.

Sadar was sitting at the hotel table, hunched over a journal. Now and then, he would write something down. Most of the time, he stared off at the wall. Alicia had tried to catch a glimpse of the journal earlier, but it was not written in English.

"You have a great kid." Alicia was startled when Sadar had spoken.

"Yes, he is pretty amazing."

"Most people wouldn't have kept him."

Anger flared through Alicia at the comment, so she took a moment to move the bags at the end of the bed and then sat down next to her son before facing Sadar. "I don't know what most people would have done. There was no choice for me but to keep him. He wasn't responsible for what happened."

"He looks so much like him."

"He is not him. My son does not deserve the consequences of other men's actions. He is innocent in all of this. It sounds like you need to work on your conscience."

"What do you mean? I didn't do anything." Sadar closed his journal and stood up from the table. He looked around the small room like he was trying to find somewhere else to go. When he did not find a place, he stayed standing next to the chair.

"You were there. You watched the king take me outside. You knew what was going to happen, and you did nothing." She tried to keep her voice down. Kenny was sleeping right next to her, and she did not want to wake him. He did not need to hear this conversation, but she needed to have it. She had been traveling all day with this man who had let her get raped, and she didn't think she could go another hour without bursting from the pain.

"I don't remember."

"Bullshit. There is no way you don't remember what

happened to me."

"You don't understand. I don't remember you. There were so many that I stopped seeing the faces."

The comment hit Alicia as sharp as a physical blow. Anger and humiliation flooded through her. "Then you are just as much of a monster as he is."

"I had no choice." Sadar moved towards her, his hands as aggressive as his voice.

There was a time when Alicia would have cowered under that movement. She was so sick of being scared. So, she stood up, making herself as big as possible, letting him know that she wasn't going to back down. "What would have happened?"

"I would have died. If I had moved against the king, if I had made a move to stop him, I would have forsworn the oath given to me as an infant, and I would have died." As he said this, Sadar moved back and sat back in the chair. His hands clenched in fists at his side, but his gaze never left her. It seemed to Alicia like he was trying to convince her to absolve him of his part, or worse: that he honestly did not think that he played a role at all. Alicia had no intention of letting him off that easily.

"Did this oath forbid you from telling him that he was an asshole and a rapist? Did it make you quiet as you watched him walk off with me?"

"No."

"Then I guess you are a monster."

"If you believe that, then maybe you should just go."

"You have value to my son at the moment. He needs you to teach him, so I will let you teach him. But do not make the mistake of thinking that I trust you. I know that when push comes to shove that you will pick the king over my son. So, the only question is, why are you not with him right now?"

"You are right. I don't know where he is. His behavior had been growing more erratic until he left, taking only those that he trusted. He didn't take me—he didn't even tell me of his fear that sent him into hiding. I have devoted my life to protecting him, and I cannot do that if I am not by his side. I was looking for him, to help keep him safe, when I heard about Kenny."

Saying this seemed to break Sadar. It was the first time his face had made any expression. He stood up and walked to the hotel room door. He paused with his hand on the door. "I won't hurt your son. You can believe that."

"Why should I trust you? The only reason you saved us was to take my son to your king. Do you plan to trade him to get back into his good graces? Are we pawns to you?"

"My oath isn't to the king. My oath is to the royal line. Your son is part of that line. He and the king are all that are left. I will do everything in my power to make sure that your son stays safe."

With that, Sadar opened the door and left. Alicia stood up and went and locked the deadbolt. Then she closed the safety latch on the top of the door. She hoped that would at least give her notice when he came back in.

She lay down next to her son, leaving the other bed free. She drifted into a half-sleep, waiting for Sadar to come back, waiting to have to go and unlock the door to let him in. Eventually, she must have drifted off completely. When she woke, it was still early in the morning, but Sadar had not been back.

# Chapter Nineteen

Alicia watched as the sun started to shine through the hotel curtains. She glanced at the empty second bed and their packed bags on the chair. The conversation from the night before had been replaying through her head nonstop. She looked at her son, still sleeping peacefully, and felt a pang of jealousy.

She took stock of what she knew. Her son could do magic. Sadar could help her son with his magic. Sadar himself was uncertain. She believed that he would protect her son as he saw fit. But she also knew that she was a horrible judge of people. His own track record was not very positive. Her son had managed before Sadar had shown up, and that was before she knew about his gifts. They would leave.

Once the decision was made, the anxiety decreased to a dull hum in the background. Now she could focus on practical matters. She got dressed and then woke up her son to do the same. Then she made sure they had picked up everything and grabbed their bags. She flung her duffle bag over her shoulder so the strap bit into her chest. Then she scraped her son's backpack on her back.

They paused at the door. She glanced through the peephole, but it did not show much more than the railing outside the door. Some part of her expected Sadar to be waiting for them on the other side, but either way, she knew they had to face it. So, they walked out and let the hotel door click behind them.

There were a few more cars in the parking lot, although it was still less than half full. The only people outside were a couple that were loading up their car. The car they had arrived in was not in the lot, but she did a quick glance in each one and let out a small sigh of relief when they were all empty.

"I'm hungry," Kenny said, still half-asleep.

"Let's go over to the gas station and pick up something for breakfast."

"But I'm so hungry. Can we get pancakes? Can we get some cereal? Can I have both?" He looked up with pleading eyes.

It was then that Alicia really thought about how much Kenny had been eating. He had always preferred picking at his food more than eating it, although some of it made it in his mouth eventually. But the last few days he had eaten everything put in front of him and most of her food as well. It was horrible timing for him to start to develop an appetite. "All right, we can go to the diner and see what they have."

The street between the hotel and the diner was a two-lane road. They waited for a car driving to the freeway from the gas station and then crossed. Alicia's heart started to race as they got closer, and she started to scan the booths through the window. There were a few families sitting in booths and a couple of men sitting up at the counter. None of them were Sadar.

A bell jingled as they entered the door, and a waitress greeted them. It was a different woman from the night before, although it was hard to be sure with the uniforms. "Go ahead and sit down anywhere. I'll be with you shortly."

"Is there any chance we can order food to go?" Alicia asked.

"Sure, here is the menu." She placed it up on the counter by the register. Alicia grabbed it and helped Kenny to sit up in one of the stools. She gratefully put the bags on the floor as she opened the menu. She became very aware of their situation when she thought back to the amount of money she had on hand.

"Excuse me," Alicia said when the waitress, Mabel according to her name tag, went to refill the men's coffees. She waited until Mabel was done and looking at her before continuing. "Is there a phone booth anywhere near here?"

"I haven't seen a working phone booth in years," Mabel said

with a chuckle. "Don't you have a cell phone?"

"It broke. I was just trying to get ahold of someone that could help us."

Mabel took a long look at her son and then down to the floor at their bags. "If you know the number, I can let you use the restaurant's phone."

"I don't," Alicia sighed. "It was saved in my phone. You wouldn't by chance have a computer? I could look it up."

"I'm sorry. I don't have much use for a computer here. There is one in town in the library though."

Alicia brightened at the answer. "Oh, that would be perfect. Can you tell me which way it is?"

"It is just down the freeway about ten miles. You can take the frontage road straight there. Do you have a way to get there?"

Alicia thought about asking if there was a riding service available, and then remembered how much money she had. Maybe she could have asked for a ride, but her mind kept reminding her that she didn't want to stand out any more than they already did. So, she lied. "Yes, I have a car over at the hotel. I just didn't want to leave the bags in there to get stolen."

The waitress paused, staring them over, and then shrugged and moved off to refill more coffee cups. Alicia looked through the menu. There was not much they could eat while walking, and the prices were a lot higher than she liked. When the waitress walked back over, she finally ordered two breakfast sandwiches and a side of pancakes. Alicia handed over more than half of their money, but they just had to get to the next town. Somehow, she would find help.

Alicia looked for Sadar, expecting him to turn up at any moment. Every time she looked out the window and didn't see him, she felt a sense of relief, but it was short-lived. She immediately started wondering where he was. Part of her hoped that he had left them. Then she wouldn't have to worry about trying to get away from him. A smaller part of her wasn't happy at that idea. That part she didn't understand, so she decided she would try and figure it out later.

She decided to chance the short walk to the gas station while their food was cooking, and she spent the rest of the money on water bottles, snacks, and gas station sandwiches. When they returned to the diner, their food was packed up in environmentally unfriendly Styrofoam containers.

"Can we eat now?" Kenny asked as they walked out of the dinner.

Alicia did another glance around to make sure Sadar was not nearby. In all, they had been up for about an hour, and she did not want to push their luck on him returning. She really wanted to get on their way, but Kenny's face was puffed up with frustration. It looked like he was about to break into a tantrum.

"How about I cut your sandwich up and you can eat part of it while we are walking? If we find a good place to stop, we can sit down and eat it there, like a picnic." The frontage road ran alongside the freeway. There was just a field of browning grass between it and the diner. From the back of the parking lot, Alicia found a path that was worn down with bike and footprints. She started towards it, with Kenny at her side, while she opened up the container and tried to cut one of the breakfast sandwiches with a little plastic knife.

"Mommy, where is Sadar?" Kenny asked.

"I don't know," Alicia said. "We are going to go for a walk into the town and find a phone so we can call Master Kang. We can see if he can come and pick us up."

Kenny looked up at her in confusion. "But if we go back, won't the bad men get us?"

"What bad men?"

"The ones at the house that were screaming. Sadar can help protect us from them."

Alicia handed him the sandwich wrapped up in a napkin to help keep it together. Even cut up, it was large with scrambled eggs, ham, and cheese trying to escape in his hands. She hoped it would fill him up for a bit.

"I think we are both pretty strong, maybe we can protect ourselves for a bit. I saw your flying sidekick in your last class. It was pretty amazing."

Kenny let out a laugh with bits of eggs falling out of his mouth. "It was pretty cool. But Sadar has magic. He hasn't finished teaching me yet."

"I know kiddo, but I'm not sure Sadar is the best person to be around. Wouldn't you like to see Master Kang again?"

The path curved as it got closer to the road. There was a worn-down section that ran next to the road. It would come and go, but it was enough that they could follow it. The area was flat with the freeway running on one side and more grass on the other. Alicia was afraid it would be too easy to see from them the town, so she kept them walking handing Kenny quarters of sandwiches until he had eaten them both.

"Is it much longer?" Kenny asked. The sun had started rising in the sky, shining down on them fully.

"We still have a long way to walk. Do you want to take a rest?"

They had been walking for over an hour, and Alicia knew they were probably not even halfway to the town. They were still following the frontage road, walking along-side it, with the freeway racing on one side and fields on the other. The only change was a wire fence that now separated the road from the field. The road was quiet; only a few cars had driven past them since they had started walking. Each time she heard one approaching, they had moved off the side of the road and kneeled down waiting until it had passed, although there really wasn't much that would hide them.

"Yes, please," Kenny said as he dropped directly to the ground.

"Let's at least get off the road. There is some shade there." Alicia pointed a little further up on the side of the road nearest the freeway where there was a tree. Kenny sighed and got back to his feet. He stomped forward like each step was a personal affront. When he reached the tree, he dropped again.

"Do you want something to eat?" Alicia put the bags down on the ground and sat on top of her duffle bag, her mind busy contemplating all the bugs that were crawling around everywhere.

"I'm too tired to eat." Kenny had already started playing with the grass around him, incapable of sitting still. This lasted a few minutes before he opened the backpack and pulled out a bag of chips.

Alicia tried to use the time to come up with an idea. She did not know if they would be able to get home without her wallet. They didn't even have enough money to get a hotel for the night.

"I don't like it out here," Kenny said.

Alicia noticed that he had found some rocks hidden in the grass and had started to stack them up like blocks. None of the stones were smooth, and yet he had them all balanced without being wobbly. She was sure that he had to be using his magic somehow.

"It is OK. You know I won't let anything happen to you. We

are a team, right?"

Kenny nodded his head in agreement, but the movement was not very enthusiastic.

"Here, have some water." Alicia reached in the backpack and pulled out one of the bottles.

Kenny took the bottle and managed a few swallows before handing it back. Then he gave another deep sigh.

"Do we have to keep walking?"

"We do unless you want to spend the night out here."

Kenny's eyes lit up, then he looked around at the overgrown grass and the freeway off in the distance. There was nothing but two roads, one empty and the other close enough to see the image of the speeding cars. "OK, I'm ready." He got up, and they continued on their way.

They had only walked another ten minutes before Alicia watched Kenny begin to glance around. He even stopped walking ahead and grabbed her hand.

"I want to go back," he finally said.

"It isn't safe," Alicia answered him. "We are going to go find somewhere safe."

Alicia started to notice a few small rocks rising off the ground. She looked around in shock while more began to rise off the ground.

"Are you doing that?"

"Doing what?"

"You know everything is going to be OK. It is still early, and we will get to the town and find a place to stay the night. Then we will find a way to get to the Grand Canyon. Maybe we can even go camping there."

She knew Kenny wasn't listening to her. Alicia looked around in shock as rocks began to float up from the ground, hovering around them until there wasn't a rock anywhere in one hundred feet that wasn't floating a foot off the ground. She stood momentarily frozen before she shook herself out of it. "Kenny." She went down on her knees and looked at her son. "I need you to take a deep breath. Do you remember the practice that Sadar taught you?"

"Yes," he whispered. His eyes were open wide, shimmering like amber, and beads of sweat started to form around his chestnut hair. His hands were clenched at the side of his thin frame. He looked so small and fragile, but Alicia noticed that there was now a layer of dirt and rocks that rose just above his sitting frame.

"Close your eyes, and remember what he told you."

Kenny closed his eyes, his hands now in tight fists at his side.

"Deep breath, you need to calm down. You control your powers. They do not control you."

Except that Alicia could see that it was not helping. Small dust tornados had started to form around them. She could see six of them swirling around.

"It isn't working," Kenny said. "I don't... it's too much."

Tears fell down his face, and the dust tornados grew around them until each of them were over a foot wide.

"Kenny Bryant Henry, everything is going to be just fine. You've got this. Just let the rocks go." Her voice came out with a faked confidence. Her own heart was beating wildly as she looked around, trying to come up with a way to control this situation. The area was empty, the cars on the freeway driving too fast and too far above the ground to notice them. They were on their own, so she knew she had better come up with something.

Then the tornados started heading their way, coalescing on them, and panic filled Alicia. She picked up her son and held him in her arms, trying to do her best to shield him as they were pelted from all sides by flying rocks and dirt.

The impacts started slowly at first, just the feeling of sand brushing against the skin like tiny pinpricks. Then it quickly picked up speed and intensity. The dust began to clog her mouth and nose, making it difficult to breathe. Then the dust turned to pebbles that began to pound into her back and sides until she collapsed from the pain, her body still wrapped around her son. Her skin was on fire, but the impacts kept coming until it was all she could think about.

"It's OK. You are safe. I am right here. You need to let the rocks down. Do you remember how Sadar taught you to let everything go?" She tried speaking over the whooping of the rocks.

"No." His voice moved from whimpers to a scream. He threw his hands over his ears, pushing his head further into her body. "I can't. I can't. I can't." He started to yell, the words lost in her shirt.

She did not notice the arms wrapping around her at first, helping to shelter her son. When they tried to pull him from her, she held on tighter, protecting her son.

"Kenny, do you hear me? You need to let it go. Let me help you." Sadar stopped trying to pull Kenny away and instead reached into Alicia's grasp until he found Kenny's shoulder, and all around them, the dust and rocks fell instantly to the ground.

"What did you do?" Alicia yelled as she backed away, her son still in her arms.

"I helped him release it." He took a step back away from them, his hands held where they could be seen. "That is all I did. I just helped him to let it go."

Alicia stopped when her back hit the tree. Kenny had wrapped his arms around her neck and his legs around her waist, although he was too big for it to not be awkward. Alicia did her best to hold him as he cried, his head buried in her chest.

"What was this?" she asked. "How could he do something like this now?"

"It was always in him. It always would have come out, but after working with him, he learned how to access his magic better. He still hasn't learned control. I can help him if it gets out of control, but for now we need to go."

"No." Alicia shook her head weakly. The adrenaline was starting to leave her system and pain was racing all over her body. "We are not going with you. We are going to town, and I am calling a friend to come and pick us up."

"If you do that, whoever is after you will find you. If they are anywhere within ten miles of here, then they will have felt that display of magic. Even if they are not, someone else could have seen it. We need to get out of here now."

Alicia looked around. The ground was covered in a thick layer of dirt that had pushed down the grass. The asphalt was no longer visible on the road. It spanned at least fifty feet in either direction of them. Then she looked at Sadar. He stood there patiently, waiting for her to make her decision, even though there really was only one decision to make, at least if she wanted to keep her son safe.

"We will come with you, but only if you keep teaching my son."

# Chapter Twenty

"Do you think that I could lift a rock that is bigger than this car?" Kenny asked. He was riding in the back seat of a blue hatchback sedan. Alicia sat next to him.

"Yeah, I bet you could," Sadar muttered.

"Do you think that I could lift a house?"

"I don't think so. Houses are not made out of rocks."

"Some of them are. I can feel some of the houses more than others." They were back on the freeway, heading towards the west coast, trying to get as far from Kenny's outburst as possible.

"You can feel the houses?" Sadar asked. He looked at Kenny in the rearview mirror, trying to gauge if he was exaggerating or not.

"Yes, can't you?"

"Yes, I guess I could if I was close enough." Sadar turned his head back to glance at Alicia, looking concerned. "Unfortunately, the houses are a bit too far away for me."

After Sadar had helped Kenny get back under control, he had rushed them to the car and taken off. They were all silent, the anxiety building as Sadar drove as fast as he could away from the area. He slowed down to near the speed limit after a few miles, but the anxiety did not decrease. It was Kenny who first broke the silence. He spoke quietly at first, but when Sadar's grunts turned into words, he talked like the event was one grand adventure that was now over.

Each time the car rocked, pain shot through Alicia's body. Bruises had already started to sprout up on her arms, turning them a dull red. She had used her back to shield most of her body. She sat rigid in the back seat, trying to minimize jostling. Sadar had not relaxed either. His body was stiff, and his face seemed locked in stoic concern.

"Do you think I could lift the Grand Canyon? Are we going to the Grand Canyon?"

"I don't think lifting the Grand Canyon would be such a great idea," Alicia said.

"Why?"

"Well, if you lifted it, when it came back down, it would smash everywhere, and then the canyon would be filled with rocks. There wouldn't be a Grand Canyon anymore."

"Oh, right." Kenny stared out the window, lost in thought. Alicia imagined him dreaming of the Grand Canyon. She hoped that dream did not involve him plotting on how to lift it. Alicia wasn't sure he had that much power. All she knew was that her son was capable of a lot more than Sadar had thought that he was, and what he could do had him concerned.

"Do all elves have earth magic?" Kenny asked, still staring out the window.

"No, all elves have magic. Some have earth magic, but not all of them."

"What other kinds of magic are there?"

"All elves have at least one of the three types of elven magic, although some are so weak that they will never be able to do much with their magic. Rarely do elves have two types of magic."

"Some elves have three types," Kenny interrupted, trying to match Sadar's lecturing tone.

"Some elves have all three types, but only elves that are of the royal line. Even then, most still have only two types."

"I'm of the royal line. This is why I can have all three types."

"Yes, but your other magic is not as strong as your earth magic," Sadar said.

"Why?"

"Your earth magic is pretty strong. You can feel the houses

that are pretty far away."

"My other types of magic could be that strong."

"Do you think that they are?"

"How would I know?" Kenny asked. "I didn't know feeling houses meant I am strong."

Alicia couldn't help but chuckle at her son. Sadar shifted in the driver's seat but otherwise ignored her.

"You said that you did illusions at school."

"Yes, do you want to see my dragon? You already saw healing when I healed your arm. Oh," Kenny turned and looked at his mother. "I'm sorry, I forgot." He reached out his hand and laid it on her arm.

Alicia's body started to hum, like being filled with an energetic bright light. She felt better, like she had just lay down and taken a long nap. The pain had taken up so much of her awareness that its sudden disappearance was shocking.

"Is that better?" Kenny asked, taking away his arm and yawning.

Alicia held up her arms. The bruising was gone. All that was left was the dirt and the dried blood.

"Are you OK?" she asked.

"Yes, just a little tired. But I could still show you my dragon if you want."

"How about later? You have already done a lot of magic today."

Alicia glanced at Sadar for the first time since they had entered the car. He looked back at her, concern in his eyes. Her son had done magic. Could they could find them again?

"Thanks for healing me. I feel much better, but you should probably not do magic anymore."

"Oh, the bad guys." His eyes grew big, and he looked at both adults with concern. "I'm sorry, I forgot." Alicia reached over and moved the ends of his brown hair out of his eyes and rubbed her palm over his dimpled cheek.

"I think it is good you healed your mom," Sadar said, keeping his gaze on the road. "I bet she feels much better now. Don't worry about the bad guys. I will stop them from following us. I think it is probably best that you take a nap now."

"OK." Kenny yawned again and then laid his head on Alicia's arm. He was asleep instantly.

"When he healed you in the bathroom," Alicia said, "he was so tired he fell. He has used magic twice in the last hour, and he is just now taking a nap."

"Magic is like anything. The more you practice, the better you become."

"That seems like a big increase."

"It is, but he is also a prince."

"Even you don't seem convinced by that." Alicia looked out the window watching the cars driving next to them on the freeway. In front of them was a family with their SUV packed with suitcases. She could see a teenager, their phone reflecting back the noon-day sun. They took out their earbud to talk to someone on the seat beside them that Alicia could not see, then they put it back in, their concentration back on their phone. Alicia looked down at the top of her son's head and leaned over to plant a kiss on top.

"He is the first halfling." Sadar's voice broke into her reflection. "I am surprised he has magic at all since he is part human. His control is lacking, but his strength is astonishing."

"If there has never been a human elf before, then how would you know?"

"Humans cannot do magic, not compared to elves. It seems combining the two bloodlines together has given him more magical strength. I wish I could really test him to really understand his limit."

Alicia watched Sadar as he spoke. She felt like she had begun to see the subtle changes in his face as he went from confusion to almost fascination. Looking at him, she supposed others would find him attractive. He had a strong jaw and symmetrical face that others enjoyed, but always made Alicia nervous. His silver hair next to his olive skin gave him a sense of exoticness.

"What do we do? How are we going to keep my son safe?"

"He has to go see the king. The king will be able to give him tutors and guards."

"No. You will not take my son to see that monster. You said you would keep my son safe. There must be a different solution."

# Chapter Twenty-One

The car jolted as it navigated the one-way dirt road. They were now driving in an SUV that Sadar had acquired during their stop for a late lunch. Yet the larger frame did not seem to do anything to help them over the uneven road full of large rocks and potholes.

They had driven off the freeway onto a highway an hour ago. Sadar had been tightlipped about where they were going. Alicia held onto hope that he had come up with a safe place for them to hide until they could work out what to do. When they turned off the paved road onto the dirt road, the late afternoon sun became hidden behind the trees that overtook them, and the car was enshrouded in shadows.

"What are we doing out here?" Alicia demanded. The car bounced, causing them to rocket up towards the roof. Alicia, for the third time in the last five minutes, checked to make sure that Kenny was safely buckled in his seat. "Tell me where we are going."

The car slowed, and Sadar twisted back in his seat to look at Alicia, his face tight as he spoke. "This is not the easiest road to drive on. Would you please let me focus on driving so that nothing happens to either of you?" Then he turned around and put all his focus on the road in front of him.

Alicia sat, quiet. It had been a reasonable request, one she had to have made many times while she was behind the wheel as well. But the way he spoke the words sent a shiver down her spine. The atmosphere didn't help either. The trees had grown over the road, so their limbs now hit the roof. The car echoed with the pattering of their light touches, offset by the high-pitched screech of a branch desperate to tear through.

Kenny's slim arms wrapped around Alicia's arm, holding her in a death grip. His head tilted away from her, so all she could see was the mop of his hair as he looked out the window watching the trees crawl past them.

They broke free from the forest, the trees releasing them with a suddenness that was startling. Before them was a small brown house, wrapped around by a porch with sections of railings that were missing. The windows were caked in dirt so thick that you couldn't see through them. The roof was in disrepair with a giant hole where a tree limb was growing through it.

"What are we doing here?" Alicia asked in confusion.

"I am hoping to talk to someone that can help us."

"You can't be serious," Alicia said. "No one could possibly live in that."

"Not everything is as it appears." Sadar turned off the car, cutting off the headlights as he opened his door. "I think it is best that you both wait in the car."

"I don't want to stay here," Kenny said, his voice quivering. He was still clinging to his mother, his brown eyes lit up with fear. The area around the house was surrounded by trees so high that it was hard to see the sky above. What light of the day remained was no longer visible to them, and with the headlights off there was very little light to see by.

"I think we should go in with you," Alicia said, her voice wavering.

Sadar looked at them huddled in the back seat and then grunted "Fine," before he got out of the car, slamming his door behind him.

Alicia hurried and unbuckled herself and Kenny. She grabbed her son's hand and got out of the car, hurrying to catch up to Sadar. They had reached him just as he was knocking on the door. The knock gave back a deep solid thunk that echoed in the silence. It was at odds with the door, which looked to be made of wood so rotten it was ready to collapse.

They waited in the near dark for an answer that didn't come.

"Are you sure there is someone here?" Alicia asked.

As she spoke, the door opened as if on its own. Sadar pushed it open further and walked inside. Alicia followed, Kenny still in her arms, and then stopped in awe. The door revealed a large living room with vaulted ceilings. There was a large wraparound couch in the middle of the floor with plenty of walking room between it and the walls, littered with bookshelves and a small piano. On the far side of the couch there was a reclining chair next to a fireplace with a full blaze. In the chair there was an older man, a book held firmly in his slender bronzed hands. He looked at them from behind a set of glasses that did nothing to hide his penetrating glaze.

"Why are you here?" His voice was deep and loud, filling up the room.

"I tried to get ahold of you," Sadar said.

The man looked at Alicia, her mouth opened in shock as she realized that there were rooms connecting from this main room. "How could all this fit?"

"Why have you brought a human into my house?" His gaze slid off of Alicia and onto the boy in her arms. The book dropped from his hand, and he half rose from the chair. "What is this?" he demanded.

"I need to find the King. I know you are aware of where he

is."

"I don't have dealings with him," the man said.

At the same time, Alicia spoke, "I told you we are not going to him." Her attention was now completely focused on the conversation.

"The human has more sense than you do." He had managed to make it to his feet and grabbed a cane propped up on the chair arm. He walked slowly but steadily towards them until he stopped a foot away from Kenny. He reached his hand up as if he were going to touch the child, and then stopped in midair. "Who is he?"

"We need to find the king. Tell us where he is." For once, Sadar's voice did not sound certain, and Alicia looked at him in concern. Sadar began to move between them and the man, pushing them towards the door.

"You could stay here," the man said. "The house is hidden behind walls of illusions. They would never be able to find you. I could help the child." The man began to leer as he spoke, his voice full of possessiveness.

"If there is magic, they will be able to sense it." The words fumbled from Alicia as she began to slowly move back towards the door. One hand supported her son who clung to her. The other reached behind her, searching for the doorknob.

"Have you taught them nothing?" The man let out a cackle, a sound that ripped through her soul. A sound no human could make. "You would be safe here from the king. I have enough power to mask this child so they wouldn't sense him, more than what this blood bound has managed. When the king finds you, there is no way he will let that child live. He looks too much like him to not be his blood, and all his relatives have met untimely accidents in the last few years."

Alicia's hand wrapped around the doorknob as she opened it. Sadar blocked their way from the old man as they slipped out the door. "What are you talking about?" she heard Sadar say before the door closed again and his words were cut off.

Alicia sprinted towards the car. She opened the driver's door and put down her son. "Get in your seat" she commanded. She waited just long enough for him to climb into the back seat before she was in the driver's seat, throwing on her seatbelt and closing the door. She didn't even have time to be relieved when she found the keys in the ignition. She started the car, trying to turn the car around fast enough to be gone before the men inside could notice.

"Are you clicked?" she asked her son.

"I'm clicked," he said.

She sped up, going down the dirt road as fast as she could without blowing out a tire. Their bodies danced in the seats, but it still seemed too slow. She kept glancing in the rearview mirror, expecting to see Sadar looming above them. She didn't remember letting out a breath until they made it back out to the paved road, and then she drove for all the car was worth.

# Chapter Twenty-Two

Night had completely fallen shortly after they had hit a highway. Alicia had made a random turn and started driving. The area was secluded with only their headlights to light up the road. She was so focused on trying to figure out where they were and where they should go that she didn't notice the changes at first.

It started small. The chair that she was sitting in was not as comfortable as she remembered. She pushed it off as exhaustion. Then she glanced back at her son, still wide awake and staring out the window, and noticed that the seat was a faded blue color. She could have sworn it had been a light brown.

She kept driving, looking for signs to help point her way. The small highway led to a larger four-lane road, and she happily turned onto it, hoping that it would lead her somewhere with people. The night seemed to be playing with her mind.

Not long on the new road, they passed houses pushed far back on long driveways. The light was too far away to do more than provide reassurance as she drove, using the headlights to look for creatures on the side of the road.

When the car gave a sudden lurch, they both jumped in their seats. The noise was louder in the silence.

"What's that, Mommy?" Kenny asked.

Alicia brought her attention from the road back to the car. Around her the car had shifted. The inside looked like a beat-up sedan with faded blue interior. The passenger seat had morphed from a brown faux leather to a blue cloth worn completely away in some sections. Her son was no longer completely buckled into a strap that was adjusted across his shoulder. Now, there was just a buckle over his lap. The dashboard was a cracked dark blue plastic with a large radio console with a manual radio selector and a tape player. Even the exterior of the car had changed. They were no longer driving in an SUV. The car was long, with a light blue hood that stretched out in front of them. The trunk had morphed from a hatchback to a large compartment off their back end.

"I don't understand," Alicia started. She looked around again as if expecting it to look completely different again. "Kenny... the car... do you see..." She didn't know how to finish.

"It changed," Kenny said. "It's like the house."

The house that had looked abandoned from the outside but inviting inside. Except, now their car had morphed from something safe and modern to an ancient artifact. As if sensing her thoughts, the car sputtered and then caught again.

On the side of the road, Alicia caught a sign—the ones they lay out to announce cities. She hadn't caught the name, but they were only thirteen miles away. So, she kept driving.

Alicia thought back to all the times that Sadar had come back with a different car. She had thought that he was stealing them a new one, but maybe he was just changing the way this one looked. He had said he took a car from someone who wouldn't miss it. She had assumed he meant they were financially well off, but maybe he had meant that one no one would want, a car that barely ran.

"Did you know it was an illusion?" Alicia asked. "Could you sense it?" When he didn't answer, she looked back at him. His eyes were filled with tears and his shoulders were slumped. "It's OK. I didn't know either."

They drove on for another few minutes before the car caught again. Alicia looked forward, willing the city to come into view.

"If Sadar could make the car move with illusion, then maybe you could as well? We just need to make it to the next city."

"You told me not to do magic. I don't want the bad men to come."

"I think maybe we left the bad men back in the house. If you couldn't sense the magic to illusion the car, then maybe others can't sense it either. We don't have far to go."

Alicia watched in the rearview mirror, her attention split between the road and her son. Kenny reached his hand out over his car seat and put it on the bench. Around them the car began to shift from the broken-down blue beast back into the light brown SUV they had been riding in most of the day. Alicia let out a small sigh.

"Way to go buddy. Thank you." But as soon as she spoke, the car made a loud knocking sound followed by another sputtering sound. Alicia looked back at Kenny in confusion, but he sat there, tears forming in his eyes.

"I'm sorry. I tried to make it look right," he said.

"It's OK, Kenny. You did good. We are almost there." She realized her mistake as soon has he had spoken. How could he illusion a functioning engine when he probably had no idea what one even looked like?

They continued forward, pushing the car for all it was worth, while it continued sputtering and knocking. When it finally died, Alicia had just enough momentum to steer it to the edge of the road. She tried starting it again and again, but the engine didn't even pretend to turn over. She shut off the headlights and sat back, uncertain what to do. But as she looked forward, she saw the outline of the lights. They were just outside of the city.

# Chapter Twenty-Three

Kenny clung to her hand as they walked off the road. There was a four-foot strip between the road and a field of long grass. The side had been mowed enough that the grass did not go above their shoes. They had made the most of the walk in the dark, only receiving light when a car drove up towards them, its headlights flooding the area, before rushing away again. They probably had not been walking all that long, but it had already been a long day, and they were both tired. The bag's straps were digging into her shoulders. As much as she wanted to collapse and give up, she had to keep up her son's morale as well. So, they sang songs as they walked. The silly tunes did nothing to take away her anxiety.

On the outskirts of town there were shops closed for the night, but ahead of them was a shopping center, still awash in light. The bright neon sign of a fast-food restaurant beckoned to them. When they finally reached the restaurant, Alicia dropped their bags into a booth with a sigh. Kenny climbed up on the bench with them, laying his head down and closing his eyes. Alicia dug in her pocket and pulled out the money they had left. There were only a few dollar bills and a small collection of coins. It would have to do.

The woman behind the counter seemed to be in her mid-forties. She had brown hair tied up in a bun, with strands of hair falling out after a long shift. She looked tired, but she also looked friendly, and Alicia hoped that she would help them.

"Can I have a hamburger kid's meal please?"

"Will there be anything else?" The woman's voice had a slight twang to it, more nasally than a Southern accent.

"Can I have a glass of water please?"

"I have to charge you ten cents for the cup."

Alicia looked at their money again, making sure there was enough before nodding in acceptance. As she handed over their last bit of funds, she asked, "Is there anywhere around where I could access the internet? I need to find a phone number to call someone."

"Are you driving through?" the woman asked.

"Yes, our car broke down outside of town. I just need to call someone to help us."

The woman looked at her and then to her son asleep on the bench. "You don't have a way to call anyone?"

"No, he threw my phone out the window." She was so tired it took her a second to realize the truth slipping out of her mouth. "I mean… I lost my phone while we were driving." But the cover-up sounded fake even to her.

"Where is he?" the woman asked.

"We left him, when we stopped. I took the car with my son. But the car was old, and it broke down. We walked the rest of the way into town." Alicia clamped her mouth shut. She was too tired to lie, so she knew she shouldn't speak at all.

"There is a hotel up the street. It isn't the prettiest place, but it is clean. My cousin runs the place, and I am sure they could find a room for you."

"Thank you," she managed, "but that's all that I had."

The woman, Jennie, by her name tag, nodded like this was to be expected. "If they control the money, they control you. Don't you worry, none. My neighbor's son works for a driving company. It's this app thing, but I'm sure I can call him and get you to pick you up. I'll call my cousin, too. He'll put you up for the night and help you get ahold of family tomorrow. You can both use a rest."

Alicia didn't answer at first. She wasn't sure what to say. Finally, she managed, "Are you sure it's OK?"

"Don't you worry none, I will take care of it. I'll give them a call and sort the whole thing out. My cousin is a good man, he will help. And my neighbor's kid, well he isn't the fastest, so I better call him now. It will give you plenty of time to eat your food while you are waiting for him."

Alicia thanked her and walked back to the table with Kenny. She had barely sat down before the same women brought out the food. Next to the happy meal was another burger and fries. Alicia looked up at the women, her mouth unsteady and words unable to come out.

"It's OK. There were extra, anyway. Get some food in you, it looks like you need it."

Kenny had woken up when the food arrived. He tore into his kid's meal and went straight for the toy. It was a little action figure that stretched when pulled as he shoveled down his food. It seemed like ages since Kenny was able to act like a kid, even if it had only been a few days. She watched as he walked the little figure over the table. He was just eight years old and was having to deal with assassination attempts and magic powers. She stared at him, trying to figure out how she would give him back his childhood. Then she took a deep breath and pulled herself together.

It wasn't long before Kenny had finished his food. Alicia had already decided to split her own meal in half. She put half in front of him and finally began to eat her own.

"Thanks," he said. His giant smile was contagious, and she relaxed a little.

When the door opened, Alicia looked up, wondering if it was the neighbor's kid who was coming to drive them to the hotel. Instead, there were two men dressed in jeans and t-shirts. They both had brown hair and light skin that had seen a lot of sun. They looked enough alike that were most likely related. Alicia was about to turn her attention back to her food when they looked directly at their table and then did a broad sweep of the restaurant. They started whispering to each other and then finally went and ordered some food.

"Have you used your powers at all?" Alicia asked.

"No, not since the car."

*Could illusions be sensed or couldn't they?* The rules of magic did not make sense.

"Are those guys human or elves?" Alicia asked Kenny.

He stopped eating, and his face scrunched up in concentration. "They are human."

"You're sure?"

Kenny nodded his head in assent and went back to eating.

Alicia turned and looked at the men. One of the men was on the phone and was looking directly at their table. The other man kept glancing at them and turning away like he was trying not to be noticeable.

"Hurry and eat. We need to leave." Alicia gathered up the

pieces of her food and began dumping everything onto a tray. Before she could stand up, the woman, Jennie, was over at their table.

"He should be here soon. Follow me." She gestured at them and opened her arms wide to herd them out the door. She walked with them to the edge of the parking lot and stopped. "Are they friends of yours?"

"I'm not sure," Alicia admitted.

"I had a sister that got married very young. She loved her husband, but we all knew that he was good for nothing. She wouldn't listen to us and ran off with him. She came back five years later with two kids and bruises all over her body." She looked at Kenny. "Make sure to keep him safe."

"I will," Alicia said. "Thank you."

Alicia looked back into the restaurant and noticed that the men were standing, not even bothering to hide that they were watching. They started to walk outside when a black sedan tore into the parking lot. At first, Alicia thought that Sadar had come to save them again, but she realized her mistake when Jennie went up to the car.

"Get in," she told them.

While Alicia helped Kenny buckle into his car seat, Jennie whispered to the driver, who couldn't be much older than twenty. All Alicia managed to hear was the word "go," then the car sped away.

Alicia turned and looked out the back window as they drove out of the parking lot. The men were outside, watching them leave.

# Chapter Twenty-Four

Kenny sat strapped in next to Alicia. The car was clean, with shiny black upholstery. On the back of the driver's seat there was a plastic organizer with breath mints and tissues organized in the pockets. A handwritten sign was slipped in the top that read: "Take what you need, and don't forget a five-star review."

"Thank you for picking us up," Alicia said. "I hope it wasn't too much trouble."

The driver was young, in his early twenties. He was wearing a backwards baseball cap and a wrinkled t-shirt.

"It's no problem. Ms. Jennie promised to make up a batch of her cinnamon rolls. They are so good you'd hug a cactus for them."

While he talked, Alicia was glancing out the back of the car, looking for headlights following them. They were driving through a residential area without streetlights. The houses released a glow of light from the porch lights.

"We still really appreciate it," Alicia said.

Next to her, Kenny seemed to be nervous as well, or maybe he was mimicking her. He kept glancing over his shoulder through the back window and then through the side windows. She thought about telling him that everything would be OK, but she had not lied to her kid before, and she wasn't going to start now. She had no idea if everything was going to be OK. All she knew was that she would do everything she could to protect him. She settled on putting her arm around him and rubbing his arm like she used to do when he was little. He calmed and leaned his head against her.

Alicia tried to be more discreet as she glanced outside.

Suddenly, there was a loud crash against the driver side of the car, pushing the car off the road and into a mailbox. Their seatbelts clenched up, and Alicia's head flung forward. Before she had settled, the driver's door had been flung open, and a hand reached in and dragged out their driver.

He started screaming, a loud hysterical scream that soon turned into one of pain. Alicia instinctively reached for Kenny, covering his ears and eyes. Her heart hammered against her chest. She glanced around, trying to understand what was happening, but the headlights only showed empty sidewalk. Then, abruptly, the screaming just stopped.

Alicia tried to frantically open her door, but it was jammed up against a fence post. She climbed over her son, glancing around in terror of what was outside of the car. On the way, she unbuckled his seatbelt and told him to hide on the floor. When he didn't move, she turned on her mom voice and told him to "Do it now." Kenny climbed down fast and crouched on the floor as far away from the door as he could.

"I love you." Alicia's voice cracked as she said it. Then she opened the door.

When she stepped out, she saw three men. They were all watching her as she got out of the car. She held her hands up, trying to look like less of a threat. She also left the door open. Then, without looking back at her son, she whispered to him, "If you get a chance to run, run, and don't look back."

She began to walk away from the car, her hands still raised. She walked towards them slowly. She tried to see if anything was lying around that she could use as a weapon. It was so dark, and they were standing away from the headlights. The men were stocky, but they stood light on their feet, ready to act. Their eyes tracked her as she walked. They were twice her size and dressed in slick black suits that looked untouched despite the broken body in front of them. She could take down one, maybe, and only because they would underestimate her. She needed to keep a path clear from her son and let him get away.

"What do you want from us?" she asked.

"The men looked near identical in the limited light. Their stance and dress mimicked each other, until the middle man differentiated himself by speaking. "We want the boy." His voice rang in the darkness.

"What do you plan to do to him?" she asked.

The same man smiled and then looked to the ground where the young driver was lying, covered in blood. Yet they looked like they hadn't moved. Alicia realized that they must have used magic. It looked like they had used their magic to force the boy's blood out through his pores. It was such a horrible way to die, and it was all because of her. Alicia pushed down the guilt. Right now, what mattered was keeping her son safe. She focused on the men. There was no way she was taking any of them down.

"If we come with you, will you not hurt him?"

"We just need the boy," the man answered.

"What about my son? If he goes with you, will you spare him?"

"That isn't our decision. Our job is to bring him."

"Why? Who sent you?"

"The king. He wants to see the boy claiming to be his son."

"Run now," Alicia screamed and then rushed at the men. She managed to get her knee in the groin of the man closest to her before the pain started. It felt like needles were stabbing her in every one of her pores. A scream tore through her. She saw the blood beading up on her arms, and then her knees gave way. She collapsed to the ground.

The pain became everything. Never could she have imagined something could hurt so bad. She wished that they would finish so she could die, so that the pain would leave. Her son. Kenny. She had to hold on to give Kenny a chance to get away.

The pain left as suddenly as it began. Alicia gasped for air. Her world expanded to include breathing and then the pain that came with each breath. Then she realized that she was still alive. Kenny. What had happened to her son?

"Kenny." She tried to speak, but her throat was raw. No sound made it out.

She heard crying over the pounding in her ears. She tried to speak again. "Kenny." Her son moved just into her field of view. He was too afraid to touch her and too scared to leave her.

"It's OK," she whispered. She wasn't sure if any sound had made it out. Or if it was louder than the tears that continued to wrack his small body.

"I think… I think I killed them. They were hurting you, and they tried to hurt me, and I got so angry and so scared, and I copied what they did. They screamed. Just like the driver screamed, just like you screamed. I kept going, and they stopped screaming."

Kenny started crying even harder. Alicia tried to reach out to him. She tried to move to see what had happened. All she felt was pain. Her vision started to fade. She focused on one more breath and managed to speak. "It's OK. You did OK. You saved me." The effort took so much out of her, but he heard. He moved towards her, curling up by her side. She knew he was trying to be careful, but the pain of him next to her made her vision fade again. She couldn't black out. That much magic had to have been like a beacon to every elf around. They had to go now. She tried to lift her head. Then there was darkness.

# Chapter Twenty-Five

She woke up screaming.

"Gently, not so much power." The voice sounded familiar, and she knew she would be able to place it in a second. But for now, she just needed to rest. Then she felt a wave of calm pass through her. The pain was still there, but it had slightly decreased in intensity.

"Very good. Can you do it one more time?" She did not hear an answer, but she felt the response as another wave of calm passed through her. "You've healed her enough to move. We need to go."

"I can do it again." This was a new voice. She knew this voice. It was a part of her.

"You have already done more magic tonight than I have ever seen. If you keep at it, then you are going to be just as sick as your mom." Mom—that word called to her. She knew that one of the voices belonged to her son and that he needed her. "Listen to your own body, it needs to rest, and we need to move."

"I can heal her some more. I'm OK." Kenny was crying now. She knew that she needed to reach him. She was so tired.

"Maybe, but you've used too much power already. Sometimes, the best way to help someone is to take care of yourself."

"I'm OK. You fixed me." She managed to push the words out. She felt a little more connected but still so tired. Someone pressed up against her. She lifted her arm and wrapped it around him.

"Time to go." The voice was urgent. She felt her son move away. She felt arms picking her up and carrying her. She lay her head against him.

# Chapter Twenty-Six

When Alicia woke up the second time, she was slumped against the window of a car's passenger seat. A blanket wrapped around her. It clung to her skin, damp and sticky. To her amazement, she felt alive. Her body still hurt, and her throat was raw, but it was nothing compared to the pain when she passed out. *She was alive. How was she alive?*

"Good morning," Sadar said.

Alicia turned her head. It was too fast a movement, and her head started to pound. They had left Sadar, yet there he was, back driving the car. She was more careful when she moved her head to the back seat. Kenny was sitting there, smiling at her.

"You're better, Mom." Alicia knew that it was a statement

and not a question.

"I have you to thank for that, don't I?"

Kenny nodded, his grin getting more prominent.

Alicia turned to face Sadar, the Sun brightening his silver hair. She watched him as he continued driving. He looked different, and it took her a minute to realize that he seemed almost relaxed. His mouth was not clenched, and even his hand held the steering wheel lighter than before. He stayed silent, allowing her time to adjust to being awake.

"You're back," Alicia managed.

"It seems that I am."

"Where are you taking us?" They both knew the question was a test.

"To a friend's place. You should be safe there."

"A friend…" Alicia let the doubt creep into her voice. "You are no longer looking for the king?"

"Those men, the ones the prince took down: they were the king's guards."

"I thought you were his guard."

"I am. Those were thugs hired by the king. They went with him when he disappeared."

Alicia shot him another look. Her head hurt too much to get into the same argument.

"The man at the house, he served the old king, Kenny's grandfather. He was the type of person who got his hands dirty.

Before I left to track you down again, he told me some things about what is happening in our world. Things I should have seen on my own, but I can't change the past." Sadar took one hand off the steering wheel and rubbed it through his short hair. "Kenny is important, more than I imagined, enough that the king tried to kill his own son. If he could do that, then I have to question everything. I wasn't there for the prince. I let him down, and I am sorry."

Sadar used the rearview mirror to look into the back seat, a deep sadness in his eyes as he continued speaking. "Kenny, it is my fault that you had to learn so much so young. It is a debt that I must always carry. I will never let you down again. You are the rightful heir to the throne, and I swear that from here on out, I will be there to protect you."

"The king, my father, is a bad man. He hurt my mother and tried to hurt me. We won't go to see him. We need to stop him from hurting people again. You will help us with that?"

"I will," Sadar said.

"Good," Kenny said, tears in his eyes, then turned to watch the scenery out the window.

"What exactly do you mean by rightful heir to the throne?" Alicia questioned.

"The In-Between is magic, and we must have someone ruling us who is strong enough to wield that magic. The king has made sure that there is no one left to challenge him, except your son."

Alicia glanced between Kenny and Sadar, trying to digest the words. Any hope of going back to their home and being safe was now gone. She took a moment, letting herself feel with pain and mourn her old life. Then she turned her focus to what was ahead. "What's the plan? How do we keep my son safe?" Alicia asked.

"I have a friend. He has no connection with the king and will keep you safe. I am driving to them now."

"Where are these friends?"

"He lives in the city of Saeluna in the In-Between. It is the elven world."

"How far away is it?"

"We will stick to the back roads, and there are a few areas that we should avoid. If we don't make long stops, we should get there sometime tomorrow."

"Is that safe?" Alicia asked. They were driving on another two-lane road, sandwiched between farmland with some sort of brown stalks shooting up from the ground. It felt like they were only a moment away from someone finding them. Her breath started to catch at the thought, but then she saw Sadar sitting next to her and for the first time his presence brought a sense of comfort. "Shouldn't we go to the In-Between here and make the rest of the journey that way? At least then, Kenny's magic will not be as noticeable."

"There are no cars in the In-Between. Technology does not

work there. It is faster to come to the human world to travel between cities."

"Couldn't you just make an illusion of a car and use that instead?"

Sadar looked at her briefly, then moved his head back to the road. "Illusionary magic does not work in the In-Between. The In-Between *is* illusionary magic. You cannot put an illusion on top of an illusion."

Alicia sat back and tried to wrap her mind around that, then realized that she would probably never understand magic.

# Chapter Twenty-Seven

It was a few hours before they stopped. It was a simple stop to put gas in the car and accommodate an eight-year-old's bladder. Alicia was still covered in the gory remains of the attack. Sadar had wrapped her in a blanket without wiping off her skin. Now she felt like an extra in a horror movie.

Sadar made Kenny wait in the car, currently a gray hatchback, until he had filled up the gas. Then he pulled the car around, so it was closer to the convenience store. He left Kenny in the car while he ran in. It seemed like only moments before he returned with two full bags and the code to the bathrooms. Even then, he dropped off the bags and had Kenny wait until he opened the restroom and made sure it was safe. By the time

Sadar allowed the eight-year-old to get out of the car, he nearly ran into the stall. Sadar positioned himself outside the door.

Alicia moved slowly, easing her body out of the car, the blanket still wrapped tightly around her. There was only one other car at the station, and he was focused on filling up the tank, so she didn't worry too much about her shuffling gait attracting attention. Once she made it inside, she leaned back on the door, trying to get the room to stop spinning. Finally, she locked the door and made it a few feet to the sink.

The mirror was a tiny square attached to the wall in a picture frame. It only allowed her to see her face. It was blotted with rust color splotches. She pulled out some of the thin paper towels from the silver holder and got them wet. Then she attempted to scrub. Her skin burned where she touched it, but some of the blood wiped off easily. Other parts looked like it had dyed her skin.

She pulled out more paper towels, dousing them with hand soap and gripping onto the sink for support, continuing to clean. By the time she had a mountain of wet reddish paper towels covering the back of the sink, she had only managed to wipe down her face and neck. Her skin was still too pale with a pink pigment in splotches across it.

Next, she ran her arms under the sink, scrubbing them with soap and water. The water shut off after less than ten seconds, and she was constantly having to pound the button to continue.

Her head was swimming, and her legs were ready to collapse, but she looked a little less frightening. She gathered up the paper towels and buried them in the trash can. She did her best to clean up traces of the blood before she finally left the bathroom, the blanket still stuck to most of her body.

Sadar sat in the driver's seat, watching her make her way out. When he saw her slow steps, he got out of the car and wrapped an arm around her, helping her back to the side of the car. He opened the door for her and allowed her to hand on to him as she sat back down.

Before he went back to his seat, he opened up one of the back doors and rummaged through the plastic bags. Alicia had closed her eyes and could hear the shuffling of the plastic and then the slamming of the door. Then she felt the movement of air as the driver's door opened and Sadar slid into his seat.

"Here, this will help." She felt something cold through the shoulder of her blanket and opened her eyes to look. He was holding a light-blue sports drink out to her.

"Thank you," Alicia said. She grabbed the bottle, enjoying the cold against her hands.

"It should help keep you from being dehydrated."

"I'm hungry," Kenny said, breaking in from the back seat.

"I think Sadar may have gotten some snacks," Alicia said.

"But I'm hungry. I want real food, like a hamburger."

"What did Sadar say?" As Alicia was speaking, Sadar started

the car and started driving out of the gas station.

"He said it was best to wait to eat for an hour or two since I will probably have to stop again anyway. He said something about a small bladder, but I don't think I want to eat that."

"I think it would be a good idea to try to find a truck stop," Sadar said. "Someplace that has both burgers and a shower for your mom."

"That sounds like a good idea to me," Alicia said. The blanket was starting to pull against her legs, causing her skin to hurt more. "I mean, if you do not want the food Sadar bought in the gas station, then I guess I can eat it. I bet there are lots of tasty things in there."

"I don't think I got anything he would like."

Alicia jumped when Sadar spoke, as his serious tone was replaced with one that was almost playful, and she had to look to make sure he was still the right person. He continued, "I could only pick up what they had, which was mostly junk food like chips and candy bars. Nothing I'm sure you would be interested in."

"No, I want it." Kenny reached over his seat and started searching through the bags.

"So, you can wait a little longer for real food?" Alicia asked.

Kenny muttered something that Alicia couldn't understand, his mouth already full of something.

Alicia turned her attention to her own drink. She attempted to remove the top, but her hands refused to maintain a grasp solid enough to twist it off. She felt a bit humiliated when Sadar took the bottle from her hand and opened it for her. But she took it back gratefully and carefully lifted it up to her lips to drink. The bottle felt like it had been made out of lead. She managed a small swallow before she put it back down between her legs. She put the lid back on just enough so the liquid wouldn't fly out.

"Thank you," Alicia said before she closed her eyes and drifted back to sleep.

# Chapter Twenty-Eight

It had taken them a little over an hour before Sadar had driven them to a truck stop with showers. Alicia felt a little better after the drink and another nap, but she still ached anytime that she moved. Kenny wanted to heal her again, but Alicia was pretty sure she would not die, and she didn't want them giving away their position. She was grateful for the shower, though.

Alicia caused a few glances as she walked in, wrapped in blankets. However, most everyone went right back to their own business. In the shower stall, Alicia had to peel off the blanket from her skin. The plasma seemed to coat her entire body, and she was again struck with gratitude for being alive.

When the water hit her skin, she flinched, not from pain but anxiety. The pinpricks as the water hit her skin reminded her of the attack. She closed her eyes and focused on the soap cleaning off her body instead. She scrubbed and scrubbed until the water reached its time limit and shut off. Her skin still had a faint smell of iron and a slightly pink tint, but she felt better than she had since the incident.

When she opened the stall curtain and walked into the changing area, the blanket she had worn was gone. In its place was a shirt with Illinois on the front of it. There was a matching pair of sweats. The material was gentle against her sensitive skin, and Alicia was grateful, although the elf did not seem to have a concept of bras and underwear.

Sadar and Kenny were sitting in the truck stop diner. Kenny was eating an adult-size hamburger with a huge milkshake. There was an extra plate of fries by him as well.

"I ordered you a hamburger as well," Sadar said. "You should probably eat some, but if you can't finish, then Kenny will help you. I'm going to order some food to go as well, so it isn't as suspicious."

"You mean how an eight-year-old can manage to eat all that food?"

"Yes, that."

"How can he? I used to have to make him finish two eggs in the morning, and now he can eat an entire cow."

At that, Kenny looked up and smiled. Alicia relaxed a little at seeing her son back to his goofy self. Then he went back to eating as fast as he could without choking.

"It's the magic," Sadar said. "He has done a lot. Eventually, his body will stabilize, and he won't have to eat as much. Unless he keeps doing this much magic all the time."

By the time they returned to the car, Alicia felt better than she had in a while. It only slightly hurt to move, and she was no longer clouded by pain. Alicia stood outside the car, between the open door and the seat, and looked at Sadar helping her son into his seat. Sadar did not look quite so well. He looked tired and even a little sad. Alicia figured that losing his worldview probably bothered him more than he let on.

"I can drive so you can catch a nap," Alicia said.

"I don't think you are fit enough quite yet for driving, and I'd have to stay awake to give you directions anyway. I'm good." He stopped by her door and held out his arm towards her. She went to refuse it, but that would just be petty. So, she used his arm as support as she eased back into the seat.

"You are anything but good," she said as he slid into his own seat. "You look exhausted and like you have just come off a long work shift or a weekend of partying. You haven't had a break in the last few days, and you haven't slept since we have met. Do elves not need to sleep?"

Alicia looked in the back seat. Kenny was asleep again, the remnants of two more take-out burgers next to his seat. He had to sleep, but he was also half-human.

"Elves have to sleep," Sadar said.

"You sure do not seem to. I have never once seen you sleep." They eased out of the parking spot and drove past lines of parked trucks. The freeway was not far behind them, but when Sadar turned into the street he kept to the frontage road.

"I am a warrior trained to defend the royal elven line. I have learned to control my sleep and not do it in front of an enemy. I imagine your human warriors have similar abilities. Besides, I have managed to take a few naps when we were not around each other."

"Am I your enemy?" Alicia turned to him with concern on her face.

Sadar glanced at her briefly, meeting her eyes, and then turned back to watch the road. He paused, considering his words before he spoke.

"I never viewed you as an enemy. However, we have also never been allies. You do not trust me. When you look at me, you broadcast your disgust and mistrust. So, I have chosen to be cautious while I am around you."

"You never really gave me a reason to trust you. Not until you started thinking about what was best for my son."

"You're right. I had spent so many years following the king that I would have taken your son right to him had I known where he was. I can never atone for what I did to you and many others.

However, I will continue to try. I will start by swearing to you that I will protect your son with my life. He is the last prince to the elven throne. He is my people's last hope. I will let no harm come to him."

Alicia stared at him. His passion and commitment were undeniable. Yet he had already changed his position more than once, and it would take more than a few hours to completely remake a person, although even nine years ago, she was able to see the good in him. Right now, she had no choice. She couldn't keep her son safe; last night had proven that. At least this way, there was a chance that Sadar would save him. Alicia turned away and rested her forehead against the cool window. Her head had started pounding again. She was not as recovered as she had thought.

When Alicia awoke, Sadar was pulling into a parking lot. They were in a city again, in a small shopping center. The sun was barely visible in the sky, and there wasn't yet much movement outside.

"Is this the place?" Alicia asked.

"No," he replied. "They will be able to tell where we cross over. We will enter here. Then we will have to travel the city on foot."

They got out of the car and grabbed their belongings. Alicia had to wake up Kenny, who was groggy. They walked over to a nearby gas station and picked up a few bags full of prepackaged pastries, protein bars, and candy bars. Alicia's eyes had widened at the selection, but Sadar insisted that Kenny would need to eat all the food over the next day or two.

Alicia picked up her and Kenny's bags. They now bulged with convenience store food shoved into every free space. The food must have weighed a lot because Alicia had to strain to lift them both and carry them after Sadar and her son. She knew it wasn't the food causing the strain. Her body still wasn't fully healed. *How was she going to manage to walk through the entire city this way?*

There was a small decorative lawn that housed a few trees and bushes. There were buildings on one side blocking it from the freeway. It seemed that no one was around. They walked towards it. Sadar checked over his shoulder continually to make sure that no one was noticing them.

Sadar knelt in front of Kenny and took his hands in his. "You have been to the In-Between before." It was not a question, but Kenny still nodded his confirmation. "You know that it can be"—he paused, looking for an appropriate word, "overwhelming when you first shift. The distortion should go away for you quickly. However, some of the humans that have come over never lost the distortion. I need you to stay with your mother no matter what. Do not lose her. You may have to help her to know what is in the elven world and what is in the human world."

Alicia stood there looking down at them, annoyed that they talked about her like she was not there. She opened her mouth to tell Sadar what she thought about putting her son in charge of her welfare, but before she got a word out, he gave her a scathing look and left to do a final circle to make sure their surroundings were safe. She would not be the weak one in their party. She had worked so hard at not being vulnerable for the last nine years. But even as she thought this, her head continued to pound, and the weight of the backpack made her want to collapse.

"When we shift, you will see both worlds," Sadar said as he returned. "You will see both the elven and human world. You will need to concentrate hard on the elven world and block out the human world's familiarity. If a car comes barreling towards you, you cannot react. It cannot hurt you. If you react, then everyone will know that you are human."

"I thought everyone would know I am human anyway."

"There has not been a human in the In-Between in over a hundred years. I am hoping that no one notices."

"Do elves see both worlds all the time? Do they have to pretend away the human world like it is some nonexistent parallel universe?" Alicia asked.

"No, most elves spend their whole lives in the In-Between. They see nothing except their world. Those of us who can travel to the human world only see both worlds after a shift. Then we adjust and see the correct world. If I try, really try, I can see between the worlds. I glimpse to make sure that I am shifting in a place where the humans will not see me. But it takes so much energy that I do not bother. I have places I have memorized that are safe places to shift. This is one of them. Are you ready?"

He looked at both of them, making sure they were ready to make the transition. Kenny reached out and grabbed Alicia's hand. Sadar reached out and put a hand on her shoulder.

"Shifting in someone else is a lot like just shifting in yourself," Sadar said. "All you have to do is include the other person as an extension of yourself."

Kenny nodded, and then they shifted.

# Chapter Twenty-Nine

Nothing changed. Alicia still found herself standing in the same parking lot hidden behind trees. She watched as a few cars drove by and a person walked down the streets.

"It didn't work," she said.

"You do not see any difference at all?" Sadar asked.

"No, it all looks the same. What do you see, Kenny?" she asked.

"It is empty. The people are gone. The buildings seem to be empty, too."

Alicia looked around her. All she could see was the human world.

"Close your eyes and tell yourself that you are somewhere

new," Sadar said.

Alicia closed her eyes and did some of her deep breathing exercises. She tried to imagine what her son saw. She counted to five and opened her eyes. It looked the same.

They walked out of the clearing and towards the street. The city had woken up, and cars were rushing on their way to work. The sidewalk was mostly empty. It was just them and a man sitting against the street side of the buildings. He didn't look at them, but Alicia couldn't tell if he couldn't see them or if he was not focused on the world in general.

When they reached the end of the block, Alicia stopped. In front of them was a road with cars streaming back and forth, and both Kenny and Sadar were going to walk right in front of them.

"Stop," Alicia screamed. They both stopped on the edge of the sidewalk. "You can't cross there. It isn't safe." She held on to Kenny's hand, pulling him tightly towards her.

"What do you see?" Sadar asked.

"There are cars everywhere. You can't let him walk into that." Her voice came out as a plea.

"There is a place up ahead that is concealed in both worlds. I want to make it there before Kenny heals you, in case you slip back completely to the human world. We need to walk across. It is safe. I will show you."

Sadar stepped off the corner and straight in front of a car. Then he disappeared. Kenny disappeared. He was no longer holding her hand. The man looked up at her in confusion and then rubbed at his face. It was overgrown with a strangely black beard and long, strangely black hair that seemed to highlight his wide eyes. He picked up his few bags of belongings, stood up, and walked away, muttering under his breath. Every few steps, the man would pause and glance back at her.

Her bags were heavy, and all she wanted to do was sit and rest, but she had to get back to her son. The world was still unchanged, but it wasn't hard to figure out that she was back in the human world. She reached out with her hand as though she could break free and reach her son, if she tried hard enough.

*Would Sadar come back for her?* All she could do was hope.

She looked around at the busy street corner. It wouldn't be safe for them to come back here in front of everyone, so she would have to go to them. She pushed the button to cross the street. She waited until she saw the green humanoid figure and walked across. *This is how you cross a street*, she thought.

The other side held more stores. These were smaller stores that opened towards the street. Alicia kept walking, trying to decide where Sadar had intended to stop. Then she saw the alley between two stores. It was filled with trash cans but not much else. She glanced around again and saw no better prospects. She walked down the alley.

She was so tired, but the ground was dirty, and the air smelled. The best she managed to find was a relatively clean wall between two trash cans. She leaned against that and hoped that they would find her.

It didn't take long. She had barely rested her head back before they strolled around the corner of the alley, looking for her.

Sadar crouched down next to her, a look of concern on his face. "It shouldn't be that hard for you to be in the In-Between."

"I couldn't focus. My head feels like someone is constantly taking a sledgehammer to it. Every part of my body is still sore, and it has taken all my energy to move one step in front of the other. Also, these bags weigh a ton. Did you slip weights in them?"

"I should have considered. I knew you weren't yet healed, but you didn't complain once. I didn't realize that you were so impacted."

"What is the point of complaining? It would not have helped our situation any, and there was nothing we could do that would have been safe."

"Most humans would have complained anyway. Elves also." Sadar looked around. There was a row of trash bins lined up against a chain link fence at the end of the alley. Some of the trash had escaped and littered the ground, filling up the space with a rotten stench. In front there was a steady flow of traffic on the road and the sidewalk. He shook his head and let out a sigh. "This is not the best place, but let's heal you. Then we can see if that will help you stay in the In-Between. If it doesn't work, then we will have to make some decisions fast."

"It will work," Alicia said with determination.

Sadar gave a curt nod and then beckoned Kenny to move closer. "I'm going to need your help. Once we shift over, I'm going to need you to heal your mom right away. You will be tired, but we are going to have to move fast after you are done. You are going to have to be strong and brave. Can you do that?"

"I'm ready," Kenny said.

Alicia felt Sadar's hand on her shoulder. Kenny wrapped his arm around her chest. She had a fleeting feeling of nausea, and then it was the same alley, complete with trash. She was still seeing the human world.

"Close your eyes," Sadar said. "I need you to keep them closed until after you are healed and we find a safe spot to regroup."

"I'm not going to be much help with my eyes closed."

"You are not going to be much help if you keep shifting back to the human world. I know I am asking a lot, but can you trust me on this?"

Alicia looked at Sadar. His face was the same emotionless mask, but there was an urgency about him. She realized, suddenly, that he had come back for her. He could have taken her son and left her, but for whatever reason he didn't.

"Fine, I'll keep them closed." As she closed her eyes, she

could hear Sadar sigh in relief.

"Your turn," Sadar said.

Alicia felt her son's hand fall on her shoulder. Then she felt energy racing through her body. She visualized white light settling in and pushing out every hurt and negative thought. The light filled her, making her feel as strong as she had ever felt. Then it left as suddenly as it had come. Her son's hand slipped from her hand, and she opened her eyes to make sure that he was OK.

"Keep your eyes closed. He is fine, just tired. Can you walk?" Alicia nodded, but Sadar paid her no attention. She closed her eyes again and felt Sadar's hand in her own helping her up. "Here, have this. It will help. Eat fast. Then we will need to hurry." There was a crinkling of a wrapper and then the unmistakable sound of her son chewing. Then she felt her body being lifted from the ground.

"What are you doing? Let me go," Alicia said.

"We need to hurry, and we can't do that if you can't see. So, you are just going to have to let me carry you."

"The pain is gone. I should be fine now. Just let me down."

"I hope you will be, but we don't have time to find out right now. We need to go."

He held her in his arms like he was carrying a baby. Even healed, she was a liability to the group. She supposed that she should feel lucky that he hadn't thrown her over his shoulder.

She could feel him running. Every time his foot hit the pavement, she felt her body jostle. There was joy in it. Her body no longer hurt. She had grown used to the pain, and now she felt light in a way she hadn't in what felt like years.

Every so often, they would pause so that Kenny could catch up. Then she felt guilty. She should be carrying him, letting him rest after he had healed her. They stopped briefly, and Alicia heard Kenny unwrap and eat another candy bar. Then they started moving again.

It was hard to judge time with her eyes closed, but it felt like at least an hour before her feet were put back on the ground.

"Can I open my eyes now?"

"Yes, now should be a good time."

She saw Kenny slumped against the side of a building. He was rummaging through one of the bags unwrapping a new item before he managed to finish eating the last one.

"Look at that." Kenny stopped eating enough to point to one of the buildings. Alicia saw a store with wedding dresses in the window. Then she caught a flicker of green, and the building seemed to shimmer. Vines covered the same building. A few kids were running around in rags. A woman was sweeping out the building, and a few more adults seemed to be picking vegetables off the vines.

One of the younger children ran up to an adult and begged for one of the tomatoes. Alicia could not understand what was said, but the child went away disappointed, and the adult seemed almost mournful.

"You said they were hungry, not starving. There is food all around here." She saw some produce growing on a large section of buildings all down the block.

"Good, you can see. We need to move. We have been here too long."

Kenny looked down at his bag of food and then at the children. He stood up and moved towards them until Sadar put a hand on his shoulder. "They will remember the strange elf child that gave them human food. We cannot afford to be remembered." As Kenny put the food back in the bag, his face lost his easy grin, and a scowl took its place.

They began to walk, but Alicia found herself having problems. She could now make out the elven world, but she still saw the human world. It was so easy to see the human world, the world that she understood. But she tried to focus on the elven world. The family had taken over nearly a block for their garden. Vines covered the buildings, and plants filled any open space. There wasn't much, but they had managed to maximize what they had. The adults looked tired. The few children seemed to be going around doing odd jobs and then sneaking away to play. Since there were no cars, the elves took up more space, leaving the only place to walk in the middle of the road. The human world was quiet. There were cars parked on the side of the road, but none were driving past. Alicia was grateful. It was easier to see the elven world, but she didn't think she was ready to ignore a car barreling at her.

The elven world was so much greener than the human world. Except the greenery appeared in patches. They would pass rows of houses covered in vegetables or fruit trees. Then there would be areas of nothing but neglect, followed by acres of magnificent rock sculptures. The elves they passed by did not give their party a second glance. Everyone seemed to be busy. Yet, the people walked around in rags with tired, beaten expression on their faces.

Alicia still had to struggle to see the elven world. She had to consciously remember that the road was now the way to move, shared by pedestrians and the occasional cart. The first time a car came barreling down on them, Alicia yanked both herself and her son to the safety of the sidewalk. Except the sidewalk seemed to be the play place of young children or set aside for storage. Her sudden movement knocked them into an older elf resting on a chair. She stood up, shouting at them in a language that Alicia did not understand. Sadar spoke back in the same language, his tone apologetic as he pushed them forward and pulled them back int the road.

"Are you still seeing the human world?" he asked.

"I see it better than your world. Nothing here makes any sense."

"It is going to get worse real soon. I need you to remember that nothing in the human world can hurt you. It is not real, not here. Pretend you are on vacation in another country, and try to focus on learning the culture. Maybe that will help to connect you more."

The next time a car came at them, Alicia stopped in the road and closed her eyes. She could feel Sadar moving towards her, probably making it look like they were in conversation and not randomly stopped in the street, in the walkway.

What Alicia did not feel was the car. After a few seconds, she opened her eyes and turned to see the vehicle continuing away from them.

It was ultimately focusing on the people that seemed to help connect her. They passed one house with an elf outside, using what Alicia assumed was earth magic to sculpt rock statues. Alicia found it fascinating to see a figure being produced right before her eyes. Yet, no tools were being used.

The further they walked, the more they started to see elves. There were no crowds, and there were still stretches of abandoned land. Yet, there seemed to be enough crops to keep everyone fed.

"Why isn't every yard covered in crops?" Alicia asked.

"Not everyone can grow crops, especially not in the city. It takes a combination of earth and healing magic. Elves have to work together, and they usually cannot manage large crops."

"Even so, we have passed quite a few of these yard farms. If there is food being grown, why does everyone look so hungry? Even the people growing the food seem to be looking on it with yearning."

"I'm not sure," Sadar said, sadness flickering briefly on his face. "I think I have an idea though. Elves use a bartering system, and that includes taxes. I think the king may be taking much of what they own."

"That's not right," Kenny said. He was walking between Sadar and Alicia, watching the new world with fascination. "It's not right that they have to grow stuff they can't eat."

"I agree," Sadar said as he patted the boy on his shoulder. "Maybe we will be able to do something about that."

# Chapter Thirty

It took them a few hours of walking before they reached the metro sections of the city—at least, in the human world. It was hard for Alicia to tell where housing ended and business began in the In-Between, since the elves did not use the buildings in the same way. They nearly ran into a market held in the middle of a street of what would have been office suites.

There were stalls, made out of different shades of rock, lined up unevenly. The elves swarmed and jostled each other trying to get to the front of the stall. They were a sea of skin tones and body sizes but their voices united into a high-pitched musical song that drilled into Alicia's ears. Sadar picked up Kenny as they pushed through the swarm of bodies. Alicia managed to see through a few gaps as people shifted, but all she saw were small collections of limp colorless vegetables.

Then Alicia saw a car driving through the middle of the event. It drove straight through the hordes of people, and Alicia braced to see their bodies flung to the side. But they continued on, unaware, busy trying to get enough to eat.

When they reached what would have been the downtown area of the human city, the masses of elves had disappeared. Now there was a sparse collection of nicer-dressed elves walking around. Kenny, once again, walked between them.

"The elves here have more magic than most of the ones that we just passed," Sadar said. "There is a possibility that some of these elves have passed over to the human world before and would be able to recognize a human instantly. So, we need to be careful and stick to the shadows as much as possible. Are you still having problems sorting out the human world from the elven world?"

"A little," Alicia said. Although, in truth, it was a lot more than a little. Anytime she saw anything that looked similar to the human world, she started to see the human world again. She had to concentrate on staying focused on the In-Between. She had to keep reminding herself that she was supposed to keep seeing a world that was beyond anything she could imagine. She liked order and predictability, yet now she had to focus away from that.

Although as they had walked, the elven world had gotten more familiar. She has started knowing what to expect, and that expectation allowed her to stay focused more. But she was still afraid of slipping back, of not being around to help her son, or worse, putting him at risk.

"When we walk in the shadows, the worlds will look the same. The shadows are a bridge. It is easier to shift between worlds in the shadows as the worlds are the most similar there." Sadar turned to Kenny. "Although you must not shift. They cannot feel that, especially not here. It is not forbidden to shift in the city, but it is highly discouraged. They would be able to know it is us."

Kenny looked up at Sadar and nodded. He reached his hand out to his mother's, and she felt a slight ripple pass through her. She looked at him questioningly, but he ignored her, focusing on Sadar. Alicia was reasonably sure that Kenny was doing something to her, but she had no idea what.

"If you ever can't tell what world you are in, close your eyes," Sadar said to Alicia. "Kenny will help lead you out of the shadows until you can come to a brighter spot and help reorient yourself."

Alicia looked down at her son and then turned to Sadar and nodded. They walked closer to the buildings when possible. Sadar led them down alleys instead of on the main street. Alicia wondered how much of this was paranoia. There did not seem to be many elves around. Here in the heart of the city, there were no longer the scraggly dressed elves. Their clothes were clean and brighter. The fabrics looked softer and had designs stitched into them. Their bodies filled out their clothing. Most were still slender, but they didn't wear hunger on their face.

The buildings were different, also. In Alicia's world, they would have been shops with brightly lit windows. Here the same buildings seemed ominous: they were dark, and curtains mostly covered the windows. They did not seem like businesses, or if they were, they did not advertise. The inner city was less colorful than what they had been walking past. While many buildings had vines or other plant life growing on or around them, none had food.

The group moved as silently as possible. They walked with purpose, and Alicia had allowed herself to believe that they would get where they were going without harassment when she heard someone yell at them.

"Hey, you over there, come here." The elf was on the other side of the street a few buildings down. Alicia wondered how he managed to notice them. She paused, uncertain of the best way to handle the attention.

"Hurry, come on," Sadar urged them on. He guided them through twists and turns, urging them to hurry. Alicia wondered if he knew where they were going. To her, it seemed like they may as well be traveling in circles. When Sadar stopped, Alicia ran right into him. It took her a second to realize that they were stuck, trapped at the end of an alley. She could hear the sounds of running footprints closing in on them. The elf must have found backup because it sounded like a pack of people. Alicia turned around, trying to find someplace to go, a door, or even something to hide behind. Unfortunately, there was nothing and no time to get out.

She looked down at her son, who gazed back at her with fear and worry. She brushed at his head, wishing she could tell him that everything was going to turn out all right. Then his face shifted from fear to his mysterious grin, the one he got when he was bound to be up to no good.

"Come here," he whispered and walked over to the corner of the wall where Sadar was trying unsuccessfully to climb. He took Sadar's hand and then tugged on both of their hands, urging them to kneel to his height. When neither of them moved, he said, "It's your turn to trust me."

Alicia was the first one to kneel next to her son, but Sadar followed shortly after. She kept Kenny's hand tightly in hers and placed her body in front of him as much as possible. No matter what happened, she would go down trying to save her son. Then, maybe he could shift back to the human world. She turned to tell him to do precisely that when the elves started walking down the alley.

Alicia held her breath, then wondered what the point was.

They were staring right at them. Except they made no move towards them. Instead, they started glancing around the alley and talking together in a language that Alicia could not understand. Then one man started yelling at another, and they all walked back out of the passage. The trio waited until they could no longer hear their footsteps. It felt like an extremely long time.

"What did you do?" Sadar was the first to break the silence.

"I made it so they could not see us," Kenny said.

"Does that mean…" Alicia started, then stopped, uncertain how to continue.

"You used illusion magic," Sadar said.

Kenny nodded his head in affirmation.

"How?" Sadar nearly demanded.

Kenny ignored his tone of voice and answered him calmly. "I could feel it, not as strong as I could before we came here, but it was still there. I know you said that it wouldn't work, but I decided you were wrong. I should be able to keep it so they can't see us. If you don't walk too fast."

Sadar stared at Kenny for a few moments then stood up. The trio began to walk again. They kept to the shadows and moved slowly. No one else seemed to notice them.

# Chapter Thirty-One

It took them nearly another hour before they reached their destination. The trio crept, sticking to the shadows, but whatever Kenny was doing seemed to be working. They made it without any further incidents. However, there were some close calls. They had to hunch up against a wall while elves walked nearby. The more they walked, the more Sadar seemed concerned or mystified.

Nothing about the building made it stand out. It looked like it might be some drugstore in the human world. Except here, curtains were covering all the windows, concealing everything inside. Alicia was surprised when Sadar went to the door and even more surprised when it opened. A bell jingled on their arrival. Alicia looked and found the metallic bells tied to the door handle. The inside was nothing like the outside. There were rows of wooden bookshelves filled with books. Most of the books looked old and worn with various materials used to bind the pages together. Alicia couldn't help looking around her in wonder.

"How can it be so different inside the buildings when you cannot adjust the outside?" she asked.

"It's magic. The In-Between is a copy of the human world."

"But what happens if things change in the human world? What if they were to knock down this building? Would it still exist?"

"Our world is just a version of your world. We rely on the king to use illusion magic to update our world. The closer we are to the human world, the more we have to update. It is one of the reasons the king is so important."

"I think I get it. It's like you need to have a new operating system." Sadar looked at Alicia as she spoke, his raised eyebrows highlighted by the glow of the candles lit around the wall. "You do know about computers?"

"I know about them," he said defensively. "I just don't have much need to use them. They do not work on this side."

"And since you do not have technology, everything you have here is handmade." Alicia walked up to the bookshelf and ran her hand over it. It was solid and sturdy, like something she would have expected to come out of a carpenter's workshop. It was very different from the particle board furniture that filled their home. She felt a pain of homesickness then. Their apartment wasn't much, but she had worked hard for it.

To distract herself, Alicia picked up one of the books and examined it. It looked like it had hand stitching, although the cover was not made of leather. It was then that she realized that she had not seen a single animal on their walk here. She turned to ask Sadar about it but stopped at the sight of another man. He was nearly as tall as Sadar, with a slightly slimmer build. His olive-brown skin and short black hair were different from Sadar's almost ghost-like complexion. However, the two were locked in the most intense gaze Alicia had ever seen. There was a history here, but Alicia couldn't tell if it was hatred or happiness.

"Sadar," the new man said, ignoring both Alicia and Kenny completely.

"Rehta," Sadar said.

Their eyes never left each other. Both faces were locked in a scowl, but the men's bodies leaned slightly towards each other. The more she watched, the more she became convinced that they had had a relationship at some point. She just wondered who had broken whose heart. Although, if she had to guess, it was Sadar.

"You said that you would never return here."

"Things changed."

It was then that Rehta glanced over at Alicia and her son.

"You brought a human into my shop."

"She's an elf," Kenny spoke up, and Alicia turned to him questioningly. *Why would anyone think that she was an elf?*

At this, Rehta crouched down in front of Kenny.

"It is a neat little trick that you are doing. Don't worry. Your mother feels like an elf, but I know that she is human. You can stop and save your energy. She will be safe here."

Kenny paused for a second and then nodded in agreement, and his hand slipped from her for the first time since they started hiding in the shadows.

"You made me feel like an elf?" Alicia turned to Kenny questioningly and then to Sadar. "Why didn't you mention it?"

"I didn't notice. I was so focused on not getting caught."

"Then how did he notice?" Alicia gestured towards Rehta.

"I have spent my fair share of time in the human world. The clothes are a first sign, but it is more than that. It is the way you just don't quite fit. Don't worry, what he does is impressive. Most elves wouldn't see past it. But perhaps, most obviously, you speak English."

"Oh, yes." Alicia said. "But then that wouldn't have stopped the other elves from noticing."

"No," Kenny said. "That was different. Then I made us invisible. Well, not invisible, more like shadows. Not that we are shadows, just that others would think we were." Her son was quick to clarify.

"You used illusion magic in the In-Between," Rehta said. "Sadar, what exactly have you brought to my doorstep?"

# Chapter Thirty-Two

Sadar and Rehta were talking loudly on one side of the store. Alicia wished that she could understand what they were saying, but they spoke in elven, and there was not even a hint of familiarity in the language.

"We need to learn elven," Alicia muttered to her son.

Kenny sat at a wooden table, one that was solid and hand carved. Alicia had gawked at its beauty when they first saw it. However, she was not sitting at it. Instead, she was on the floor; the firmness of the wood tiles felt nice against her skin, and she needed that feeling at the moment. It had been a long day.

Another advantage of sitting on the floor was that Sadar and Rehta could not see her. Alicia was not ashamed of the way she calmed herself down. However, she also knew that some of her more eccentric behaviors tended to freak people out. So, Alicia kept them hidden as much as possible. She sat on the floor, flexing her fingers and slightly rocking until the talking stopped. As the footsteps approached, she closed her eyes and took several deep breaths, slipping back on the mask she wore to navigate a world not built for autistic people. Her hands fell to her sides, her rocking stopped, and she moved her body to a pose others would find relaxing. Well, as close as she could manage.

"I thought illusionary magic did not work here," Alicia blurted and then mentally berated herself for not allowing a more natural flow to the conversation. However, the question had been consuming her and nearly demanded to be let out. Sadar, however, no longer seemed fazed by her abruptness.

"It does not. At least, it normally does not."

"Then how does Kenny manage it?" Alicia asked.

"I think we should probably let him tell us."

Kenny looked up at them, and Alicia saw that he had been drawing, using paper had given to him when he ushered them away so that they could talk. It was a pretty impressive drawing of farms going up the side of a building. He even attempted some elves—at least Alicia thought they were elves.

"I know you said that it wouldn't work. But I still felt it. It doesn't feel the same, but it is still there. None of the magic feels the same here. Although, the other two are stronger here, I think."

"Fascinating," Sadar said.

"All you have to say is fascinating?" Alicia turned on Sadar. "I thought you were supposed to teach my son."

"It appears that he is teaching me, as well. I do not know why he can still feel illusionary magic. To me, it is like a giant brick wall. The only time I can access it is to shift out of the In-Between and into the human world. Then it is released. We have to take our illusionary students to the human world to train. There is even a small school set up for the most powerful of them."

Alicia glared at him. "What does that have to do with anything?"

"It was just meant to emphasize my point that he should not be able to use illusionary magic. But your son should not necessarily exist either. I have no idea how Kenny was conceived. Rehta has never even heard of a human and elf child, and nearly every elven book has passed through his doors at one point or another."

Alicia stared at her son, who was still sitting at the table and now back to drawing. He was her pride and joy. Her son had changed her life in so many ways, and all of them for the better. He made her step up and often step out of her solitary life. She had to learn to advocate to make sure he had what he needed and learn to navigate the world to ensure that she cared for him.

Now she felt like she was failing him. They had lost their home, they were stuck in a world that shouldn't exist, and the world had gotten so far away from logical that she was having a hard time coping. She liked things to make sense. She wanted them to be in order. She enjoyed doing the same thing day in and day out. Now all of that was out the window. But the worst of all of it was that she had no answers for her son. Alicia had no way to explain to him what was going on or even how he could exist. Although, looking at him calmly drawing, she had to admit that this was probably more of a problem for her than it was for him.

"I do have a theory," Sadar said. "I think the reason that Kenny can use illusionary magic in the in-between is due to his human blood."

"Why would that make a difference?"

"Being half-human is bound to have some impact on his magic. I would have thought that it would have depleted his magic, making him a less powerful elf. But, watching him, I think it is the exact opposite. His human half seems to heighten his elven half. Since his elven half is of the royal line, it is already some of the strongest elven magic. But he is stronger as a barely trained eight-year-old than anyone else alive."

Alicia watched her son add fluffy rounded clouds to his picture. It would be so much easier, for her, to go on pretending that this world didn't exist, and her son wasn't the most powerful magic user in generations. Even the thought made her want to laugh in an unstable fashion. Instead, she took a deep breath and moved forward. "So you think that this extra power helps him to use illusionary magic in the land of illusions?"

"Only partly. I think that Kenny can still connect to illusionary magic because he is only partly in the In-Between. You have seen how hard you have to work at seeing the elven world. Earlier, when you stopped focusing on the elven world and only saw the human world, you fell out of the illusion. You basically shifted all on your own. It is easier for you to be in the human world than the elven world."

"I shifted? You don't think I am at risk of shifting anymore?"

"What do you see when you look around you?"

"I see you. I see bookshelves and a lot of books."

"Exactly. You see the In-Between. You have finally accepted that you are here. You could still shift back, but it would be harder now. You would need familiarity, and it would have to be a choice. Although, most humans allow themselves to drift back as soon as they understand they are not trapped here."

Alicia looked at the sconces on the wall, each with flickering handmade candles. On the table there was a lantern filled with oil. This was not the world she grew up in, but it was one that her son belonged to, at least partly. "I am not most humans. I am the mother of the elven prince, and by that fact alone, this is my world now. At the very least, it is where I need to be to keep my son safe."

"I'm leaving. I talked with Rehta, and you can stay here with him. He is upstairs making space for you. I shouldn't be gone long. I just need to see what has become of this world myself. I need to see what I am responsible for, so that I can determine the best way to help."

"We could come with you," The response was almost desperate. Sadar was the only familiar thing in the space and the thought of losing him made anxiety crawl up her spine. Over the last few days, he had become familiar.

"Rehta is a good man. I promise you that. He will keep your son safe."

"You love him?" Alicia asked. Then she immediately realized that she had overstepped. "I'm sorry. You don't have to answer that."

"Over the last several days, there have been times that you have baffled me about how little you seem to understand the world around you. Then there are moments where you see more than most people would."

"We will stay, because you trust him, and because you think this is the safest place for my son. But what happens next is not a decision that you will get to make alone."

Sadar didn't answer her. He just gave her a brief glance and turned and walked around the bookshelves. She heard the jingle of the door opening and then nothing. For the time being, they were alone. Alicia went and took a seat next to her son, looking at the progress he had made on his picture. "Well, it is a good thing we are in a bookstore," she said. "Maybe we can find answers in some of them."

# Chapter Thirty-Three

The bookstore was quiet and dark. It was nothing compared to the excitement of the last few days, much to Alicia's delight. Alicia enjoyed the chance to regroup, but Kenny soon grew bored. A room full of books and none that he could read.

Alicia moved out of her chair enough to whisper in Kenny's ear. "Want to go on an adventure?"

"Yeah," he said back. His face spread into a grin.

Rehta had returned back downstairs, and Alicia could hear him shuffling around on the other side of the store. She wasn't sure what he thought about them being dumped on his lap, and wanted to stay out of his way as much as possible. She soon got an idea. "Out there," Alicia pointed to the rows of bookshelves, "there are two carnivorous beasts that live in the jungle. They are protecting a famous artifact. We brave explorers have to explore quietly until we find the right artifact and make it back to our camp without being caught."

"What artifact are we looking for?"

"I'm not sure. It is hidden by magic, but when we find it, then it will reveal itself."

They set off crouched down low and walking slowly. When Kenny would burst into giggles, Alicia would put her fingers up to her lips, but she laughed along with him.

The books were varied. Some spines were blank. Others were labeled with writing that almost looked like runes. More books had a script that looked like fancy calligraphy but with unrecognizable letters. There were even scrolls on the shelves. They walked row after row. Alicia was looking for something that would help her make sense of this world. She wasn't sure what exactly, but she did now it would to be something that she could understand.

They passed a set of stairs that led to a second floor. Alicia thought about going up and seeing if there was anything that would be entertaining to an eight-year-old. Then she decided against it. It was one thing to be sneaking around a public space. Upstairs was probably private. It was most likely best not to upset the person who was harboring them.

Instead, they went forward, down the last row of shelves.

Here they were rewarded. One side of the shelf was full of human books for all age ranges. The books were mass-produced and came in multiple languages, but most were in English. The other side was full of elven books written for children. There were stacks of picture books that looked like grade school primers piled upon each other. They looked like the most used books in the shop.

While Kenny wandered over to the human books, Alicia picked up one of the picture books. It looked just like the books that she had used to teach Kenny how to read. It was even shaped the same, just paper folded over and sewn at the binding. She opened it up and marveled at the pictures. It seemed to be hand-painted. The pictures showed a boy who grew tomato plants. Under the pictures were words made out of a circular script with lots of lines leading the way from the loops. They were just unrecognizable symbols on a page, especially since she didn't know the sounds. Though, as she stared down at the words, there was a faint tingling in the back of her head. It was similar to when Kenny did magic.

Alicia looked around, hoping to see a book that would translate English to elven. She knew it was a long shot, but it seemed her only chance. There didn't seem to be one, but she did find a book of pictures with the elven words next to them. She picked up her small pile of books and went over to Kenny. He was sitting on the floor, reading a book with a teenage wizard on the cover.

"Look what I found." Alicia showed him the books.

"This is elven?"

"I'm pretty sure. Too bad we don't know any of the sounds. Maybe we can ask Sadar later."

Kenny put down his chapter book and picked up the book with the painted objects. He peered at it intently. Then he flipped through the pages until he stopped on a page with a tree illustrated across two pages. The roots reached across the bottom of the page, and the lush greenery of the top dominated the left side of the page. On the right side, floating in the sky, there was a word. Kenny began moving his mouth like he was trying to sound it out. Alicia recognized the gesture from helping him to learn to read. Then he burst out, "Alda. The word says alda. It means tree."

"How do you know that?"

"The words speak. You just have to listen closely."

"You mean the words speak as the earth speaks?"

"No, well, maybe. They both speak magic. But the earth's magic is different. The words seem to have word magic. It's like they want people to know what they say, so they help them out."

Alicia looked at the word for tree and thought, *alda*. She tried to clear her mind of everything but the tree and the elven word. The buzzing was there, almost like an itch in her mind, but then it flittered away out of her reach.

Alicia sat back down and focused on her son. He seemed to have moved on from the small pile of books and had trapped a book with more words than pictures. He was struggling with it, but he seemed to be reading it.

"Do you understand it?" she asked.

"Yes, but it is still hard. I have to learn to read all over again."

"You are picking it up fast. It took you much longer to learn to read English."

"That was hard. I had to practice. This is almost like the words are reading themselves. Can books be magic?"

"I don't know." Alicia sat down next to Kenny. The shelves were close together, but there was enough room for them to sit down side by side. She looked at the story he had picked up; it was a picture book with hand-illustrated pictures and several handwritten sentences on each page. "What is the story about?"

"It's about a unicorn that wants to be a rainbow. Do you think there are unicorns?"

"I don't know. There doesn't seem to be many animals. So I would guess no. However, I've recently learned magic is real, so I guess anything is possible."

She reached out and tickled Kenny. His giggles echoed through the store. Alicia went to tell him to be quiet but stopped, wondering if it really mattered.

"Do you think you can read me the book?" she asked.

Kenny started reading in elven. The words were coming out of his mouth in the same high-pitched tone used at the market. She winced and put her hands to the top of her head squeezing gently to settle herself. There was the normal noise drilling into her brain, but there was something else. Like her body was rejecting the words as they were spoken.

Kenny seemed to realize her discomfort. He switched to speaking English. His finger pointed to each word as he spoke. He spoke fast, seeing the words in elven and pronouncing them in English without hesitation. The reading level of the book was fairly young, but it still seemed impossible.

When Rehta walked down the aisle, Kenny closed the book. They both sat up, guilty.

He said something to Kenny in elven. Kenny nodded his head in agreement.

"He can understand elven," Rehta said to Alicia.

"Yes, a little. I don't understand how he could have picked it up so fast."

"The elven language is magic. Since Kenny is such a strong magic user, he will naturally connect to the language. He will be fluent soon. You will be able to learn it, I think, but it will probably fight you at every turn. It has been quite some time since there have been humans here. But I may be wrong. This whole situation is unique. There has never been a half-elf before. That is bound to be a factor."

*There has never been a half-elf before*, Alicia thought. "Why…" Alicia halted, unsure of how to continue. "Why do you think it has happened now, if there has never been a half-elf before?"

"I think that is a really good question, and I wish I had an answer for you. All I can say is that magic has rules like any other system, but that doesn't mean we understand all the rules. There is something about your son that needed to be, and here he is." They both turned to look at Kenny sitting and reading. At the attention, he looked up and smiled at them, and when they did not talk to him, he went back to reading. "I came over here to tell you that I have some errands to run, and I think it would be a good idea for you both to come with me."

Alicia was shaking her head in dissent before he had even finished speaking. "I think we should stay here. It took a lot for us to get here, and I'm sure it's safer if we stay."

"I assure you that I am capable of protecting both you and the prince. Although, from what I hear, you are both formidable yourself."

"I didn't mean to insult you. I'm sure we will be safe with you. It is just that every time Sadar leaves, trouble comes."

"Trust me when I say he can bring his own share of trouble to your life." He sighed dramatically, but it was offset by the dreamy smile on his face.

Alicia looked at Rehta questioningly, but not wanting to

push.

"It is hard to love someone with different ideological principles." The words flowed freely from him. He seemed so open after spending so much time with Sadar. "Yet maybe that is how love is. Two fates separated by their destinies, fighting to be with each other. Unable to stay apart."

"Do you ever think that maybe you spend too much time with your books?"

"You don't believe in love?"

"I don't understand it. I've never needed to be around a lot of people, and I've never felt an attraction to anyone."

"Everyone is different, and it is our differences that make us great. I am a romantic. I knew the first time I saw Sadar that we were destined for a tragic love story. I was visiting a warehouse uninvited. It was full of food, just sitting there unneeded." As he spoke, Rehta's hands flowed as if acting out the story. "So, I decided it would be best to help make sure that it didn't go to waste, for a reasonable price.

"I ran with a local group. We had been quite busy and were causing a nuisance to the nobles." Rehta chuckled to himself, lost in his own reminiscing. "So, they sent in their blood sworn. We managed to escape, and he thankfully never saw me. It was all quite dramatic. I managed to arrange to run into him a few nights later, and the attraction came quite easily to both of us."

"How long until he realized you were a thief?"

"Oh, I like you. Nice and direct! He knew right away, of course. He helped me move away from that group, but I could never quite live up to his noble expectations. And he could never understand what it was like to grow up outside the palace."

"Where do you want to take us? Tell me the truth."

"Like I said, I have some errands to run." Rehta's voice turned serious, the easy humor gone. "There are some people I think you and your son should see. No one dangerous, no one too important, just people trying to survive."

Alicia looked down at her son. Although she was sure he had listened in on everything that was said, he was still focused on the book. So it didn't surprise her when he spoke.

"I think we should go. I know you are worried, but Sadar wouldn't have left if he didn't think Rehta could keep me safe. Besides, I can do magic here."

"I still don't know," Alicia said.

"You have always taught me that it is important to help other people. So how can I know how to help unless we go see what the people need help with?"

"Maybe it is not our place to help." But the words rang hallow to Alicia's ears as she said them.

Kenny finally put his book down and looked up. His lips quivered as he spoke. "I belong here. I need to be around the elves to help me figure out what is happening and how to keep everyone safe. Before, I was so different from everyone, and I didn't know why. Now I know. They need me as much as I need them. Maybe it is not my job, but I want to help. There are bad people here, and because of that, I had to do something bad. I want to help stop them. I want to help the people, so they don't have to do bad things and make up for the bad things I had to do. I know I had to save you, but I still want to do more good things than bad."

Alicia sat down next to Kenny and wrapped him in her arms. He climbed into her lap and snuggled like he used to do when he was smaller.

"We're going to get this figured out. We will find a way to get you safe. Then we are going to go home. You can go back to school, and I'll find a new job. We will go back to see Master Kang. Don't you miss him?"

Kenny nodded. "I do," he said in a tearful voice. "But it was so hard there."

The words hit Alicia deeply. She remembered her own school days that she spent watching all the other children laugh and play. Every time she tried to join in, she did something wrong. They taunted her, ridiculed her, until she thought she would break. She never belonged—she just tried to find a way to survive. How could she ask the same of her son, if there was a place he really was a part of?

"If we go with you, he will be safe?" Alicia looked up at Rehta for reassurance.

"I promise that if anything were to happen, I would protect him with my life." He said it with such intensity that Alicia did not doubt his declaration.

"OK, we can go."

"Good. We need to leave soon. We need to make sure we are back in time."

"In time for what?" Alicia asked.

"It is just best not to be outside too late at night. You can get changed now." Rehta gestured for them to stand and then ushered them towards the stairs that they had found earlier. "If you walk up the stairs and enter the first door, you will find outfits that I left out for you. You can also take a shower."

"You have running water?" Alicia asked.

Rehta glared at her for a few seconds and then sighed. "It is only technology that does not work here. Plumbing, while a marvel, is not actual technology. However, the water may be a bit colder than your world. We have to use alternate means of heating the water. We are quite fortunate as humans have put in all the work of creating the piping for the building. We get to enjoy it. There are also the workings for electricity here. The wiring is in the walls. Even the switches are there. But if you were to flick a switch, nothing would happen. So, many elves chose to cover them up instead. Now get ready. I will be waiting for you down here."

# Chapter Thirty-Four

At the top of the stairs, there was a short hallway with three doors off of it. The wall and doors were both wooden, and Alicia couldn't help wondering if they were an elf addition. What she couldn't do was move. Space up here was more intimate, and even though Rehta had given her direction to come up here, it still felt like an intrusion. After everything, this was where she froze, but knowing her actions were illogical did nothing to alleviate the anxiety coursing through her.

Alicia paused, took a deep breath, and resisted finding something on which to tap her fingers. Instead, she mapped out one thing she could bring herself to do.

"That door is open," Alicia said. "Let's see if that is where

Rehta wants us to go." The sentence was a release for Kenny, who had waited patiently at her side. Now he bounded off into the room. Before Alicia could even make it to the doorway, he had raced back out.

"This is it. There are clothes on the bed and a giant tub. I think it is made out of a type of rock. But it is so big someone probably carved it with their power. I could probably make a tub. I wonder what else I could make."

Kenny continued talking while Alicia got acclimated to the space. They were used to this routine, and Alicia found comfort in it, allowing her to decrease her anxiety.

The walls of the room were a mixture of wood and metal. Alicia began to see how the bedroom was shaped from what was a stockroom or something similar. The bathroom had a toilet and a bathtub that appeared to be marble. The fixture for the tub was metal and came directly from the wall. It was amazing what transferred to this world and what didn't.

Alicia started filling the tub with water, delighted when it worked. Despite Rehta's assurance, Alicia hadn't been optimistic. Then she had to wrangle a squirming eight-year-old into the tub. She located a bottle of very human shampoo and a bar of soap that was probably handmade in the In-Between. Once Kenny was settled in the tub with his hair washed, Alicia went and looked at the clothes on the bed.

Kenny's clothes looked reasonably easy to understand. The

232

pants were a drawstring. The shirt seemed to have two triangle pieces that overlapped and tied on the sides. It was almost like their taekwondo uniforms. Her clothes were another matter. It looked like a dress cut down the middle and then cut up into shapes. Then the shapes were sewn back together, except now the sides weren't even. There were ties everywhere, and Alicia had no idea how it was supposed to go on. She hated dresses—they left her feeling vulnerable, and, most importantly, she hated fighting in them.

Alicia checked in on Kenny and then took a better look at the room. The bed took up the majority of the room. It was large, probably bigger than a king-size. She reached down and touched it. The bed was soft but not built in a factory.

On the walls, there were various pieces of art that all seemed to be vegetable-themed. Alicia shook her head at the choice and moved to the last item in the room. There was one more door, although this one was closed. She took a deep breath and opened it.

It was a large walk-in closet. There were piles of clothes stacked on shelves. The floor held shoes in various sizes. There were boxes of items that came from the human world. Some looked like canned food. Others were first aid supplies. Alicia was surprised to see so many human goods stacked above the bookstore. Then, thinking back to Rehta's story, she decided it was best not to think about it too much. Instead, she picked through the clothing and located pants and a shirt similar to her son's.

She closed her eyes, trying to remember the walk here, trying to remember what people were wearing. She came up blank; she had been too busy, focused on the empty houses and the growing plants to remember the people all that much. She couldn't help wondering how women were even treated here. For the first time, it sunk in how far away from home she was and how she could no longer rely on her own set of rules. She sank to the floor of the closet and, clutching the clothes, began to rock back and forth. Her mind flared with anxiety, and she let it overwhelm her. Then she focused on what was important: her son. She let herself enjoy the sensation of moving back and forth with the press of the floor into her body. Then she stood up and went to get her son out of the tub.

It took a while to wrangle Kenny into the new clothes. Then she had to get herself cleaned and washed. She knew that Rehta was on a timeline, and she did not want to make him late. It was probably fine, well, hopefully. If he wanted them to hurry up, then he would probably shout at them, and he hadn't done so.

When they walked downstairs and saw Rehta was still working on bagging something up, Alicia relaxed a little. She hated being late.

Rehta had several cloth bags laid out on the table. Each of them seemed to be the size of a plastic shopping bag. Rehta was gathering the bags into two larger canvas bags.

"Do you want me to help carry anything?" Alicia offered.

Rehta looked up as if startled by her request. Then he shook his head and put one of the canvas bags on each of his shoulders.

"If this is some male pride thing, then I assure you that I am capable of carrying a bag. It won't emasculate you either."

"No, it would not. I'm just concerned about what would happen if we were stopped."

"If anything were to happen, carrying a bag would be the least of my problems. I'm human, and I think if it came down to them searching bags, they would notice this. Besides, you said it is safe."

"It is safe. You will both be fine."

"You have to decide. It is either too unsafe for me to carry a bag, and we really shouldn't go out at all. Or, everything will be fine, and I can help you carry the bags."

The streets were empty when they left. Rehta locked the door with one bag on his shoulder. Alicia was carrying the second. The bag was a little heavy, and she was glad Rehta didn't have to hold both of them.

They walked for long enough that the bag had dug into both of Alicia's shoulders. Kenny was getting bored and trying not to show it. His attention would wander, and his steps would slow down. He would open his mouth to speak, probably to complain, and then glance at Rehta. His mouth would close. His body would slump, and he would straighten and pay attention again.

Alicia was trying to gauge the time. It had taken them hours to get to the bookstore. They had to have spent hours in the bookstore as well. Yet the sun was still up in the sky like it was only a little after noon. The sky itself was clear, not even clouds to be seen. *Were there clouds here? If not, then there wouldn't be rain. If there was no rain, then how would they have water?* Her mind was caught up in the endless loop of questions. She was about to ask Rehta when they stopped.

The downtown area had transformed into a place that had seen better days. The building they were in front of looked like a supermarket. The set of doors framed glass that, for some reason, did not exist in this world. The trio stepped through the empty frame.

The front of the store was lit from the sunlight streaming in. The front of the store was glass, glass that did exist. The building was empty of all the shelving. However, the register counters were present and looked like they had been turned into bedrooms with cots set up in the middle of them. Some of the other counters existed as well. The one in the back had fabric hanging above it from the ceiling, cutting off the view.

There was a giant pit in the center of the store with a handful of elves breaking off parts of the hole and lifting them into a large metal container.

"They are mining?" Alicia asked.

"The throne has assigned them to dig the earth for organic rock. Our people prize it as it can be a vessel for magic. They will bring up the earth and then sift through it, making sure to find even the smallest piece. This is dangerous and tiring work, but the quota keeps growing, and now most are unable to stop unless they wish to be tried as a traitor."

Rehta started walking back to the closed-off section. Alicia stopped and looked at the elves. They were covered in sweat and dirt. Something bothered her. It took a second of watching before she realized that they looked defeated. Like they had lost all hope. Kenny started to pull on her hand, walking towards Rehta. She followed, but she couldn't take her eyes off their work. They were going so fast, and dirt and rocks were going in all directions. No wonder it was dangerous.

"What is organic rock?" Kenny asked.

"I guess that it is rock that is alive," Alicia said.

"How can rock be alive?"

"I have no idea."

"I believe you would call them fossils," Rehta said. Then he slipped between the folds of the material and the wall. Alicia watched Kenny follow and then did so herself.

Inside there were more cots scattered around. It was not a large space, and most of it was already taken up with a young child playing with some rocks on the floor and a woman mixing something on the counter. On the cots, there was a man with his head wrapped up in bandages and a young woman who had her leg wrapped and propped up.

The entire place was dirty. Fine silt covered the counters. There was dirt smudging their faces and coating their clothes. The air seemed as full of dirt hidden behind the curtain as it did out in the open where they were working.

Rehta walked up to the woman. They embraced and started talking in Elven. The woman's face brightened suddenly, a smile cracking open her expression. Then she took one of the bags from Rehta. She looked through it, full of gratitude that needed no translation.

Then she removed a small pouch from her apron and held it out to Rehta. She seemed apologetic and a bit frightened. But he took the pouch with only a quick look inside and tucked it away under his waistband.

Rehta had walked back their way and pointed at Alicia's shoulder. She looked and saw the straps for the bag. With all that had happened, she had forgotten that she was even still holding it. Alicia slid the straps off her shoulder and handed the bag over to Rehta, trying not to show her relief at the missing weight.

Rehta reached into the bag and pulled out a plump orange. He walked over to the child sitting calmly [AA1] on the floor and handed the orange to them. A smile sprouted on the young child's face as they reached up and wrapped their arms around Rehta's neck. When Rehta stood up, the child's focus turned to the orange. They held it up to their nose and gave it gentle squeezes.

It was then that the woman seemed to notice that Rehta had brought company. She talked to Rehta in confusion, her words becoming faster and more frightened. But he talked to her reassuringly until she seemed to calm.

Rehta walked back to Alicia and Kenny, putting his arms around them to turn them around and pushing them towards the exit. As they left, Alicia turned around for one last look and met the woman's eyes. They were full of suspicion and fear.

# Chapter Thirty-Five

Alicia's mind was turbulent as she walked on autopilot, following Rehta and Kenny. So much had just happened, and she felt disconnected, like she was missing context. So, her mind whirled and turned until she realized there was so much she just didn't understand. She only knew that Rehta had taken them to a place without hope. She just wasn't sure of his intentions.

When Alicia next focused on her surroundings, they were in a new part of the city. The streets were cleaner with no dirt on the sidewalks or the people. The clothing was brighter and made out of softer materials. There was not a lot of foot traffic, but those who were out were not alone. There tended to be one or two people strolling with sun umbrellas to provide shade. Behind them was at least one person carrying their belongings. They even passed a litter being carried down the street on the shoulders of elves dressed only in light vests and a layer of sweat.

They gave the trio a wide berth as if they could catch poverty even though Sadar had explained that a person's station in this world depended on their magic level. Finally, they slipped off the main street they were on, and Alicia found herself outside a red-bricked building. The building was rectangular shaped with large windows spaced out regularly down the side. The front of the building held two large glass doors. Above them, in block metal letters, read *King Elementary School*.

Rehta walked up to the door and then knocked in what Alicia assumed was a secret code. Looking through the glass, Alicia could see nothing but the next set of doors, so she jumped when there was a slight fluttering just inside. Then a lanky teenager stepped out of the shadows. They wore a dark short cloak with a hood over their head. It cast a shadow over their face, giving them a sense of mystery that seemed dramatic. They made a point of looking over the trio and then pulled one of the doors open a fraction. Rehta indicated for Kenny and herself to go in first. Kenny walked right in with Alicia hurrying behind him. She quickly pulled her son behind her before she had even consciously registered that two more youths were hidden in the shadows. Both had pulled out knives on them.

The teenagers stared at Kenny and her with distrust. Alicia's entire body tensed up, and her mind kept running through the moves on how to disarm an opponent. It was something she had practiced thousands of times but never actually had to use. Any movement and she was ready. Even if she were hurt, it would give Rehta time to get her son out of here.

"Lizza, Airek, Santh." Rehta turned to each youth as he said their name, making sure to look at each in turn. "Do not be daft, boys. Put away those weapons. You know who I am."

"We know you," the first youth said in a nasal tone and hesitant in a language he was not native to. "We don't know them, though."

"Lizza, they are my friends, and you best leave them alone. This young man is stronger than Santh, by a lot."

"Not a chance," Lizza said. "Santh is the best rocker flinger in the entire city."

Rehta turned and gave a slight nod to Kenny. Alicia noticed that in each of the corners of the vestibule there were piles of small pebbles. They started to rise, causing the teenagers to jump. Then the smallest of the youths turned excitedly to the second youth, talking rapidly in elven and pointing at the rocks.

The piles continued to lift until Kenny had combined them all together in a giant ball that rotated above their heads. The trio stood with mouths open and eyes wide. When the ball began to separate and form four separate piles, which were then sent back to the corners of the room, their eyes opened even wider.

"Have you come to drop him off?" Lizza asked. "We will gladly take him."

"No, that's his mother. They are just passing through."

The three seemed to stand a little straighter at this answer. The two with knives immediately tucked them away. "Is she here to adopt more?" the shortest youth asked, his English thick with an elven accent.

"No, Airek. He is not adopted, that's his birth mother."

The three youths started talking to Rehta in elven, each speaking faster than he could respond. Alicia could not understand any of it, but Kenny reached and put his hand in hers. Finally, Lizza opened the second set of doors and motioned them through. The three teenagers stayed guard on the other side. The two had disappeared back into the shadows, but Lizza stood facing them, his face still hidden in the cloak.

"What did they say?" Alicia asked Rehta as they walked down an empty hallway with closed doors lined up on each side.

"They were just confused and curious." Rehta reached down and mussed up Kenny's hair. Kenny moved even closer to his mother, holding her hand tighter.

"Was it a good idea to tell them about Kenny? What if they go and tell someone?"

"I'm counting on it, but don't worry. No one here will tell anything to anyone related to the king. You will not find a group of people that hates him more than in this building.

"Why are we in a school anyway?" Alicia asked.

Rehta reached out and opened one of two large doors in front of them. It opened into a school gymnasium full of children. There had to be at least a hundred camped in the small room. They ranged in age from teenagers to infants, and it was easy to tell that the older children held a lot of responsibility for the younger children. But for containing this many children, the room was too quiet. It was the occasional squeal of delight that was followed by whispers to be quiet. Even the footsteps seemed muted in the room, like they had all figured out how to walk by making as little noise as possible. It was disconcerting.

Once they entered, Rehta stopped and held onto the door, helping it to close quietly, but even that click caused the room full of children to freeze and turn their heads towards the group. Alicia looked back at the children, staying still until they gradually lost interest and went back to their quiet activities. Alicia looked down at Kenny who seemed to be studying all the children. Rehta had left them, already walking towards the only elf that seemed to be of adult age, if barely. Rehta beckoned them over. Kenny let go of Alicia's hand and started walking through the various groups. He watched one group of children about his age playing with a group of dolls. When a young boy looked up, he smiled at Kenny and Kenny tentatively smiled back. The boy went back to playing, and Kenny turned away and finished walking towards Rehta.

"Alicia, I would like you to meet Sisha. They run this orphanage." Rehta's voice was barely a whisper.

Alicia looked at the elf. Sisha was taller than Rehta, and thinner. They seemed to have been whittled down to almost nothing. Sisha was dressed in a shirt and pants similar in style to the ones Alicia now wore, except the color had faded out of them and there were patches made in the coarser clothing. Their face was narrow, just shy of being gaunt, and their hair was dark but cut close to their scalp.

"It's so nice to meet you." Their voice was almost musical. They held out their hand, their face full of amusement. "I've never met a human before."

Alicia held up her own hand, and awkwardly shook the unmoving elf's hand. "It is nice to meet you as well. Do you run this entire orphanage?" Her voice came out loud, and many of the children looked at her with startled expressions.

"I have help from some of the older children." Their voice was clear but quiet. They knelt down and spoke to Kenny. "What do you think of our home?"

"I think it could use more toys so that the kids can smile more. If it is all right, I would like to bring some next time we come to visit." At this, Kenny looked up at Rehta. "Do you have any toys in your shop we could bring?"

"No, not there. But I will find a way to trade for some."

Kenny gave a brief nod as if to accept his words as acceptable. Then he turned back to look at the children until he noticed a group around his age that seemed to be quietly playing a game that looked almost like duck, duck, goose.

"May I go join them?" Kenny turned first to the young elf and then to Alicia before running off to join them as quietly as he could manage.

"Why are the children so quiet?" Alicia asked, her voice a whisper.

"Our last home was raided because some of the children got too loud. We lost twenty-three children that night. Those that were there remember, and those that have come after have been told by the other children. No one wants to be found again."

"Oh," Alicia gasped and then brought her voice back down. "Who would want to hurt children?"

Sisha shared a brief look with Rehta before asking, "How much do you know about our world?"

"Not enough, apparently."

"The children here all have parents that were sentenced by the king. They are all in prison or dead. At least, these are the ones that we have managed to help escape or have found on the streets."

Alicia looked to her son, checking to make sure that he was safe. He was currently walking around a circle of children, quietly tapping on their heads. The youngest held her shirt to her mouth to soften her giggles, her black curls bouncing silently as they played. "Why would the king want to hurt these kids?"

The elf looked at the children, then at Rehta, as if deciding if to speak. "I think," they said then hesitated. "I think he is afraid that someone will challenge him, even though none of these could. Most are the children of farmers and merchants."

Rehta opened some of his bags, showing Sisha the contents as Alicia detached from the other adults and watched Kenny playing with the children. They had been running from Kenny's father for less than a week, but all the families here had been running for much longer. She was so focused on her son that it was a lot to adjust to all these other children being cared for by one young adult.

"I don't have all the payment this week," Alicia heard the elf say. "I know we are still behind, and we are working on it."

The children were now pointing at objects and speaking, the words too quiet for Alicia to hear. Kenny appeared to be copying what they said.

"I know we said that we would catch up this week. It is just that Niko came back and said the market had been closed down in Ettyburo. We don't have someone who can shift anymore, not since we lost Mat. Niko has gone to Jelik to sell, but it will be a while before he can make it back."

Alicia turned around, realizing the conversation that was happening behind her. "You can't possibly be selling to them."

She tried to keep her voice low so none of the children could hear.

"It's what I do," Rehta said. "I wouldn't be much of a merchant if I didn't sell things."

"I'll figure out a way to help clear their tab. I still have a little money in my bank account, if I can get to it. Just give them what you have now."

Rehta looked at her, as if lost in thought, then he turned and continued his transaction with Sisha.

# Chapter Thirty-Six

Alicia stood outside of the school, trying to determine how to get back to the bookstore. Kenny stood next to her, his gaze moving between Alicia's still form and that of Rehta walking away.

"We're going to get lost," Kenny said.

"We are not going with him anymore. I won't have him dragging us around as he swindles people that cannot afford it."

Alicia finally took off, in the opposite direction to Rehta. She glanced down at her son to make sure that he was following, then kept her gaze focused ahead of her, acting like she knew what she was doing.

"You're going in the wrong direction."

Alicia ignored Rehta and kept on walking until she realized that Kenny was no longer at her side. She looked back and saw him stopped between the two adults, an uncertain expression on his face.

"The bookstore is this way. I just need to make one more stop and then we will head back," Rehta said.

"We're not going on any more stops with you. I am not going to participate in you taking advantage of all these people. They need help, not overpriced goods."

"Trust me when I say that my next stop will have no problem paying."

"That's supposed to make me feel better?" Alicia turned towards Rehta, still not moving.

"I don't care how you feel. This is my job. This is how I don't starve. It is how I make sure all those people you saw today do not starve. It isn't exactly easy to get food around here, and I make sure that they have it. I didn't need you telling me to leave the food for the kids. They haven't paid their bill in over a year, and I keep delivering."

"Oh," Alicia said. "Why are you taking us to all of these places anyway?"

"I thought you should see what our land is really like. Sadar has been gone too long from the people, and I figured the prince should know." Rehta let out a sigh. "Maybe it was all a mistake, but I have one more stop and then I will take you back to the bookstore."

Alicia looked at Rehta. There was a lingering sadness in his brown eyes. His face fell in momentary grief before he caught himself and put on his usual grin. "One more stop, and then we head back."

Shortly after, they stopped at a large building. It was extravagant with white pillars across the front and white marble stairs leading up to them. Behind the pillars there was a porch that looked to be marble except for the carpeting leading up to the doorway. The entryway was two large solid wooden doors with beautiful metal handles. Alicia tried to imagine what it would be used for in the human world. Maybe it was a small museum. That, or it could just be a house for someone who had a lot of wealth. Regardless of what it was in the human world, it was almost certainly a rich elf's house. Why were they bringing food to someone who had this much already?

Rehta didn't enter the front doors. Instead, he walked around to the side of the building and through a fence gate. There was a less gratuitous door there. It was the same wood, but not quite as thick and only one door.

Rehta knocked several times and then stepped back.

They waited and waited. Alicia expected Rehta to knock again, or to turn around and walk away. Instead, he stood calmly and patiently. Alicia admired his self-assurance. Even if it was all an act, Rehta came across as completely in charge of every situation. Well, every situation that didn't involve Sadar. Alicia tried to mimic his poise and wait just as patiently. She tried to look like her mind wasn't being swarmed with a constant stream of thoughts about why they shouldn't be here. Or about how they were going to be caught at any moment. She tried not to think that maybe they should not have trusted Rehta since he seemed to be delivering them up to the very people they were trying to stay away from.

Alicia looked around, wondering if she was contributing to their own capture. She took her son's hand and was trying to think through the anxiety when the door opened. She stared at it, willing herself to run while, at the same time, telling herself that she had every reason to trust Rehta. Finally, the door opened enough to reveal another elf. He was dressed in clothing that was well kept but did not seem to be as fine. He wore gloves on his hands and had a rag hanging out of one of his pockets.

"I have a delivery for the count," Rehta said.

The elf gave a nod and stepped aside to let them all in. The house was stunning. There were hand carved tables and chairs of a rich brown wood. The counters looked like they were brought over from the human world, but they had been adapted for elven functionality. The countertops were granite placed atop thick brown wooden counters. Shelving had been added to the areas that would have housed a fridge and stove in the human world. The kitchen area was larger than Alicia's entire apartment.

"Welcome, welcome to my home." The elf swept into the room. His hands were spread open like he was trying to encompass everyone in a grasp. It caused his robe-like clothing to flare. With his bright coloring, he almost looked like a butterfly. He looked healthier than the rest of the elves they had visited. "I am sorry for the wait. But I expected you earlier. There was a visitor that had best not see my delivery. Now what have you brought today?"

The man walked over to Rehta and pulled the bag off his shoulders. Then he placed it on the table and quickly checked the contents.

"Good, good," he mumbled. "I may have to go to his new court and I will need to have supplies." He pulled out a bottle of ketchup from the bag, cradling it like it was made of gold. "I'm trying to put it off, but I will have to go."

"You know where he is?" It was the first time Rehta had spoken. Alicia noticed that he held himself stiffly. In all other locations he was relaxed and reassuring, yet here was different. He seemed uncomfortable, maybe even angry.

"No, like he would trust anyone with that information. There has just been word that he may be requesting my presence. I've tried to evade the summons for as long as I could, but what am I to do? He is the king, after all."

The man turned and looked in Alicia's direction, but his gaze moved right past her and straight to her son. He stared so intently that Alicia took an involuntary step in front of Kenny, blocking his view. He turned and looked at her then. It was a quick glance that took in her entire presence and then moved on.

"What have you brought to my doorstep?" The man talked to Rehta, but he had moved to better see Kenny. "It cannot possibly be." He turned towards Rehta then, his eyes wide. "Does anyone else know?"

"There are not many I would trust enough to let them know."

"Interesting that you trust me." He moved then, his robe fluttering as he dashed. He was in front of Alicia before she registered his movement. His hands clasped her arms to her sides. He was shorter than her, and she could see the bald spot on top of his head, but his grip was firm. He looked at her face, as if searching for something, then as quickly let her go.

"This can change everything," he said. "I think it is time I went to court."

# Chapter Thirty-Seven

Alicia woke up to light from the window falling on her face. Over the last few days, she had become used to waking up in unfamiliar places, and she took her customary moment to reorient herself. The memories of yesterday hit her hard.

Her son was still fast asleep on the bed. She paused and looked at him. He was so sweet and innocent and young. Voices from downstairs drifted into the room. It sounded like Sadar was back. Alicia rearranged the blankets so that Kenny was covered. Then she slipped out of the elven clothes she had fallen asleep in and back into her human clothes before heading downstairs.

Rehta and Sadar talked in loud whispers like they were trying not to wake them up but had gotten a bit carried away with what they were saying. Sadar had his arms folded and his customary scowl on his face while Rehta moved his arms around as he spoke. They were both standing between the stairs and the back room Rehta used as a kitchen.

They did not notice Alicia walking down the stairs. So, she tried clearing her throat loudly. Neither of the men seemed to hear. Instead, they continued talking, focused only one each other. Finally, she spoke up: "Good morning."

They stopped talking immediately and turned to watch her finish walking towards them. When they continued to stare, Alicia decided that now was as good a time as any to get her answers.

"How can this place be in such disrepair? We saw people being worked to death and children orphaned by the hundreds." Alicia walked up to Sadar, her voice nearly yelling. "If you knew, I know there is no way that even you could not have blindly followed this king."

"I have not been in the city for quite some time. I didn't know how bad things had gotten," Sadar said.

"Things have always been bad," Rehta said. "You have just chosen not to see it."

"It is my duty to serve the royal family. I do not have to agree with their decisions." The men continued the conversation that Alicia had tried to interrupt. Sadar stood frozen with his hands folded, his feet braced and his face impassive. Rehta talked with his hands and face as much as his voice. His face broadcast every expression and his hands flared with every word.

The two men were opposites. Sadar with his fair complexion and stoic manner. Rehta with his darker complexion and passion. Yet, as Alicia watched them, she got the impression that they were less two distinct individuals and more two halves of a whole.

"Your duty comes before everything," Rehta said.

"Yes, it does. It always will. It was a decision made for me as a child, but it still binds me as an adult."

"We are all pawns in the king's world," Rehta said. "We have to choose how we plan to die, either slowly starving to death out here or faster in the king's prison."

"How do you get the food you feed them?" Alicia asked, once again trying to break up their argument.

Rehta turned and glared at her. "It is best that you do not know that."

"What food?" Sadar asked.

"It is best you do not know about that either," Rehta said. "I get food because someone has to. I just happen to be good at it."

"What do you mean?" Sadar asked. He slumped against one of the shelves of books, looking lost and conflicted. Then it vanished, and Sadar crossed his arms again and scowled, more than usual. Alicia wished he had been with them and seen the things that they did. Then maybe he would do something. There was no way that he could stand by and watch all those people suffer.

"You brought us here for a reason," Alicia said.

"I brought you here to keep you safe," Sadar said.

"You want something from us. You want something from my son." Alicia felt small next to the two men. It wasn't that they were so much taller; it was that the two men dominated so much space.

"I just want to keep Kenny safe," Sadar said. "I'm not sure what our next move is, but he should be safe here for now."

"I didn't mean you." Alicia turned and glared at Rehta. "He wants us for something, or at least my son. He led us around yesterday, showing us the desperation of this world. He wanted to get our sympathy. I just don't understand why."

"I didn't show you anything that wasn't true." Rehta walked to a table near the kitchen door and sat down in one of the chairs.

The movement was so casual that Alicia was sure it was calculated. She tried to copy him by strolling over to the table and pulling out a chair opposite him, but the chair was heavier than expected and didn't move. She pulled it again, making a large screeching noise across the wooden floor. By the time she sat down, she was done trying to be strategic and ready to just hide. Flushed with embarrassment, her words came out more pointed than intended. "I am sure it was all true. You probably didn't have to alter your plans any to pull at our heartstrings.

This world has problems, I get that. What I don't understand is what it has to do with me and my son."

Sadar was still standing, his gaze was fluctuating between the two, but otherwise he was silent.

"There is no heir to the throne. People are putting up with the king because no one can take his place. Did Sadar tell you how the In-Between is made?"

"I think he mentioned something."

"The worlds are connected. Every so often a new version of our world has to be created. The closer the contact we have with the human world, the more often this happens. If we get too out of synch, our world will start to collapse and the illusion will not hold up. We need the king for that." Rehta had folded his hands on top of the table. He was trying so hard to come across as calm, but Alicia could see how tense his fingers were lanced together. It was something she did herself when she was anxious.

"Is there another solution? Maybe if multiple illusionists worked together?"

"This isn't the first bad monarch we have had. They've tried in the past, but only royalty can keep the In-Between going. It isn't just the refresh. It requires a constant connection. We have to have a ruler to survive." Rehta nearly spit the words out.

Alicia tapped her fingers on the table, thinking long and hard. "We will help you, and then we will go back to the human world where my son can grow up and lead a normal life."

"You think that you will be safe just by going back to the human world?" Rehta asked.

"We will if we help you take down the king."

"There are no other heirs left. If your son doesn't take the throne, then the entire In-Between will fall. Humans will have hundreds of thousands of refugees that are hungry, tired, and full of magic. You've seen the devastation that happens when unethical magic users interact with the human world. Even those we call magicless will have complete power over your world. We are not the same people who tried to coexist thousands of years ago. Now we are just as bent as the human world. We will be the ones who try to rule. Then what will happen to your son having a normal life?"

"There has to be a way. What if the veil did come down? What if there was a sort of treaty that your people would agree to follow? Maybe integrating elves back into the same world would be a good thing. If they agree not to harm, not to take over, then it could work out for everyone."

"Except it would take someone powerful to make them fall in line," Rehta said.

"You could do it. I saw you with the people. They respect you. They would listen to you."

"Elves respect power." Rehta stood up, pushing the chair behind him, and started pacing on his side of the table. "I have enough magic to slip between worlds and not enough for the guards to suspect me of doing so. I am not this figurehead that you want me to be. People will respect your son. He comes from the royal line and has the magical ability to protect the people. He is the strongest magic user we have seen in generations, maybe even ever. The people will only turn from the king to follow your son."

"Why does it have to be her son?" The sound of Sadar's voice startled Alicia—she had forgotten that he was even there.

Rehta stopped walking. When he looked up his face was full of grief. "It has to be her son because everyone else is gone."

"What do you mean?" Sadar stepped forward, reaching out to Rehta instinctively. When he realized, he dropped his hand and stood still. Rehta closed the short distance, wrapping his arms around Sadar. Sadar embraced the other man, holding him while he silently cried. Rehta's head was buried in Sadar's chest.

It took a minute before Rehta composed himself enough to speak. They separated slightly, both men leaving an arm around the other as if afraid to let go.

"They're gone, all of them. First it was the distant cousins," Rehta said.

"There were a string of accidents," Sadar said. "The king and queen sent me to investigate, but there was nothing out of the ordinary. Just bad timing."

"Then the king and queen died," Rehta continued.

"They died while I was away," Sadar said.

"No one blames you. No one saw it coming." The two men were lost in their own world again, talking like there was no one else around.

"I made it back for the funeral, but I was ordered not to attend. He sent me away, as soon as I returned, on a mission to the human world."

"No one knows what happened." Rehta's voice cracked as he spoke. "All we have are rumors. The royal healer said that they died of an illness crafted especially for them. One that only a handful of people had to skill to create. No one can confirm if it is true because he went missing."

"The king kept me away. Every time I completed one mission, there was something else to do. He kept me away for the last two years, until recently when even his orders went silent." There was a hit of anger in Sadar's voice as he spoke.

"They tried to hide, once it became apparent what was happening." Rehta looked directly at Sadar desperately. "Anyone who was of the royal line with a spark of magic ended up dead. I tried to hide a few. I smuggled them across, but they were found. There is no one left, no one but his son."

Rehta tucked his head back against Sadar's chest, his sobs audible. Sadar wrapped his arms around him, but his face looked forward in shock.

# Chapter Thirty-Eight

Alicia watched through the kitchen door as Rehta demonstrated to Kenny the correct way to cut up an onion. Kenny had come down the stairs uncertain about what he was walking into. Rehta had wiped off his tears and taken the young boy into the kitchen to help cook. Alicia and Sadar both sat at the table watching them at a distance.

"You love him." Alicia turned towards Sadar.

"I have only known him a few weeks. He is a great kid though."

Alicia paused, uncertain if Sadar was joking. His face was unmoving, and his body was stiff. "I wasn't talking about my son. You love Rehta. How long have you two been together?"

"It isn't that simple."

"It never is." Alicia slumped in her seat, turning back to watch the duo cut up vegetables.

"How dare you speak about how I feel?" The verbal attack was sudden and so full of venom that Alicia froze at Sadar's words. "How could you possibly know anything about emotions? You're practically a robot. You talk so easily about love, but you are incapable of it yourself. You talk about saving my world when you were incapable of navigating your own."

The words hit Alicia hard. She shrank back and tried to keep the tears from falling on her face. She knew he was angry and confused, but he also wasn't wrong. Even now, she knew the emotion that coursed through her did not show on her face.

Sadar let out a disgusted sigh and stood up suddenly, his chair crashing to the floor. "I need some air," he said as he stormed towards the bookstore's door.

Alicia turned back and saw Rehta staring at her. He finished putting the rest of the cut vegetables in a pot on a wood burning stove. Then he picked up a tray of muffins and brought them to the table, Kenny trailing behind him.

"Kenny," Rehta said. "On the shelves by the entrance I have a few games that I have collected. Why don't you go and pick out something for us to play?"

Kenny stood unmoving, eyeing the plate of muffins. Rehta picked one up and handed it to him. "You can take this one with you."

"Thank you," he said as he grabbed the muffin and nearly ran through the shelves of books to find the one with the games.

"Thank you for working with him this morning," Alicia said.

"We should get packed and ready to move to a safe house. We want to be ready in case he brings the guards back." Rehta's words were so sudden they threw Alicia off.

"Who is bringing the guards back?" Alicia asked, confused.

"Sadar. I saw him leave here—he was angry. We should be ready to move." Rehta's voice was matter of fact. Alicia had problems connecting it to the man that had cried in Sadar's arms less than an hour ago.

"He is not going to bring anyone back here," Alicia said.

"I wouldn't be so confident. Sadar is very loyal to his ideals."

"That is why I am confident. He has already wrestled with his loyalty to the king and decided to support my son. He vowed to protect him, and bringing the guards here would break that vow. So we are safe, at least from him. Him storming out of here was all about whatever is between the two of you."

"He arrested me once. We had already known each other for over a year when I had traveled to the capital to protest the rights of the magicless. Protesting of any kind was illegal, even then." Rehta took a muffin off the tray and split it in half. He looked at it, but didn't make a move to eat it. "When I was released, I tracked him down. He was sitting at a bar alone. He had a drink waiting for me, like it was all planned. I was so angry at him. I wanted to scream and yell, and he was sitting there, waiting for me to do just that. Then I realized that Sadar is loyal to a fault, and I knew if I made him choose between duty and me, that duty would win. So, I took the drink and sat down and never spoke about it again."

"It is not exactly the romantic relationship that most boys dream of."

"Perhaps not, but I am not most swooning bachelors. I want someone who can hold their own against me, and there is a certain romantic appeal to knowing that someone finds you so irresistible that they skirt their lines of morality."

They stopped talking as they heard Kenny making his way back to them. He was carrying an armful of boxes that were precariously balanced in his arms.

"Do you want some help, Kenny Bean?" Alicia asked.

"I've got them." His voice was muffled by the pile that climbed up to his eyes.

She watched him as he made his way to the table. When he was close, she reached out and took the pile from his arms. There were boxes of board games, the same ones they had played back home. There were also some unlabeled wooden boxes that seemed to be games she was unfamiliar with. On top of it all was a small package that was wrapped in cloth. She took it and unwrapped it, finding a pile of handmade playing cards. It was the same cards that she was familiar with, except they were hand painted on some sort of handmade card stock. On each of the face cards there were intricate pictures of people in crowns. They all bore a striking resemblance to her son.

"It's time to make a plan," Alicia said.

"We have to get Kenny on the throne."

"That's not an option. He is just a kid, a human kid."

"The orphanage is full of kids. The difference is he's the only one that can help them."

"I want to help them." Kenny's voice broke through their discussion, causing them both to pause. "It isn't OK that they have to live like that. They were hungry, and they couldn't even play."

"I know you do. You're a good kid, but you don't understand what that means." Alicia looked at her son and then around the bookstore. She realized suddenly that she had stopped seeing the human world. It was apparent that this was not the same city that she lived in, even though it shared the same general shape. "I think that no matter what we decide, there has to be a way to help these people."

"I want to help them," Kenny said, more adamant.

"Sometimes, when we help people, it means that we have to make sacrifices of ourselves. It would be very different if we were to stay here. You would have to learn a lot, but you wouldn't get to go to school like you used to. You may have to do boring things, even if you would rather be playing. There are no TV or video games here."

At the last comment, Kenny froze up a little. They hadn't been here long enough to appreciate the implications of not having electricity. "I don't want to be different anymore, but those kids were like me. I could do magic and they didn't get scared. I want to go home, but I also don't want to leave here. I can be myself here. Maybe there is a way that we can watch TV here." His eyes brightened at the idea.

Alicia wasn't quite as sure as her son. There was still so much about this world that still didn't make sense, but she also knew how hard it was to try and fit into a world that didn't accept any differences.

"I think we have a lot to figure out. There has to be another way without making him king," Alicia said and sank into a chair. She did not want her son pulled into this life, but she also did not see a way around it.

Kenny had stopped fidgeting with the games and looked up at the two adults. He walked over and climbed into her lap. Then he placed his hands on her face and moved her head to look at him.

"You know we have to help. You taught me that we help people who need it. All these people need it, and I am the only one that can help. How could I walk away and grow up knowing that I didn't help them when I could?"

"My job is to protect you. Being king is not fun. The responsibility is too much, and you're still so young."

"I wouldn't be king, at least not completely and not until I am older. You will help me until then. Rehta and Sadar will help as well."

# Chapter Thirty-Nine

They spent the afternoon poring over the political science books in the bookstore. They were all written in elven, and Alicia could not understand any of it. She hated that she was dependent on others to read it for her. Sadar had returned in time to finish eating breakfast with them. The men seemed to have decided to ignore each other and instead took turns translating passages for her.

Lunch had come and gone, and Kenny had long since gotten bored and was sitting on the floor, playing the board games with himself. One of the elven games was a remake of a game made entirely out of rock pieces. Kenny was attempting to play it without using his hands.

Alicia was looking at her notes, calling back Rehta and Sadar when she needed their help answering a question or translating another passage. She could tell that Rehta was not very happy with her unwillingness to jump up and risk her son's life at his demand. Alicia knew that Rehta had good intentions, but his intentions were mainly for the elven world. Alicia planned to help, but her focus was on making sure her son made it through safely. To do that, she had to understand the elven world better.

During her time flipping through books, she caught glimpses of Rehta and Sadar. They would look up at each other and lock eyes. They seemed to orbit around each other as if they were afraid of being seen together even though it was just the four of them in the store, yet they seemed to be aware of each other at all times.

When Kenny went to bed, it did not take long for the pretense to end. They started huddling in the corner, whispering. When they slipped away together to the bedroom, Alicia stayed with her books.

At some point she had fallen asleep at the table, her head cushioned by an open book. She woke to Sadar coming down the stairs, but she had a plan all laid out. It was not a perfect plan, and she was still worried about her son. The only problem was that Sadar and Rehta were going to hate her.

Before telling her plan to them, she needed to run it by her son. The two had always been a team, and if he was going to step into an adult role, she wanted him to have the first chance to veto everything that was about to happen.

They moved into their shared bedroom, and Alicia let him look at her notes while explaining what she had in mind. They spoke quietly. They spread papers around them as they both laid down on their stomachs with their chins propped up on their bent arms. Alicia couldn't help grinning. It was so familiar, like they were back home having another family game night.

"How will you handle all the people?" was the first concern that Kenny had.

"What do you mean?" Alicia asked.

"You don't like people. You said that leading a nation would mean lots of meetings and lots of talking with people. If you become my regent, you would be doing a lot of that until I was old enough to do it myself. It seems like it would make you very unhappy."

"Here is a secret, kiddo. No one should enjoy being in power. If I start to enjoy it, then that is when you should start to worry. I have to hang on for the next ten years. You will have to hang on for the rest of your life. Although, you know I will still be at your side, ready to help you when you need it."

"And we will have Sadar and Rehta, too."

"Yes, hopefully, we will have them also. I hope that they understand."

"We need them."

"Yes, we need them. But remember that they do not need to know the whole plan right away. It is the only way that I can see it working."

"I understand."

The two walked down the stairs to the bottom floor, where Sadar and Rehta waited for them. Alicia thought they might have walked in on something as the two seemed to spring apart from each other. Their hair and shirts appeared to be in slight disarray.

"We have a plan," Kenny announced.

"Oh, please do tell," Rehta said. He sat down at the table and faced them. Sadar stood behind him, as if guarding Rehta from unknown harm.

"Kenny will take the throne, and I will be his regent," Alicia said.

"Finally, you have come to your senses," Rehta said.

"It is not possible," Sadar said at the same time. "You are a human, you lack any power, and you are not of royal blood."

"There is precedent." Alicia flipped through her notes and handed them a page. "It had happened before that there was a younger king on the throne. His mother acted as his regent after the king and queen were both lost in some battle. She was not a queen, and she had very little magic ability of her own. Her son was the king's only known offspring. She was the king's concubine and not of noble birth. She ended up marrying the king's brother, who was next in line for the throne. The king's brother knew that his magic would not hold the throne, and some third cousin or something would probably overthrow him. By marrying, they solidified the throne. She ruled as regent until her son was of age and then served as his advisor until he married. He was Kenny's great-great-great grandfather if I am not mistaken."

"There is no one left of royal blood that is strong enough to ensure such a position," Rehta said.

"They do not need to be of royal blood, especially since no one is left to challenge Kenny's claim. If there were, we would let them have the throne. I have two choices. I can marry someone who has enough magic to protect Kenny's claim, or I can marry someone of the royal line who has a little magic."

"That could work." Rehta turned around and looked at Sadar as he spoke. "We have to do something, and if this is what she wants, then I'm all for it."

"Is there anyone left that would be willing to marry a human?" Sadar asked him.

"We'll find someone," Rehta said. "If we do nothing, then we will be left with this king on the throne, and that's not an option."

"What if we fail? What if Kenny gets kille? We cannot go off on some halfcocked plan."

"Am I going to die?" Kenny's eyes were wide and full of tears.

"Enough." Alicia stood up from her chair, her hands smashing the table. "I've worked out a plan that you haven't even fully looked at. If you think it won't work, then we can revise it. But do not go traumatizing my son. I'm doing all of this to keep him safe. If I had my choice, we would go back to our old lives right now, where the biggest worry we had was making sure rent was paid on time."

Alicia pulled out the outlined plan that she had developed and threw it on the table. Then she picked up her son, who was much too big for carrying, and went with him up the stairs. They stayed in the room all morning. After Alicia had calmed down Kenny's worry, they played games and explored. It wasn't until Kenny started complaining about being hungry that she ventured to go back down stairs while Kenny stayed in the room.

She walked as silently as she could, but soon realized that it did not matter. Both men were sitting at the table waiting for her.

"Did you read it over?" Alicia asked.

"We did," Rehta said. "We should probably discuss some of the plan. We have some ideas on how it can go more smoothly."

"Are you onboard?" Alicia turned towards Sadar.

Sadar looked back at her, his face impassive. She waited until the pause went on awkwardly, and he started to speak. "I still have concerns."

"Do you have a better idea?"

"No." The word was said grudgingly. "However, this plan

still needs work. I am blood sworn to the throne. I can do nothing to hurt the future of the In-Between. I will not betray your son. There is also an obvious flaw. We do not know how to contact the king."

Alicia slid into a seat at the table facing the two men. She gathered up the pages of her notes and picked up her pencil. "OK, let's make this work. As for how to contact the king, I was thinking that Rehta's friend, the count, could help us with that."

# Chapter Forty

"Having second thoughts?" Rehta asked. They were standing near the front of the bookstore, waiting. Alicia and Kenny were both dressed in their human clothes with their bags on the ground. Alicia, full of anxiety, tried to stop her right arm from twitching by focusing on moving her thumb against her pointing finger. Apparently, this movement had still been noticed.

"Do you think that Sadar will be able to pull it off?" Alicia asked. She watched Kenny slump to the floor by one of the covered windows. He took one of his toy cars out of his pocket and started running it around the ground.

"I know he seems all tough and rigid, but that is just a front he puts on. He has done so much to defend the king that now he sees a way to make amends. He will not fail you, I promise."

"You do not have the most unbiased opinion of him."

Rehta laughed. "Maybe not, but my opinion is the most relevant. I can assure you that he is committed. He not only finally declared his love, but he promised to spend the rest of his life with me. We just need to get Kenny on the throne."

Alicia felt her stomach drop at the news, her guilt outweighing their excitement. "Wait, he proposed, during all of this?"

"Yes." Rehta's smile was radiant. Alicia tried hard to fake a smile.

"Did he give you a ring?" Alicia asked.

"Elves do not exchange rings. Our ceremony is simple. We bind ourselves together, showing our joining as one soul."

"Wait, is that what I will have to do?"

"Yes, you will stand before the nation and declare your union."

"I guess I should have asked about all this earlier. Is there anything else?"

"What else would there be? There is nothing more magical than a marriage. When you get married, you are married for more than life. You are married for eternity."

"I have one more question," Alicia stammered. "Do elves ever have more nontraditional marriages? For example, say my future partner meets someone while I was in this political marriage."

"Elves have divorced, but it is not something done lightly. If you are planning on a divorce, then it is best not to go through the marriage."

"No, not divorce. That cannot happen. This marriage is too important. But what if either one of us wanted to continue another relationship while we were married? If both parties agreed, would it be allowed? It isn't like we are going to be consummating the marriage. There will be no other offspring, and the point of the marriage is completely political."

"It is not unheard of for such an arrangement to happen. But it seems like a horrible way to start a marriage."

"The whole situation is horrible. I do not want to condemn a man to a sexless relationship because I have no desire to engage him that way. If there is someone that he is interested in, then he should be allowed to continue that relationship after we are married."

"That is very noble of you."

"Nothing about this situation is noble. This is just about survival. When my son was born, I told him I would do anything to protect him. Just because I didn't realize what that meant does not mean that I should not keep my promise."

"It is time to go. He should be ready for you, and you should have some distance before I make the call." Rehta leaned down and pulled Kenny into a hug. "You got this, little man. Just remember to be brave for your mom."

"I will," Kenny said.

"You don't have to do this," Alicia said.

"We don't have a choice," Rehta said. "None of us do. You've seen what is happening to my world. We have a chance to fix it and we have to take it. Besides, I have the easiest task of you all."

Alicia nodded her head in acknowledgment and reached down to pick up her bag. She turned to her son. "Are you ready?"

Kenny picked up his backpack and, with Alicia's help, slipped it on. Then he put his hand in hers and they headed out the front door. They walked quickly, trying not to stand out even though there did not seem to be anyone around. They passed neighboring store fronts, all of which appeared to be vacant, until three buildings down there was a small alley, just like Rehta had described. The alley was clean and empty. They walked down it to the end until they were hidden in shadows.

"Do you know what to do?" Alicia asked.

Kenny concentrated and held her hand tighter. "It's clear," he said.

Alicia felt a familiar tingle. The smell hit her first, like a strong odor of urine. Then she saw the rows of trash cans and the garbage littering the alley. The walls were covered in painted over graffiti, and Alicia knew they were back in the human world.

# Chapter Forty-One

After they had slipped back to the human world, they walked to a gas station a few blocks away. It was their agreed-upon meet up location. As they waited, hand in hand, Alicia could not help but see the similarity to their journey's start. She had learned so much and changed so much, yet they were still here waiting on Sadar. They were always putting their faith in him. She just hoped that she was not wrong to do so.

"Don't worry, Mom. Everything will work out just fine. Sadar will protect us."

Alicia wished she could have his blind faith and optimism. But then, if she did, they would have already been shipped off to the king. Someone needed to be a realist and plan for the worst.

A nondescript silver suburban pulled up on the street in front of the alley they were hiding in. It was precisely the type of car that Sadar would acquire, but she waited to be sure. Finally, the window rolled down, and Sadar appeared, gesturing for them to hurry and get in the vehicle. They both ran and climbed in. In the back, there was a booster seat for Kenny. Alicia glanced up at Sadar quizzically.

"Well, we can't have the kid getting hurt. So I made sure to grab one."

While they drove, Alicia was still on edge. "Do you think he made the call yet?"

"Don't worry, everything is fine. There is no way they could have caught up to us this quickly."

Alicia, sitting in the front passenger seat, looked out the window. They were still in the downtown area. Traffic was heavy, causing them to stop before moving only a short distance. It felt jarring to be by so many people again after the sparseness of the In-Between. She looked at her world and saw how dark and dingy it was. Pollution filled the sky, dimming the sun. Instead of random gardens there was trash floating everywhere. "Maybe the In-Between is not the only world that needs saving," she muttered.

"It is hard seeing what humans are doing to this planet. Maybe, once the throne is secure, we can reach out and find ways to help the humans, too."

Alicia held on to this thought as the anxiety filled her—maybe they could do good for more than one world. They just had to make it through the next part. The downtown area started to slip away, and Sadar jumped on a road headed out of town. As the buildings started to become suburbs, Alicia looked back at Kenny and saw him reading one of the books that he took from the bookstore.

"Are you doing OK, kiddo?"

"Yeah, sure," he said, lost in a different world.

They drove on until even the houses started to become scattered. Alicia wasn't sure how long had passed, but it looked to be at least noon.

"Do you think we should stop soon?" Alicia asked.

"There is a spot a few stops ahead. If you're hungry I would recommend eating something now, just in case."

Alicia reached in her bag and pulled out a stack of muffins that Rehta had packed. She passed them around and watched to make sure her son ate. She kept her own muffin in her hand, her stomach too full of nerves.

"Do you trust me?" Sadar asked.

Alicia looked at him but did not answer.

"I think we have been followed. Everything will be fine. This plan will work. All that matters is that the significant parts happen. The little details can change. You need to be flexible."

"I am not a very flexible person."

"I've noticed."

They pulled off the freeway. There were a few gas stations and restaurants. Sadar pulled into the parking lot that was biggest. He drove around the gas pumps to the back end of the building, as if trying to be unnoticed. The area they parked in was a small strip of pavement that extended back into gravel. There were a few large trucks parked further back. They sat, facing the back door of a restaurant.

"Should we go in and order some food?"

Sadar turned and looked at Kenny then faced her. "It's time. Just remember that you trust me." He opened his door, slid out, and shut his door fast. Before Alicia could follow him, the locks clicked into place, trapping them. Alicia's breath caught as panic began to overwhelm her. She undid the lock and attempted to open the door, but it would not move. She frantically went to the driver door, but it wouldn't open either.

"This wasn't part of the plan," she screamed. She pulled on the door handles, willing them to open. "This wasn't part of the plan." The words came out of her mouth on loop as she pounded on the window. They had talked this part through, how they would be handed over. It didn't involve Sadar locking them in the car. She felt helpless, the plan already spiraling out of control. All the anxiety that she had been holding on to overwhelmed her. "This wasn't part of the plan." The words were now a desperate plea.

"Mommy, what's wrong?" Kenny's voice was scared. Alicia knew she needed to calm down for him, but the thought had barely registered before their car was surrounded by a hoard of black SUVs.

Alicia started crawling over the front seat to reach Kenny when the car door opened. A burly elf saw her, said, "Oh no, you don't," and then grabbed her, pinning her arms at her side as he pulled her out. She kicked and screamed, but none of it seemed to bother him. The elf placed her in the back of one of the SUVs, her head barely missing the roof.

As they closed the door, she saw them taking her son out of the vehicle. He looked at her with fear, tears streaming down his face, but went with them without a fight.

"It will be OK," she screamed, uncertain if he could hear her. "You're going to be OK."

There was a group of four men gathered around her son's door. They were all muscled with black suits and ties, looking like they learned how to dress from Hollywood movies. Their voices picked up. The words were elven, but they were unmistakably arguing. Sadar came to them, trying to push some of the men away from the car door. His figure seemed almost small next to the imposing elves in suits.

One of the elves pulled one of Sadar's arms behind his back and walked him to the back of another car. Alicia turned to follow them and caught a brief look of fear in Sadar's eyes. She watched Sadar try and struggle with the bigger man. At the same time, he was talking desperately in elven. A second man opened the door to a third SUV and, between the two of them, managed to get Sadar in the back seat.

The men left at her son's car started yelling. Alicia, desperate to divert their attention, started to scream. She half lay back on the SUV's bench seats and lifted up her feet trying to smash through the window. The screaming stopped as they turned their attention to her. One of the men said something to the group and shut her son's door. Then he walked around to the front of the SUV. Another man joined him right after and the car took off.

A third man walked away, joining the SUV they had taken Sadar to. Alicia stopped kicking as the two remaining men started glowering in her direction. They exchanged a few brief sentences and then moved to the front of her SUV.

# Chapter Forty-Two

There was a divider between the back seat and the driver's seat. Alicia wondered if they had managed to find cars like that or if they had put it in themselves. The divider went from the ceiling down to the floor and looked to be welded to the car somehow. It seemed to be made of some sort of clear, durable plastic or plexiglass.

It wasn't soundproof, because there was a row of holes that ran about head height between the driver and passenger seat. The holes were too small to stick one of her fingers through, or even a pencil. Not that she had one on her to try. But the holes were big enough for sound to go through, which is how she knew that the two men in front were ignoring her.

She spent the first part of the trip asking the men where they were going and why they were arguing earlier. She asked about her son and even asked how they managed to find them. About an hour into the drive, according to the bright green lights of the dashboard, she finally decided that the elves did not understand English.

The next hour she just talked randomly. She figured it didn't matter what she actually said if they could not understand her anyway. She told them some funny stories about her son. Then she talked about her last boss, a life that seemed so long ago. She even talked to them about Christian. She was hit by a wave of loneliness when she brought him up. She wondered how worried he was. Then she thought about how she needed to reach out and tell him that she was OK and would, she hoped, continue to be OK. She said each word as she thought it, letting her filter go completely.

The men stared ahead, continuing to ignore her. About three hours in, her voice started to go. She continued talking as her voice caught, and it seemed this was what finally broke through the men's calm. The passenger reached over and turned on the radio. The car was full of classic rock so loud that even she couldn't hear herself talk. She sat back and continued trying to watch the road signs to know where exactly they were headed.

The car finally pulled into the parking lot of a nightclub. The parking lot held a few vehicles, but it contained a lot more people. They huddled in groups, watching as the elf pulled her from the car. They stood passively and without reaction as Alicia stared back at them. They watched like this was a performative art piece that they were forced to witness. Alicia recognized their clothing as those from the upper elven class, yet most of the outfits were dirty and creased. The people looked helpless and without hope. Yet, they seemed to accept it. In the crowd, Alicia noticed the count they had visited a few days before. All life seemed to be drained out of him. Even his clothing seemed dimmer.

More cars pulled up, and Alicia saw her son pulled out of another vehicle. She tried to reach for him, but her escort held her arms as he started walking her to the door. Alicia strained to see her son and let him know that everything would be OK, but she could not see past the elf.

The elves forced her down a small set of stairs in a back room. At the bottom of the stairs appeared to be a sort of makeshift prison. Two rows of wire mesh cages took up most of the floor, with just a narrow walkway separating them. Each row was divided into three cells with a wire divider. The walls looked held together by leather ties. It seemed so flimsy that Alicia supposed that there must be magic somewhere helping to make them secure.

The elf holding her opened one of the doors and pushed her inside. As the elf closed the door and moved away, Alicia heard more footsteps on the stairs. A second elf appeared, carrying Kenny. Her son appeared limp in his arms, and panic shot through Alicia. Then she saw his eyes open and alert. She realized he was offering as little resistance as possible. He was still sticking to the plan. The second elf moved to put her son in the cage in the opposite row. "Put him in with me," she pleaded to the two elves. They both pretended to ignore her, but they put her son in the cage connected to her. At least that was a small comfort.

"There has to be some mistake. I am blood sworn to the prince, not a criminal to be thrown in a cage." Sadar's voice carried down the stairwell. He followed soon. His arms were wrapped in some sort of restraint, and the elven guard was half-carrying him down the stairs. "I was bringing them to the king. If I knew where to go, they would have already been here by now. I am loyal to the throne. You know I am loyal to the throne because I am alive. My bond doesn't allow for disobedience."

The pair made it to the bottom of the stairs with a second guard trailing behind. Sadar was putting on quite a show, and as Alicia watched she realized that he hadn't said anything that wasn't true.

"Have you told the king I'm here?" One of the guards opened the door to an empty cage, and the other guard threw Sadar in. Alicia watched as Sadar fell into the ground, a bit too dramatically, his cheek scraping on the concrete floor. "You must tell the king that I am here. There is a plot on his life. He needs to be informed."

Sadar did not stir as they flipped him over and removed his restraints; however, as the elves turned away, never once uttering a word, Sadar lifted his head off the ground and gave her a quick wink. It was over before she could process it. If it wasn't so out of character for him, she was sure she would have missed it altogether.

As Sadar continued screaming to be released, Alicia rushed to the side of the cage that connected with her son. She tried to reach her hand through, but the mesh was too close together, and she was only able to get a few fingers to him. "Are you OK?" she asked.

Kenny grasped onto her fingers. He looked unharmed, but the fear was evident on his face. "I'm OK."

Alicia turned and glared at Sadar, fueled by her own fear. But Sadar did not notice. He had finally stopped screaming and was now lying down on the floor, staring up at the ceiling while ignoring the other two prisoners. So, Alicia turned back to her son. "Remember what we spoke about when we left."

"I remember," Kenny said, his eyes starting to tear up. "I remember all of it."

"Do you remember what you promised? Do you still promise?" Kenny kept his face down, refusing to look at her. "If you do not still promise, I will send you back right now; we will end it all. I need to make sure that you will do what I say if the time comes. Nothing matters to me more than keeping you safe."

"Keeping you safe matters to me," Kenny whispered.

"Hopefully, I will keep safe, too. But if I do not, you have to go, no trying to save me. I will try to save myself, and you follow the plan." She spoke in a whisper. They had agreed to not talk about the plan here. They agreed to keep up the pretense at all times, in case they had people watching or were using human electronics. But this was too important.

"Yes, Mom," Kenny finally agreed.

When Kenny had agreed back in the bookstore, Alicia knew that it was easy for him then, when this was still some grand adventure rather than the reality where they could all be hurt or killed. But here, actually seeing the danger, she knew it was harder for him to agree to leave if things got dangerous. Her son always seemed to believe that he had to look out for everyone, but especially her. So, while she loved his sweet nature, she was not prepared for her son to get hurt here. She just hoped that when the time came, everything would work out as planned. Alicia hated when plans changed, especially ones she worked so hard on and ones that could kill them all.

# Chapter Forty-Three

Being stuck in a cage was maddening. You lost control of every fundamental decision. You were fed when someone decided you should be fed. You had to wait until you were allowed to use the restroom, although both men had taken to using a section out of their cell as a waste facility when they needed to pee. Alicia worried that she would need to do so if the guards did not arrive soon.

The excitement of being caught wore off after the first night, and then Kenny just grew bored. There was not much to do in the cells, so Alicia tried to make up games to entertain them. They did physical challenges to see who could do the most push-ups or run in place the longest. They practiced kicking and blocking, and Alicia reviewed self-defense basics, so it was fresh in Kenny's mind and her own. Alicia felt comfort from the practice, like they were back in the Taekwondo studio with the family they had created.

They played mental games. Kenny's favorite was I-spy, where they would find an object in a room, and the only hint was the color. Unfortunately, the room did not have a lot of decoration, and they ran out of items fast. They played a math game, taking whatever concept Kenny was learning in school, and Alicia would make up problems for him to solve. They also took turns telling stories.

Kenny was excited to tell her about all the new adventures he had discovered in the elven children's books. She tried to listen, but her mind would start to drift away with worry. None of them anticipated being kept in a cell for days. They had all assumed that the king would deal with them quickly. The purpose Alicia had felt when she brought her son here was starting to fade. Instead, she questioned her decision. He should be in school playing with his friends. They should be back in their own life. She missed the predictability of it all.

At times, Sadar tried to join in, and Kenny accepted him readily. Alicia either ignored him or told him to stay away from her son. Whenever a guard came down, Sadar tried to negotiate with them to get out of his cell. He told them loudly about how they should not be keeping a blood sworn soldier in prison with criminals. He once told them that he had information that could save the king's life, but the guard had entered the cell and started pounding on him instead. Alicia flinched each time she heard the sound of a fist connecting with his flesh. He was quiet for a few hours after, laying on the thin mat that was in their cell. Alicia wasn't sure if he was really hurt, and she was too afraid to show concern.

Unfortunately, the guards did not come down too often. They were lucky to be brought two meals a day, and those were often stale leftover club food. Alicia ate as little of hers as she could while keeping up her strength and then passed what she could to her son through the bars. There just wasn't enough food for a growing eight-year-old. Thankfully they brought them a jug each of water every morning. It was a good sign that they were at least trying to keep them alive. Alicia was concerned that they might start drugging their food at some point, but she wasn't sure how to handle that. Ultimately, they were at their mercy either way, and she wanted them as healthy as possible when the time came to face the king. So, she made sure that Kenny drank every drop of his water after it became apparent they would replace it the next day.

They were on their fourth pitcher of water, and their millionth made-up game, when they heard footsteps coming down the stairs. It seemed too early for their evening meal, although stuck in the basement with only fluorescent lighting that

---

never changed, it was very hard to tell.

The two guards that came down were not the goons that they had seen up to this point. One of them had deep brown skin, and the other was pale, tall, and lanky. Even though they wore the same black suit and tie that seemed to be the requisite uniform, they were not the standard short brown-haired front linemen they had seen to date.

The elves came to Alicia's cell and unlocked it. They motioned at her to hold out her hands. She did so, and they placed a leather binding around them. It was tight enough that she was afraid she would lose circulation in her hands.

Then they walked over to her son's cage and motioned him out. They tied the same leather strap around his hands and then told him to stand next to his mother. Alicia looked at her son and was relieved to see he wasn't bound quite as tight as herself.

The two elves started to lead them up the stairs when Sadar began shouting.

"You should take me as well," he said. "I am blood sworn to the king."

"Shut up," the skinnier man yelled and then hit his hand against the wire mesh of Sadar's cage, causing him to jump back. "We are just here for the bastard and the woman. The king will deal with you later."

Alicia startled when he spoke. She had started to believe that the guards were incapable of speech.

"You will want to bring me. There is a conspiracy against the king. Someone threatens his life. The other two guards didn't listen to me, and now their duties have been put on you. I know who the traitor is, and I need to tell the king. Let me come and you will be rewarded, or ignore me and see what happens."

The two guards exchanged worried looks. Alicia wondered if Sadar was guessing that something had happened to their previous guards. There couldn't be any way for him to have known. Either way, the plea seemed to feed enough to the guards' fears.

"You'll come, but we will bring you in dishonor. You'll walk up in binding, a prisoner to stand before the king."

"I live only to serve. If I must face dishonor, that is a small price to pay for ensuring the throne." Sadar looked at Alicia when he said this. His gaze drilled through her. Then he turned to the guard and waited for bindings to be placed on his wrists. Then the guards put a chain around his neck. Sadar seemed to be expecting this as he lowered his head to allow the shorter elf to secure it.

"What does that do?" Alicia blurted out, forgetting in her curiosity that she was supposed to be upset at Sadar.

"It will stop him from accessing his magic."

"Oh, good," she managed to get out. She was relieved that they did not put one on her son. However, she was going to have a word with Sadar and Rehta after this was all over, since they had forgotten to tell her such a device even existed.

# Chapter Forty-Four

The group was escorted up the stairs and through what looked to be a back room and a small kitchen before they arrived in an open converted warehouse. The room was large, easily holding over a hundred people. The ceiling was tall and unfinished. Panic threatened to pull Alicia under as she realized that this place was nearly a twin of the club where she had first met the king. It seemed he had a preferred type of venue.

Loitering around the walls was the king's court. The faces were dirt-covered, and the clothing had gone from fine linen to a desperate need to be washed. The room was gloomy, built without a way for natural sunlight to enter and covered in limited fluorescent lights. It reflected off the people's faces, washing out their natural pigment. The entire room of people was focused on their group's entrance. The crowed watched them with a mass of expressionless faces. No, not expressionless. As Alicia studied the people more closely, she saw signs of fear and exhaustion that they were trying to hide.

Alicia's eyes were drawn to the back of the room where a spotlight highlighted parts of a stage. In the center of the spotlight the king perched on an armed wooden chair. The chair was generic, the type that one would find at a kitchen table or chain restaurant, yet the king perched on it like it was a grand throne. His legs were spread wide, taking up as much space as possible. They were covered in a ridiculous pair of purple striped slacks. His hands, the same hands that had once grabbed her long ago, were clasped in between his legs as he leaned forward slightly. When Alicia finally managed to pull her eyes up to his face she froze with anger, bile filling her mouth. Her hand reached out instinctively for her son, fumbling until she found his shoulder and pulled him closer to her.

The king was looking at them like he was examining an interesting bug or some curious anomaly, even though he was the one dressed in a purple silk shirt with puffed up sleeves and a V-neck that went clear down to the middle of his chest. He wore several necklaces in an emulation that had not gone well. Instead of gold links, he wore gold lockets, diamond pendants, and even a few sets of pearls. Yet the ridiculousness of the outfit did nothing to offset the look he threw their way. Like they were garbage barely worthy of his time. It was so much harsher than the look he had given her last, before he had torn her entire world apart.

Sudden movement caught her eye and two elves in black suits and ties walked in from the shadows. In between them a man was draped, one arm over each of their shoulders, although they were holding on to each arm to keep him up. They dumped him on the floor next to the king, and Alicia let out a gasp when she finally recognized Rehta. He crouched on the floor. His shirt was missing, and bright red bruising stood out across his olive skin. When Rehta looked up, Alicia could not help but let out another gasp. His lip was split, with dried blood covering the lower half of his face. His eyes were nearly swollen shut and an entire ear seemed to be missing.

This wasn't the plan. Rehta wasn't even supposed to be here. He was supposed to slip over after them and make the call to turn them in. Then he was supposed to use his resources to get away and go into hiding until, one way or another, this day was over. If they didn't make it out, he was supposed to find her son when shifted in between the worlds. Rehta was her back up plan, her way of knowing her son would be safe even if she wasn't. Yet here he was, broken almost beyond the point of recognition.

Alicia turned to Sadar, uncertain what to do next, but he stood stoic and unmoved. He looked directly at the king, not even acknowledging his fiancée. Suddenly he moved, slipping easily out of the grasp of his escorts, through the open floor, where he bounded on to the stage. Two more suit-wearing goons slipped out of the shadows, but Sadar was already laying prostrate on the floor, bowing to the king.

"My body, blood, and life are hereby bound to the throne," Sadar said quickly but loudly. In the silence, the words seemed almost to echo. Sadar lifted his bound hands as if worshipping the king as he spoke. Alicia could not keep the betrayal off her face at the display, but soon she noticed that the nobility had begun murmuring. A few were even openly gesturing as if their own hands were bound, their eyes wide with disbelief.

"Isn't that the blood sworn?"

"He has to bind his own blood sworn?"

The words flittered around the crowd, bringing the people to life. Alicia was startled to realize that some of the crowd was speaking English and not elven, but given his emulation of human culture, it probably wasn't that surprising.

Sadar kept to his knees. His head stayed bowed, but his hands remained raised so all could see. Alicia was not sure what he had done, except that he had done something. After the king did not react, the murmurings started getting louder. Alicia heard more rumblings about the blood sworn being a prisoner.

As near as Alicia could tell, Sadar had just made the king look bad by showing that he had to keep him under guard, the one person who had to protect the throne at all costs. Alicia realized in that moment how much having someone strong enough to hold the throne meant to these people. After years of his abuse, it took just the thought of his weakness for them to start to revolt. She started to have hope their plan would work. It had to work.

The king must have felt the growing change in the court as well. He stood up from his throne and gestured towards Sadar. "Rise," he said and then raised his hand as if making Sadar do just that. Sadar followed the prompting and rose. It all seemed over the top to Alicia, but then she supposed the king was trying to save face in front of everyone. He had to earn back the respect that Sadar had just cost him. The worst part was something so simple seemed to be working. The people had stopped murmuring and had turned expectantly towards the stage.

"Untie him. The blood sworn should never have been brought to me as a prisoner. He is my trusted guard and should be at my side." He talked as if he had not been the one to command Sadar to be in prison in the first place or to keep him away from this makeshift castle. Alicia had to try hard not to roll her eyes at how overdramatic everyone seemed to be. Sadar seemed to take it all in stride. He waited while they removed his bindings. Then he moved to stand at the side of the king. Seeing Sadar back at the king's side was the ultimate betrayal. Alicia found herself again unable to hide her distaste.

Alicia turned to her son. She was afraid to speak, so she gave him her mom look, which he instantly recognized. He unhappily gave a slight nod. If the time came, he would leave, she hoped.

The king finally turned his full attention towards her and Kenny. He looked at her and then gave a slight nod. "Yes, I think I remember you. It is hard to be sure. There have been so many." There was a round of laughter from his court, but not everyone joined in. The crowd was not as devoted to him as he would want. "Bring them here."

Alicia felt one of the suited men put his hand on her shoulder and push her towards the stage. She pulled her son in front of her before the guards could touch him and walked towards the king. Kenny looked up at her with fear, and she managed to give him a reassuring smile. She hoped that he could not see her own panic.

When they had made it to the front of the stage, the king turned his attention to his son."He's not much to look at." The crowd let out another polite laugh. "Kill the boy, but not the mother. Not yet, at least. Bring her up to my bedroom."

"No," Alicia screamed. "You cannot harm him. He is your son."

"That is exactly why I must harm him. The throne is mine, and I will not have any son of mine trying to take it from me." The king had publicly declared Kenny to be his son. Alicia hoped that it was enough.

"You would order your heir and prince of the In-Between to

be slaughtered like some common criminal. If he is your son, then shouldn't he at least receive death by your hands? Doesn't your law state that the punishment for killing a prince is a gruesome death?"

The guards paused and looked towards the king. They seemed unsure of which was worse: the fate of killing the prince or the consequences for disobeying the king. Alicia felt guilty for the fear in their eyes.

"The great thing about laws is that I can change them. All I have to do is flick my wrist, and poof, the law is gone. Kill him."

The guards took a hesitant step towards her son.

Alicia glanced towards the king. "It would help if you changed the law. I am sure these guards do not want to die for obeying you."

"Kill him," the king roared.

"You are going to send two innocent guards to kill the rightful prince, your heir? I didn't peg you for such of a coward."

That got the attention of the court. They began to murmur again. Alicia thought that she saw a few elves slip away, maybe heading back to the In-Between. The king must have noticed it as well.

"Cowards," the king bellowed. "If you will not kill them then you will pay. Kill them." The king turned to one of the men that had carried in Rehta.

The man moved to the front of the stage and took out a gun

from under his suit jacket. He held it up and waved it around, accidentally firing off a shot. The bullet pinged off the metal ceiling. What happened next was lost in a sea of screaming. The crowd started scattering, some disappearing right from the spot they stood in. Alicia had grabbed Kenny and wrapped herself around him, shielding him as much as she could.

"You need to go," she sobbed in his ear, but Sadar started talking over everyone, his words transported directly to everyone in the room in what must have been a use of illusionary magic.

"Surely, you do not need to resort to using human weapons to maintain the In-Between. I am so happy that I was able to find you so that I can help bring order to the throne." The room started to settle and the remaining elves, about half the room, now stared back up at the stage. Alicia glanced up over her shoulder. The king was looking at Sadar with such hatred. He picked up a sword that was looped over the back of his chair. Before he could do more than put it in his hands, Sadar was talking again. "Of course, the prince cannot be killed. You need an heir to the throne. I know it is unconventional that your son is half human, but you are so fortunate that he was born. While I was, well, let's say 'exploring' the human world, I heard that you had to have a human operation, the kind that does not allow you to have any more children. We are so lucky that your son was found."

"What type of operation?" The voice sounded familiar, and

Alicia was not surprised when she saw the count walk out of the crowd.

Sadar turned towards the king as if he expected the king to answer the question. He just stood there, a tall purple stick holding on to his sheathed sword with tight fists.

"I won't go into too much detail because we have some children in the room, but humans have a procedure that makes it impossible to have any more children. The king is infertile. With the unfortunate accidents that have befallen the royal line, there is no one that could inherit the throne."

The entire room of people stood as if in shock. The goon with the gun put it back under his jacket and walked off the stage. The rest of the suited guards walked out after him. Alicia watched them leave, then she turned towards Sadar in confusion. He continued ignoring her. Instead, she found Rehta who gave her a small smile on the half of his lips that weren't swollen.

The people slowly had come to life again. They were pointing at Kenny now, their eyes darting towards her son and the king. Alicia stood back up, now that the gun was gone. Kenny stood still next to her, letting them look. Alicia allowed herself to think of the best case scenario: the king having to accept her son as heir, them working to make the world better without bloodshed and without her having to become regent for her son.

The king slung his sword over his head so that it lay across his back. Then he walked down the side of the stage in some steps hidden in shadows. He stopped right in front of them, his eyes a vacant gaze that never left Kenny. Then his hands reached up pulling the sword from the sheath.

Alicia watched the blade inch towards Kenny's chest. It was so close, and they had lost. He needed to get out of there now. Alicia called to her son, telling him to go. But the blade stopped as soon as it touched the prince's chest. It dropped, clattering on the ground. The king's eyes were wide. Blood was pooling out of his mouth. He looked down and saw a blade piercing his heart. He gave a final look at his son and then fell to the ground. Sadar was standing right behind.

"I have protected the prince and rightful heir of the In-Between so named by his father, King Taro the Second. His father attempted to kill him in cold blood without the benefit of a trial. As blood sworn, I had no choice but to defend the prince. I now face the judgment of the crown."

Alicia stood frozen, watching the blood pool on the ground. It had been so close to being her son. That thought brought her back, and she noticed her son also staring at the man who had tried to kill him. She turned him away from the body and towards the crowd of elves. Later they would process what had happened. They would find an elven therapist and work through the nightmares that were sure to come. But for now, they were not finished.

# Chapter Forty-Five

"How can he hold the throne? He is human and without magic." The voice came out of the crowd of remaining royals. It was just the loudest of the voices that had overcome their shock and were now screaming for attention.

However, the voices became background noise as Alicia followed her son. He had slipped out of her hands, sidestepped the body, and was already headed up to the stage. When they arrived, Sadar held Retta in his arms. Alicia froze at the sight of tears running down Sadar's face.

Kenny slid up next to Rehta and held his hand. He closed his eyes and grew very still. Alicia stood over the three males, at a loss for how to help. She stood twisting her hands looking for signs of improvement.

"It's not so bad, I think." Kenny looked up to Sadar as if for approval.

"I don't have healing magic. I can't help." The words came out as a curse. When Sadar saw Kenny flinch back, he softened his tone. "What does it feel like?"

"I think I can help." Alicia recognized the voice as the count. She watched as he walked onto the stage slowly, as if he were afraid that Alicia would not let him pass. He was dressed in a bright green silk robe with a rainbow feathered bird embroidered across the back. Unlike most of the other elves, he still looked well put together, as if he had prepared for what was coming. "I am a healer, although I am much better at using my powers to, shall I say, impact people's emotional state, rather than actually healing. I can help the boy to know what he is seeing so he does not end up hurting your friend."

It took Alicia a moment to realize that he was waiting for her permission to pass. Her mind was stuck on how he just admitted to using his powers. *Was that allowed?*

"He was my friend as well." The count's voice was so quiet that Alicia could barely make out the words. Finally, she nodded and let him past. He knelt down next to her son and started whispering directions.

It hit Alicia suddenly how quiet the room had gotten. She looked out. Standing in the spotlight, the people appeared as no more than silhouettes. Their shadow forms seemed unmoving and focused on her son. They clung together, arms wrapped around each other until they were entwined lumps. She tried to place herself in their position. They had put up with a ruthless monarch because they were so reliant on him to keep their world together. Now he lay dead on the floor, and the promised replacement was a half-human child.

"I am sure that you are all uncertain what comes next for your world." Her words came out hesitant and were half swallowed up in the high ceiling. She cleared her throat and continued. "I know you need a strong ruler, a ruler of royal blood, to keep your land together. My son has already shown strong ability in all three elven magics. He can use illusionary magic, he can use earth magic, and as you are witnessing, he can use healing magic.

"As the mother of the prince, I claim regency." The crowed stirred slightly at this, but Alicia talked over the commotion. "Once I marry, I will help my son fix the many wounds created by your former king. We cannot bring back the lives that the king already took. But we can ensure that everyone will receive a fair trial and that we can bring back the glory of the In-Between."

As she finished speaking, she felt a presence at her back. She turned to see the count escorting her son, who was trying to hold back a yawn.

"You all know me," the count said. "You know that I am

quite fond of dramatics. In that spirit I would like to present to you the proof of your new king's healing ability."

Sadar helped Rehta up, keeping one arm around him as they walked in front of the group. When they arrived, Rehta took a step away from Sadar so that he was standing on his own. He looked alive. The bright red bruising was gone, replaced by a more yellowish tone, like the bruises had had days to heal. His face, still covered in dried blood, looked healed, all except for the missing ear.

"Not much to be done for something that is missing," the count whispered to Alicia before turning back to the crowd. "The old king did a number on him. There was internal damage that the new king managed to heal. It is something that you have seen over and over again. How many of us have lost someone to his reign?" The count's voice broke at the last sentence. Alicia wondered who he had lost.

"How do we know you didn't heal him?" The voice came from one of the shadowed elves.

The count let out a hearty laugh before replying. "Anyone who knows me would know that I would be living a grand life as a healer if I had that capability. Being a count is fine and all, but nothing compared to a high healer's life."

There were a few chuckles that cared up from the crowed, but they were overshadowed by another voice.

"Can he really summon all three magics?" Another voice

asked.

Alicia turned and looked at her son. He seemed about ready to fall asleep standing, but he gave his mother a nod. The room erupted in shouts, and Alicia turned to find a red serpent dragon swooping through the crowd. It rose to the ceiling and let out a breath of fire, illuminating the room. The elves were darting behind the bar, fleeing out the door, and some were taking cover under other elves.

"That is enough," Alicia said to her son. "Besides, I don't think those kinds of dragons breathe fire."

Kenny gave her a sheepish grin and the dragon vanished out of existence. The screaming stopped, but the elves, shadows again, stayed in their place.

"Do you think we can do something about the lighting?" Alicia asked the count. However, as soon as the words were out of her mouth, small orbs of light started hovering in the air.

"You are doing that?" The count turned towards Kenny. "That is amazing. I didn't even know that light could be an illusion." The count seemed to gather himself and then turned his attention back towards the crowd. "I think we have established that the new king is very capable of illusionary magic. Now then, what about earth magic?"

"I don't think that is such a great idea," Sadar said. "I assure you that the king is very capable of earth magic. It is probably best not to have him cause an earthquake until he has gained control over his powers a bit more."

"It's OK," Kenny said. "I promise I won't make the ground shake that much."

As soon as the words left his mouth the ground began to shake. Alicia found herself struggling to stay standing as the stage lurched back and forth, threatening to buckle.

"That's enough," Alicia said.

Sadar reached out and laid his hand on Kenny's shoulder and the ground began to settled again. Alicia's stomach continued protesting at the movement. While she was trying to breathe and focus, she realized that the count was staring up at the ceiling. She followed his gaze, but all she saw were the lights that her son had already created.

"He managed to keep an illusion spell while using earth magic," the count said, his voice full of awe. His words must have been heard by those closest to the stage because a murmur seemed to go through the crowd, and soon they were all talking and gesturing wildly.

"I have been traveling with the king and the regent for a while now." Sadar's deep voice cut through the crowd. "I provided training to help him gain some control, but this is just the start of his powers. His human blood seems to amplify the elven magic, giving us the most powerful magic user we have seen in generations. I cannot tell you how it is possible that we have a half-elf for a king. All I know is that I am grateful.

Finally, we have someone on the throne who can make our kingdom prosper."

"Long live the king." The shout came from the count, but it was carried up quickly by the crowd until the room was full of the cheers. Alicia tried to stand tall in front of the people while Kenny, standing in front of her, was just trying not to fall asleep. She looked out to the crowd, making sure to let each person know that they were seen, while actively trying to avoid the old king's body, lifeless on the ground. Alicia let the chanting continue for a few moments before she cut in.

"Go back to your homes," she said. "The tyrant's rule has ended. It is time to prepare for a new king. We will announce the death of the king in one hour at the palace, back in the In-Between."

A few of the elves slipped out through the doors, but the majority stood around in confusion. Alicia looked back at her group, uncertain how to proceed.

"Most of these elves don't have illusionary magic," the count said. "The few that do are not powerful enough to cross back without an entry point. The nearest one is a few miles away."

"How did they all get here then?" Alicia asked.

"Most were escorted by the king's personal guards."

"Can you arrange to get them all home? Maybe put them in groups with someone who can shift them home. See if the guards left their vehicles outside when they ran."

The count gave her a nod and then gave Kenny a small bow before leaving the stage. He walked to the first group of elves and started issuing commands. Sadar gave a brief bow to Kenny and then left to help.

Retta was standing with one hand clutched to the back of the makeshift throne.

"Why don't you sit while we wait and make sure everyone gets back safely?" Alicia said.

"I'm fine," Rehta said. He stood up taller, pretending not to be in any pain.

"I could probably heal him again now," Kenny said.

"I'm fine, really. There is still so much to do today, and you should save your strength for that."

Kenny opened his mouth to argue, but a yawn came out instead. He sheepishly covered his mouth.

It wasn't long before it was just the four of them, the count having gone on ahead with one of the groups.

"There is one car left for us. Our capital is not too far off from here. It will be better to get as far as we can in this world. There is a doorway near the royal house that I know about. I will send someone back to clean this place up."

After they walked off the stage, Alicia picked up her son, letting him rest on her shoulder. His legs dangled past her knees and he weighed more than she remembered, but she needed to know that he was OK. It wasn't until they made it outside, the sun hitting their face for the first time in days, that it really hit her that they made it. Her son was finally safe. Now she just needed to figure out how to run a kingdom.

# Chapter Forty-Six

The room was dark, except for a thin strip of light that carried under the door. The walls were silent—the real kind without the hums of air conditioners or plumbing. Alicia sat on the floor, her back against a pile of cleaning cloths. Her knees were bent and her hands wrapped around her legs, pulling them to her chest.

Kenny was in another part of the palace being cleaned and dressed. She had left him with Sadar as she slipped away, needing a moment to compose herself. She had opened doors at random, startling staff she had yet to meet, until she found this supply closet. Alicia felt comfort in the familiarity of cleaning supplies shoved in a room. She walked in, closed the door, and broke down.

It started as shaking, all the adrenaline leaving her system. Then there was crying with muffled sobs. She wanted to scream and shout, but too many people would hear her, so she let it out as quietly as possible. When the worst of the repressed fear and anxiety had leaked from her, she sat clutching her knees, basking in the silence.

She knew that she did not have much longer. She would need to pull herself back together and go out there and be the person everyone needed her to be. She wasn't ready yet, so she sat in the dark for a few minutes more.

When the door opened, she wasn't surprised. She kept her head down, allowing her to stay in her own thoughts as long as possible. She heard the scraping of an object moving across the floor and the soft grunts as someone sat down.

"I hope you don't mind if I leave the door open some. I don't seem to be as fond of darkness as you are." The count's voice rang in the small space.

"It's alright. I know I need to get up soon." She lifted her head, wiping off her eyes with her sleeve. She reached back for one of the cleaning cloths and used it to wipe her nose.

"It's probably best to stay in here a little bit longer. They are currently trying to find you something ostentatious to wear. Sadar suggested that you might prefer a simpler outfit. I volunteered to find you so he could stay with the king."

"Thank you." Alicia reached out and took an outfit from the

count. It was an elven shirt and pants. She held the shirt up to the light to get a better look. The cloth was blue on one side and faded to black on the other. On the blue side there was a yellow sun embroidered on the chest. On the black side there was a grayish moon on the bottom of the shirt. When the shirt was tied on, they would overlap each other. Alicia ran her fingers over the embroidery, marveling at the quality.

"Well, it can't be too simple." the count said. "You are the regent, after all. I acquired them from a noble who was more than happy to provide them. He will, of course, want a personal audience with you at a later date."

"This is perfect. Thank you again. I will change and meet you out there in a minute." When the count didn't move, Alicia turned towards him, looking at him for the first time since the warehouse. He was wearing the same robe, only slightly unkempt. His eyes were trained on the ground, and she used the time to really look at him. He was older than her, but probably not more than his mid-forties. He wasn't bad looking, she supposed. He had a solid chin and feathery brown hair. He was pompous though, and his flair would be tiresome long-term.

"From the way you are assessing me, am I correct to assume that Rehta talked to you about our forthcoming marriage?"

"It was Sadar who talked to me. Does that mean that Rehta is up?"

"Do you know"—the count's voice was deflated, at odds

with his usual flair—"the king disposed of all magical users that he thought would be a threat, but he hadn't managed to take out all the high healers. He tried. A few he converted to his cause and some others he managed to dispose of. They are hard to impress since they can take life with just their magic."

"I've seen it. I've felt it. What does this have to do with Rehta?" The closet was starting to become uncomfortably small, and she wanted to escape, but she knew this conversation needed to be finished.

"Oh, yes. There are three high healers here and they fixed your friend up quite nicely. I believe the king has already learned a few things from them." His voice had returned to his normal joviality, but it felt forced.

"Do you want to marry me?" Alicia blurted out.

"Sadar mentioned you liked to get straight to the point. I will do what I need to do for my kingdom. That is what is important."

It was such an evasive answer that Alicia wasn't sure how to respond. She knew she was missing something, but she wasn't sure what it was.

"I don't even know your name." Her voice came out smaller than she intended.

"My title name is Count Headgefield, but my given name is Jaydence."

"In my head I just called you count." She knew it was a lame thing to say as soon as it came out, but she was still nervous around him, and communicating was difficult.

"Well, I suppose if we are married it is probably best to call me by my given name."

The conversation tapered off, and they both sat in awkward silence before Alicia thought of something else to say. "I should probably know more about you than just your name."

"What would you like to know?"

"Did you lose someone? You don't have to answer if it is too much."

The partial smile slipped from his face, and his eyes began to tear up. "I'm sorry. It has been a few years now. I usually have more control, but everything today seems as raw as the day it happened. I had a son. He was not much older than your son when he was discovered. He had illusionary magic like his mother. He was gifted, so gifted that he was part of a group to visit the human world. He was the youngest one to go and train. The king said the school caught fire, that it was the type of chaos that just happens in the human world. I shouldn't have let him go. We suspected, even then, what was happening. My wife didn't survive the grief."

"That's…" Alicia's voice broke in anguish. "I wish I could have done something. I know it is too late now. Marriage would probably cause too much pain."

"No, it's not that at all." Jaydence stood up and started pacing the small space, his hands moving dramatically. "I do want to remarry one day. I want to have another child. No one could ever replace my son, I just want someone to know him. I want someone to help carry his memory past me. Maybe that is a selfish thing to put on a child, but he always wanted a sibling. I know you managed to have a half-elf before, but it seems unlikely to happen again."

"I don't want more children." Alicia pushed back as far as she could to avoid getting trampled. "If I marry, it is political only. You could have relations with someone else, but it would be difficult to be a family."

"It seems like we are in predicament." He stopped and stood looking down at her.

"I have a plan." She kept her head down avoiding his gaze. "There is someone else who I think would be a good partner. I was afraid of losing your support, but if you would rather not marry me, then it will work out."

"Who do you have in mind?"

"Sadar." It came out as a whisper.

"Ah." Jaydence let out a chuckle. "That may be difficult as I hear he and Rehta are engaged."

"Yes, I know. As I said, it will be political in nature only. I have no desire to ever consummate the marriage. He and Rehta can continue their relationship."

"How does he feel about this?"

"I figured it was best not to give him much of a choice."

# Chapter Forty-Seven

The royal palace occupied what would have been the state capital building in the human world. The outside was white and surrounded by pillars. The inside was full of vaulted ceilings with elaborate paintings. Alicia had made her way to her new living quarters to get dressed in the suit that Jaydence had provided. Outside her window she saw a yard full of elves assembling, despite the short notice. So many of them seemed dirty-faced and covered in rags, but there was a sense of excitement that rang through the crowed.

Alicia moved from the windows and let her new team of elves style her hair while they made disapproving looks at her outfit. They spoke only elven so Alicia let them carry on, ignoring their more grand gestures of holding up elaborate dresses for her inspection.

However, she had timed her return well, and it wasn't long before someone else had come to escort her to her son. Kenny was adorned in a suit made out of a red cloth that looked like silk. It was split at the sides and tied all the way up with elaborate white knots with tassels hanging off them. The shirt was patterned with white embroidered starbursts. Alicia couldn't help the smile that spread to her lips.

"You look very dashing," she told her son with a chuckle.

He smiled at her and started giggling. "It's a funny shirt, isn't it?"

"I like it, I really do." She went to tousle his hair, but thought better of it. Instead, she crouched down and gave him a hug. "You're going to do great."

"I haven't finished memorizing this yet. Sadar says it's important I say it right." He held up a piece of paper written in elven.

"Keep practicing. I know you can do it."

As they started to walk, Alicia reached down to take her son's hand, but at the glare from Sadar she stopped. It probably wouldn't do to have the king seen holding his mother's hand.

Sadar had cleaned up nicely as well. He was dressed in a uniform, similar to the one wore by the guards that were escorting them through the palace. They were a traditional elven cut with tan coloring. There were embroidered elven words running down their sleeves and a gold starburst symbol above their heart. Sadar's uniform included a few extra embellishments and was a darker brown color. It set him apart while still connecting him to a whole. Escorting her and her son, he looked to be at peace for the first time since she had met him.

The group walked through the center of the royal palace along a walkway that had been sectioned off by rows of guards. Behind the guards were a mass of elves. These elves were not as disheveled as the mass outside the building. Their clothes were less worn, and they looked a little better fed. As the party past, they tried to look over the guards to get a glimpse of their new king. There were shouts throughout the crowed, all of them in elven. The rest of the party did not seem disturbed by them, so Alicia continued walking forward.

They were escorted to a hallway off the throne room. As the doors closed, cutting off the crowd, Alicia welcomed the silence. Her son slumped down against the wall and started working on memorizing his lines. Rehta appeared from a room off the hallway. He went to Sadar and started fixing his uniform and then headed to Alicia to do the same to her outfit.

"Why are all the people here?" Alicia asked. "They won't be able to hear what is said."

"The world is changing," Rehta said. "Wouldn't you want to be a part of that any way that you could?"

"I could let them see it." Kenny looked up from his paper.

"What do you mean?" Rehta asked.

"We could show them, like if they were watching it on TV." A small screen appeared in the hallway. The screen was a reflection of themselves—as Alicia moved, so did her counterpart on the screen.

"That's remarkable," Alicia said.

"I know you said that I couldn't watch TV if we stayed. But I wanted to watch some, so I've been trying to make my own. I can only put stuff on the screen that is happening here, at least right now." Kenny looked up sheepishly at his mom.

"How many can you make? How far away can they be?" Rehta asked.

Kenny shrugged. "I just need to know where to put them."

"You," Rehta snapped at one of the guards. "Go find me a map."

The guard turned to look at Sadar who gave a brief nod before the guard took off. It wasn't long before he came back with a map. Rehta started making marks on the map while Kenny kept nodding at what Rehta was saying.

"There, they should all be ready."

Rehta stood until he framed himself in the window and started speaking in elven. Then the screens flicked off.

"First thing tomorrow, I am going to need a tutor. I have got to learn how to speak elven," Alicia said.

"He told them that I could use illusion magic in the In-Between, so that everyone can watch the broadcast. He told everyone who saw it to tell their neighbors and come back in five minutes to watch," Kenny translated. Suddenly his eyes widened, and he looked down at the paper in his hands. "I only have five minutes." He went back to working on memorizing the lines on the page.

"How will they understand me if I don't speak elven? How will I understand them?" Alicia felt her anxiety spiking again, the reality of what she was about to do finally hitting home. She had been so focused on getting to this point that she hadn't thought about what it meant to actually take on the responsibility of ruling a kingdom.

"Don't worry, I will translate for you." The count had slipped through the doors and joined them. "The screens were amazing. I think you may have scared everyone in the entire kingdom."

Kenny's face lit up at the compliment.

"That reminds me. Rehta, I was hoping that you could handle something for me," Alicia said. "In the crowd I saw some familiar faces. I was hoping that you could escort them to better seats."

Rehta gave her a nod and then slipped out of the hallway.

"Alright, we probably should not keep them waiting any longer," Alicia said.

She nodded to two guards who opened the door connected to the throne room. Alicia took a deep breath and then gave a measuring nod to her son. Together they stepped out. The room was large and could easily hold a couple hundred people. It had been arranged with wooden benches that were now full of the elitist elves. They were all dressed in outfits not dissimilar to hers and her son's. They were outfitted in jewels and elaborate hairdos, and not one person looked like they had missed a meal in the last year.

In the back, Rehta was making room for new additions. There was the young elf who ran the orphanage as well as a few of the older youths. She also recognized the miners. There were a few other people that Rehta brought in that Alicia had not met, who were probably people that had he had been smuggling food to. Some of the nobility started mumbling at the newcomers, but Alicia turned away.

In the front of the room there was a raised platform. The steps were made out of a type of stone and looked like they were a part of the building that transferred over from the human world. On the platform there was an elaborate wooden throne. The deep red wood twisted and wrapped around itself, creating a braiding pattern on the legs, arms, and sides. The back was a solid wooden piece that was carved with figures Alicia could not make out. On the seat there was a simple cushion. It looked like the most uncomfortable chair ever made.

Alicia gave a nod to Kenny and a screen appeared above the throne.

"Elven people." The voice came from an older elf standing to the side of the stage. "I present you the heir apparent, King Kenny the First, and his Regent and mother, Alicia."

Alicia walked up to the stage with Kenny at her side. Behind them Jaydence and Sadar followed. Jaydence positioned himself at Alicia's side, and Sadar stood beside Kenny. They all stood together in front of the throne, a seat that Kenny could not use until his official coronation. That could not happen until after her wedding. Which could not happen until after she announced her future husband. There was so much to do, but, standing on the stage, she let it all go. She needed to be present in this moment.

The audience had stood up and the room was full of polite clapping and more exuberant cheering. Alicia looked at the nobility in the front rows, acknowledging them briefly. Then she turned her attention to those in the back, people she actually knew. She tried to meet their gaze before turning her gaze until it appeared that she was looking directly at the screen, acknowledge the crowds that were filling the streets. Most had probably never even seen the throne room, let alone been allowed to witness important events such as this. It was something she hoped to rectify. The people needed to be given a voice.

When the cheering had started to lull, Alicia spoke, "Citizens of the In-Between, I present to you your future king, King Kenny the First." The count translated her words out to the people.

The cheering started up again as Kenny stepped forward. He took a deep breath and started speaking in elven, Jaydance translating at Alicia's side.

"I am King Kenny, son of Alicia and King Taro the Second and the rightful heir to the throne. I will use my magic to protect and defend the elven people, my people. I hereby declare my regent to be my mother, Alicia Henry."

Kenny stepped back and took deep breaths. Alicia wondered if he breathed during any part of his speech. The words were spoken in a rush, but just slow enough to be made out. Yet, the people seemed to be happy with his presentation. They cheered and kept cheering even when Alicia stepped up to the front of the stage. She spoke in English, pausing long enough for the count to translate her words.

"Elven people, earlier today, an attack was made on King Kenny's life. He was recognized as heir to the throne and then attacked. Sadar, blood sworn to the throne, had to decide to allow him to be killed or to take the life of his attacker. The attacker was King Taro. He attempted to take your heir's life without trial or judgment, leaving the In-Between with no possibility of a successor"

"I understand that some of you may be concerned. Your new king is half-human and half-elf, the first known halfling in all of elven history. Let me assure you that his magic is strong enough to keep the In-Between safe. The screens you see before you, made with illusionary magic, are just one example of your king's skill." There were gasps of astonishment in the crowds, as if they did not believe what they had heard when Rehta first made the announcement. Alicia waited for the room to calm before continuing.

"I assure you that the king will use his magic to defend the people, and not to hurt them. There will be a new reign in the In-Between. It will be one of fairness. All people who have been imprisoned will be given new trials, with proper representation. The innocent will go free, and the guilty will be punished according to their crimes. Unless they have taken a life, their life will not be taken, as is the law that has been part of the In-Between since its creation."

Alicia tried understanding the crowd's reaction, but there were too many people to try to analyze all at one time. For a brief second, she envied those who could feel the energy of the crowd, then she let the envy go. Even when there were difficulties, she wouldn't trade being autistic. So, she turned slightly, just enough to see Sadar's face. He gave her a slight nod, and it was enough to let her know that things were going OK.

"I want to assure the elven people that I will not be regent alone. Therefore, today I will announce my engagement." The cheering grew louder with those words. Even the nobility seemed to scowl less.

"I will marry and will be regent with an elf at my side. However, this elf must have magic strong enough to defend the kingdom until my son becomes of age. It is someone who can aid and guide your future king and someone who has proven that he will serve the throne above all else."

Alicia watched Rehta during her speech and saw the exact moment that he understood. His face moved from confusion to fury. Alicia hoped that he understood that she did not plan on taking anything away from him. She did not need a husband. She needed someone to keep her son safe.

"In three days, I will marry Sadar, blood sworn of the throne. He will serve as regent at my side, and together we will protect the throne until my son comes of age and can rule on his own. I swear on my honor that we will abdicate regency upon his name day. We will serve as nothing but advisors after that day. After the marriage, King Kenny will be sworn in as king of the In-Between."

The crowd in the throne room cheered. Alicia wanted to be happy that they had done it; they had completed everything. Except she wondered if Rehta would ever forgive her for marrying his love.

# Chapter Forty-Eight

Alicia would have preferred that the wedding had been a small ceremony. But unfortunately, nothing seemed to be unassuming when she was the regent of a kingdom. This time they had forced her into a dress, a horrible thing with white lace. The wedding planner thought it would be great to combine human American wedding culture with elven culture. Alicia had tried to assure the wedding planner that she didn't care. She wanted everything to be as simple as possible, but it wasn't about her. Nothing was about her anymore.

The dress itched. Every part of Alicia's body felt like it was on fire. She wanted to rip it off. Yet even she knew she couldn't get away with jeans during her wedding. She would have to keep this monstrous garment on for the wedding ceremony and her son's coronation. She still had hours left of this horrible itchy fabric. It was hot, too; the heat pressed down on her. Usually, it would have calmed her, but today, it just made it so she couldn't breathe. Then there was the noise. The wedding was taking place in the throne room. It wasn't any more crowded than the night they had claimed the throne for her son, but the noise today was unbearable.

She couldn't do it. Alicia reached back, trying to undo the fasteners on the back of her dress. She felt the tears come to her face unbidden. There had been so much work to do in the last three days, and Alicia had barely had rest. How was she going to pull this off if she was already losing it after just three days? She kept trying to reach the back of the dress, becoming more and more frustrated when she failed. Her entire body was on fire. It hurt everywhere the lace touched her or the fabric pinched a little too tightly. She started hyperventilating.

Alicia felt a set of hands on her own, guiding her hands down to her side. She hadn't heard anyone come in and jumped at the unexpected contact.

"What is wrong?" Rehta asked.

"It hurts," Alicia managed to say. She was losing control. She started pacing, and her arm started twitching. Rehta reached out and held her. Then he began undoing the buttons and let the garment fall to the floor. Alicia took a breath in relief. Rehta wrapped her in a blanket, one that was soft and almost silky. Alicia took the blanket and went and curled up on the overlarge wooden chair. She tried to work on her breathing and calming her mind, bringing herself back to the present.

"I think I ruined my makeup," Alicia finally said.

"Didn't anyone think to have you try on the dress?" Rehta asked.

"I did, but only for a short time. I told the seamstress the lace was too much, but she not only insisted, she put even more on it. What am I going to wear?"

"You will wear what you should have been wearing all along. Elven wedding clothing is simple."

Rehta slipped out, and Alicia sat, enjoying the feel of the blanket on her skin.

It was good that Rehta was back. He had slipped out of the hall as soon as Alicia had made the announcement. Alicia tried to send for him, but he was nowhere to be found. Finally, last night he had shown back up, and they had talked it out. Meaning Rehta yelled to the point where the guards were so sick of entering the room to check on the situation, they just positioned themselves in her royal bedroom.

Rehta knew that Alicia had no design on Sadar beyond their friendship. He understood she had no desire for a romantic relationship with anyone, ever. However, Alicia still wasn't sure Rehta would ever forgive her for taking away his romantic ending. Finally, Alicia convinced Rehta that she needed him, and her son needed Sadar.

Rehta was still upset. But Alicia knew that he would accept this, eventually. Sadar was the best choice, the only choice. Last night, Rehta finally, grudgingly, agreed.

He also agreed to be her assistant. He would help guide Alicia, and that would give him a reason to be around Sadar. Alicia knew one thing from the two days without Rehta at her side: she had no clue what she was doing. Who in their right mind would want her to approve aspects of a party? Look at the mess it had already caused.

This time Alicia heard Rehta as he moved into the room. He held in his hand a simple silk dress.

"No pants, not today, but this is a traditional elven wedding gown."

Alicia slipped it on over her head and sighed in relief. The color was a simple light blue, with embroidery around the skirt edges. It was almost like a blue flame that rose into the skirt's folds. The sleeves ran down her arms, loose until they wrapped around the wrists. Alicia realized the irony that if they had started with this dress, she would have hated it. Yet now, it seemed like a gift.

Rehta had also brought in a makeup container. He went to work, fixing Alicia's tear-stained face. Then he redid Alicia's hair, something she didn't even realize that she had ruined.

"Are you ready?" he asked.

"Ready."

The ceremony was relatively straightforward if Alicia ignored the thousands of people watching both in the room and on the screens that Kenny had projected. Kenny watched from the side in a small chair. The throne loomed behind them all.

Alicia tried to ignore the people watching and the upcoming coronation of her son. Instead, she focused on Sadar. He was standing in front of her, holding a thin piece of leather that looked like the same binding that they used to handcuff people, except this one had decorations etched into it. *Great*, Alicia thought. *They view a wedding the same way they view prison.* Although the comparison did seem to fit.

Alicia held out her wrists and allowed Sadar to bind them together. Then she did the same to his. She figured it was apt that women always were bound first in a wedding ceremony. It made it just that much harder to get the leather wrapping around Sadar's wrists. Gender equality was going to have to be part of her regency political platform.

She looked at Sadar's face then, probably for the first time in the ceremony, and saw his expression was grim but determined. She imagined that her own looked similar. Yet, no matter how unhappy either of them looked, it did not seem to deter the people's joy. When they turned towards the people, awkwardly with both wrists still bound, they shouted with joy, and Alicia saw their faces streaked with tears.

Alicia tried to share their happiness, but her arms were shorter, and she had to stretch to reach. Sadar raised his arms so far that Alicia had to go on tiptoes to keep her arms from pulling out of her sockets. Alicia decided that this was not how this relationship was going to go. She wrapped her fingers around the leather strap and tugged until Sadar's hands lowered to a more comfortable level. *That is much better*, Alicia thought, and then turned her attention back to the people.

There were only thirteen more years of this left to go.

# Epilogue

There was a lot of routine in running a kingdom.

Each morning Alicia would wake up and be greeted by breakfast and a briefing that contained anything of importance from the night before and everything she needed for the day ahead.

After she had finished, she would get dressed with the help of her assistants.

Alicia usually spent mornings in meetings where elves argued about the state of the country. It used to be a lot of rich elven men. Not a single non-male elf sat on any of the councils. It turned out that it was an easy fix, as she had the power to remove people from their seats and replace them with whom she saw fit. The council members tried for treason for their cooperation with the former king were filled in by a more diverse group. Rehta was the first appointed. Sisha, the head of the orphanage, had become the second. It was a start, but there was a lot more to work to do before the In-Between became an equitable place to live.

Lunch was always a private affair. Alicia and Rehta would meet up with Sadar and Kenny, and they would enjoy their hour together as their own unique family. Kenny would talk excitedly about what he would be learning in his afternoon training, where he worked with the most proficient tutors they could find. Then Kenny would grudgingly listen to Rehta's recount of the council members' meetings and apply what he had learned in his morning schooling. While it may not have been as exciting as magic to the boy, he showed excellent reasoning skills. Alicia did not doubt that he would make a worthy king when he came of age.

After lunch, Alicia would go and take petitions in the great hall. There she would listen to grievances and point out the obvious to a group of people too involved in a situation. At times the elves would remember that she was a magicless human, and there would be problems, but for the most part, they respected her decisions. It was apparent she didn't want power, and she had a unique way of seeing the world that became respected. It turned out she wasn't all that bad at being a regent.

At night she visited the library that Rehta had built. They had opened it to the public most of the day. But for two hours, it was closed to everyone except for her. She lived for these hours curled up in a soft chair, escaping in some adventure.

Except not tonight. Tonight she stared at the envelope in her hands. It was made of sturdy green paper and was sealed with an old-fashioned wax embossing. It was addressed to her mailbox in the human world, delivered to the palace by one of the royal carriers just this afternoon. The return address was from Christian.

She had called him after things had settled down. She had made up a story about her informing on her old company and having to go into hiding. It hurt to lie to him, but she also knew she could not tell him the truth. Over the months they had exchanged letters. He was moving on with his life. The proof was in her hands.

Finally, she opened the envelope. The wedding was only a few weeks off. He would understand why she couldn't come. It was better, really; it was one relationship of his she wouldn't ruin. At least she could send them a nice wedding gift.

She stuffed the invitation back in the envelope and wiped the tears off her cheek. She tapped her fingers on the chair's arm. One... two... three... all the way to thirty. Then she took a deep breath and schooled her face back into her mask, becoming the person the In-Between needed her to be.

# ACKNOWLEDGEMENTS

I want to thank my kids for helping me to become the person I am now. A special shout out to my youngest who listened to me read my story aloud countless times.

I am extremely appreciative to my developmental editor who helped me shape this story into the best version of itself and my proofreader who helped me to spruce it up. Any errors are my own.

Thank you to Christin, for reading and listening to me talk endlessly about my worlds. Also, thank you to all the amazing autistic people in the world. We are amazing and we deserve more stories about us being amazing. I hope you enjoyed this one.

A huge thank you to my Bookstagram family. There is nothing more special than finding people who will talk about books with you. Thank you for listening to me talk about this book, and for reading it. You are all amazing!

Made in the USA
Middletown, DE
30 October 2022

13769105R00195